ACCLAIM FOR

"Explosive, thrilling, action-packed – meet Alex Rider."
Guardian

"Horowitz is pure class, stylish but action-packed ... being James Bond in miniature is way cooler than being a wizard." *Daily Mirror*

"Horowitz will grip you with suspense, daring and cheek – and that's just the first page! ... Prepare for action scenes as fast as a movie."
The Times

"Anthony Horowitz is the lion of children's literature." *Michael Morpurgo*

"Fast and furious." *Telegraph*

"The perfect hero ... genuine 21st century stuff." *Daily Telegraph*

"Brings new meaning to the phrase 'action-packed'." *Sunday Times*

"Every bored schoolboy's fantasy, only a thousand times funnier, slicker and more exciting ... genius." *Independent on Sunday*

Titles by Anthony Horowitz

The Alex Rider series:
Stormbreaker
Point Blanc
Skeleton Key
Eagle Strike
Scorpia
Ark Angel
Snakehead
Crocodile Tears
Scorpia Rising
Russian Roulette

The Power of Five (Book One): *Raven's Gate*
The Power of Five (Book Two): *Evil Star*
The Power of Five (Book Three): *Nightrise*
The Power of Five (Book Four): *Necropolis*
The Power of Five (Book Five): *Oblivion*

The Devil and his Boy
Granny
Groosham Grange
Return to Groosham Grange
The Switch
More Bloody Horowitz

The Diamond Brothers books:
The Falcon's Malteser
Public Enemy Number Two
South by South East
The French Confection
The Greek Who Stole Christmas
The Blurred Man
I Know What You Did Last Wednesday

ALEX RIDER

ACTION
ADRENALINE
ADVENTURE

ARK ANGEL

ANTHONY HOROWITZ

WALKER
BOOKS

For AC

First published 2005 by Walker Books Ltd
87 Vauxhall Walk, London SE11 5HJ

This edition published 2015

2 4 6 8 10 9 7 5 3 1

Text © 2005 Stormbreaker Productions Ltd
Cover illustration © 2015 Walker Books Ltd
Trademarks Alex Rider™; Boy with Torch Logo™
© 2010 Stormbreaker Productions Ltd

The right of Anthony Horowitz to be identified as author
of this work has been asserted by him in accordance with
the Copyright, Designs and Patents Act 1988

This book has been typeset in Officina Sans

Printed and bound in Great Britain by Clays Ltd, St Ives plc

British Library Cataloguing in Publication Data:
a catalogue record for this book
is available from the British Library

ISBN 978-1-4063-6024-0

www.walker.co.uk

CONTENTS

FORCE THREE

The bomb had been timed to go off at exactly half past three.

Strangely, the man it had been designed to kill probably knew more about bombs and terrorism than anyone else in the world. He had even written books on the subject. *Looking After Number One: Fifty Ways to Protect Yourself at Home and Abroad* might not be the snappiest of titles, but the book had sold half a million copies in America, and it was said that the president himself kept a copy by his bed. The man did not think of himself as a target, but even so he was always careful. As he often joked, it would be bad for business if he was blown up crossing the street.

His name was Max Webber, and he was short and plump with tortoise-shell glasses and jet-black hair that was actually dyed. He told people that he had once been in the SAS, which was true. What he didn't tell them was that he had been dropped after his first tour of duty. In his forties he had opened a training centre in London, advising rich businessmen on how to look after themselves. He had become a writer and a journalist, frequently appearing on television to discuss international security.

And now he was the guest speaker at the fourth International Security Conference, being held at the Queen Elizabeth Hall on the south bank of the Thames in London. The whole building had been cordoned off. Helicopters had been flying overhead all morning and police with sniffer dogs had been waiting in the foyer. Briefcases, cameras and all electronic devices had been forbidden inside the main hall, and delegates had been made to pass through a rigorous screening system before being allowed in. More than eight hundred men and women from seventeen countries had turned up. Among them were diplomats, businessmen, senior politicians, journalists and members of various security services. They had to feel safe.

Alan Blunt and Mrs Jones were both in the audience. As the head and deputy head of MI6 Special Operations, it was their responsibility to keep up with the latest developments, although as far as Blunt was concerned, the whole thing was a waste of time. There were security conferences all the time in every major city but they never achieved anything. The experts talked. The politicians lied. The press wrote it all down. And then everyone went home and nothing changed. Alan Blunt was bored. He looked half asleep.

At exactly two fifteen, Max Webber began to speak.

He was dressed in an expensive suit and tie and spoke slowly, his clipped voice full of authority. He had notes in front of him but he referred to them only occasionally, his eyes fixed on the audience, speaking directly to each one of them. In a glass-fronted projection room overlooking the stage, nine translators spoke quietly into microphones, just a second or two behind. Here and there in the audience, men and women could be seen with one hand pressed against their earpiece, concentrating on what was being said.

Webber turned a page. "I am often asked which is the most dangerous terrorist group in the world. The answer is not what you might expect. It is a group that you may not know. But I can assure you that it is one you should fear, and I wish to speak briefly about it now."

He pressed a button on his lectern and two words appeared, projected onto a giant screen behind him.

FORCE THREE

In the fifth row, Blunt opened his eyes and turned to Mrs Jones. He looked puzzled. She shook her head briefly. Both of them were suddenly alert.

11

"They call themselves Force Three," Webber went on. "The name refers to the fact that the earth is the third planet from the sun. These people wouldn't describe themselves as terrorists. They would probably prefer you to think of them as eco-warriors, fighting to protect the earth from the evils of pollution. Broadly speaking, they're protesting against climate change, the destruction of the rainforests, the use of nuclear power, genetic engineering and the growth of multinational business. All very commendable, you might think. Their agenda is similar to that of Greenpeace. The difference is that these people are fanatics. They will kill anyone who gets in their way; they have already killed many times. They claim to respect the planet but they have no respect at all for human life."

Webber clicked again and a photograph flashed up on the screen. There was a stir in the auditorium as the audience examined it. At first sight, they seemed to be looking at a picture of a globe. Then they saw that it was a globe sitting on a pair of shoulders. Finally they realized it was a man. He had a very round head which was completely shaven – including the eyebrows. And there was a map of the world tattooed on his skin. England and France covered his left eye. Newfoundland poked out over his right. Argentina floated around one side of his neck. A gasp of revulsion spread around the room. The man was a freak.

"This is the commanding officer of Force Three," Webber explained. "As you can see, he cares about the planet so much, he's rather let it go to his head.

"His name – or at least the name that he goes by – is Kaspar. Very little is known about him. It is thought he might be French, but we don't even know for certain where he was born. Nor do we know when he acquired these tattoos. But I can tell you that Kaspar has been very busy in the last six months. He was responsible for the assassination of Marjorie Schultz, a journalist living in Berlin, in June; her only crime was to write an article criticizing Force Three. He planned the kidnapping and murder of two members of the Atomic Energy Commission in Toronto. He has organized explosions in six countries, including Japan and New Zealand. He destroyed a car manufacturing plant in Dakota. And I have to tell you, ladies and gentlemen, he enjoys his work. Whenever possible, Kaspar likes to press the button himself.

"In my view, Kaspar is now the most dangerous man alive, for the simple reason that he believes the whole world is with him. And in a sense he's right. I'm sure there are many people in this room who believe in protecting the environment. The trouble is, he would kill every single one of you if he thought it would help him achieve his aims. That is why I'm issuing this warning.

"Find Kaspar. Find Force Three before they can

13

do any more harm. Because with every day that passes, I believe they are becoming a more serious and deadly threat."

Webber paused as he turned another page of his notes. When he began speaking again, the subject had changed. Twenty minutes later, at exactly three o'clock, he finished. There was polite applause.

Coffee and biscuits were being served in the foyer after the session ended, but Webber wasn't staying. He shook hands briefly with a diplomat he knew and exchanged a few words with some journalists, then moved on. He was heading towards the auditorium exit when he found his way blocked by a man and a woman.

They were an unlikely pair. There was no way he would have mistaken them for husband and wife, even though they were about the same age. The woman was thin with short black hair. The man was shorter and entirely grey. There was nothing interesting about him at all.

"Alan Blunt!" Webber smiled and nodded. "Mrs Jones!"

Very few people in the world would have recognized these two individuals, but Webber knew them instantly.

"We enjoyed your talk, Mr Webber," Blunt said, although there was little enthusiasm in his voice.

"Thank you."

"We were particularly interested in your comments concerning Force Three."

"You know about them, of course?"

The question was directed at Blunt, but it was Mrs Jones who answered. "We've heard about them, certainly," she replied. "But the fact is, we know very little about them. Six months ago, as far as we can see, they didn't even exist."

"That's right. They were founded very recently."

"You seem to know a lot about them, Mr Webber. We'd be interested to learn where you got your information."

Webber smiled a second time. "You know I can't possibly reveal my sources, Mrs Jones," he said lightly. Suddenly he was serious. "But I find it very worrying that our country's security services should be so ignorant. I thought you were meant to be protecting us."

"That's why we're talking to you now," Mrs Jones countered. "If you know something, I think you should tell us—"

Webber interrupted her. "I think I've told you quite enough. If you want to know more, I suggest you come to my next lecture. I'll be talking in Stockholm a couple of weeks from now, and it may well be that I shall have further information about Force Three then. If so, I'll be happy to share it with you. And now, if you don't mind, I'll wish you good day."

Webber pushed his way between them and

headed towards the cloakroom. He couldn't help smiling to himself. It had gone perfectly – and meeting Alan Blunt and the Jones woman had been an unexpected bonus. He fumbled in his pocket and took out a plastic disc which he handed to the cloakroom attendant. His mobile phone had been taken from him when he went in: a security measure he himself had recommended in his book. Now it was returned to him.

Ninety seconds later he emerged onto the wide pavement in front of the river. It was early October but the weather was still warm, the afternoon sun turning the water a deep blue. There were only a few people around – mainly kids rattling back and forth on their skateboards – but Webber still checked them out, just to make sure that none of them had any interest in him. He decided to walk home instead of taking public transport or hailing a taxi. That was something else he'd written in his book. *In any major city, you're always safer out in the open, on your own two feet.*

He had only taken a few steps when his mobile rang, vibrating in his jacket pocket. He dug it out. Somewhere in the back of his mind he seemed to recall that the phone had been switched off when he handed it to the cloakroom attendant. But he was feeling so pleased with himself, with the way his speech had gone, that he ignored this single whisper of doubt.

It was twenty-nine minutes past three.

"Hello?"

"Mr Webber. I'm ringing to congratulate you. It went very well."

The voice was soft and somehow artificial. It wasn't an Englishman speaking. It was someone who had learnt the language very carefully. The pronunciation was too deliberate, too precise. There was no emotion in the voice at all.

"You heard me?" Max Webber was still walking, speaking at the same time.

"Oh yes. I was in the audience. I am very pleased."

"Did you know that MI6 were there?"

"No."

"I spoke to them afterwards. They were very interested in what I had to say." Webber chuckled quietly. "Maybe I should raise my price."

"I think we'll stick with our original agreement," the voice replied.

Max Webber shrugged. Two hundred and fifty thousand pounds was still a great deal of money. Paid into a secret bank account, it would come tax-free, no questions asked. And it had been such a simple thing to do. A quarter of a million for just ten minutes' work!

The man on the other end spoke again and suddenly his voice was sad. "There is just one thing that concerns me, Mr Webber..."

"What's that?" Webber could hear something else, in the background. Some sort of interference.

He pressed the phone more tightly against his ear.

"In your speech today, you made an enemy of Force Three. And as you yourself pointed out, they are completely ruthless."

"I don't think either of us need worry about Force Three." Webber looked around to make sure he wasn't being overheard. "And I think you should remember, my friend, I served with the SAS. I know how to look after myself."

"Really?"

Was the voice mocking him? For reasons Webber didn't quite understand, he was beginning to feel uneasy. And the interference was getting louder; he could hear it in his mobile phone. Some sort of ticking.

"I'm not afraid of Force Three," he blustered. "I'm not afraid of anyone. Just make sure the money reaches my account."

"Goodbye, Mr Webber," said the voice.

There was a click.

One second of silence.

Then the mobile phone exploded.

Max Webber had been holding it tight against his ear. If he heard the blast, he was dead before it registered. A couple of joggers were approaching from the other direction, and they both screamed as the thing that had just moments before been a man toppled over into their path.

The explosion was surprisingly loud. It was heard in the conference centre where delegates were still drinking coffee and congratulating one another on their contributions. They also heard the wail of the sirens as the ambulance and police cars arrived shortly afterwards.

Later that afternoon, Force Three called the press and claimed responsibility for the killing. Max Webber had declared war on them, and for that reason he had to die.

In the same phone call they issued a stark warning.

They had already chosen their next target.

And they were planning something the world would not forget.

THE BOY IN ROOM NINE

The nurse was twenty-three years old, blonde and nervous. This was only her second week at St Dominic's, one of London's most exclusive private hospitals. Rock stars and television celebrities came here, she had been told. There were also VIPs from abroad. VIPs here meant very important patients. Even famous people get sick, and the ones who wanted to recover in five-star comfort chose St Dominic's. The surgeons and therapists were world class. The hospital food was so good that some patients had been known to pretend they were ill so that they could enjoy it for a while longer.

That evening, the nurse was making her way down a wide, brightly lit corridor, carrying a tray of medicines. She was wearing a freshly laundered white dress. Her name – D. MEACHER – was printed on a badge pinned to her uniform. Several of the junior doctors had already placed bets on which of them would persuade her to go out with them first.

She stopped in front of an open door. Room nine.

"Hello," she said. "I'm Diana Meacher."

"I'm looking forward to meeting you too," the boy in room nine replied.

Alex Rider was sitting up in bed, reading a French textbook that he should have been studying at school. He was wearing pyjamas that had fallen open at the neck and the nurse could just make out the bandages criss-crossing his chest. He was a very handsome boy, she thought. He had fair hair and serious brown eyes that looked as if they had seen too much. She knew that he was only fourteen, but he looked older. Pain had done that to him. Nurse Meacher had read his medical file and understood what he had been through.

In truth, he should have been dead. Alex Rider had been hit by a bullet fired from a .22 rifle from a distance of almost seventy-five metres. The sniper had been aiming for his heart – and if the bullet had found its target, Alex would have had no chance of surviving. But nothing is certain – not even murder. A tiny movement had saved his life. As he had come out of MI6's headquarters on Liverpool Street, he had stepped off the pavement, his right foot carrying his body down towards the level of the road. It was at that exact moment that the bullet had hit him, and instead of powering into his heart, it had entered his body half a centimetre higher, ricocheting off a rib and exiting horizontally under his left arm.

The bullet had missed his vital heart structures, but even so it had done plenty of damage, tearing through the subclavian artery, which carries blood over the top of the lung and into the arm. This was what Alex had felt when he was hit. As blood had poured out of the severed artery, filling the space between the lung and the thoracic cage, he had found himself unable to breathe. Alex could easily have died from shock or loss of blood. If he had been a man he almost certainly would have. But the body of a child is different to that of an adult. A young person's artery will automatically shut itself down if cut – doctors can't explain how or why – and this will limit the amount of blood lost. Alex was unconscious but he was still breathing, four minutes later, when the first ambulance arrived.

There wasn't much the paramedics could do: IV fluids, oxygen and some gentle compression around the bullet's point of entry. But that was enough. Alex had been rushed to St Dominic's, where surgeons had removed the bone fragments and put a graft on the artery. He had been in the operating theatre two and a half hours.

And now he was looking almost as if nothing had happened. As the nurse came into the room, he closed the book and settled back into his pillows. Diana Meacher knew that this was his last night in hospital. He had been here for ten days and tomorrow he was going home. She also knew that she wasn't allowed to ask too many questions. It was there in large print on his file:

PATIENT 9/75958 RIDER/ALEX: SPECIAL STATUS (MISO). NO UNAUTHORIZED VISITORS. NO PRESS. REFER ALL ENQUIRIES TO DR HAYWARD.

It was all very strange. She had been told she would meet some interesting people at St Dominic's, and she had been required to sign a confidentiality clause before she began work. But she'd never expected anything like this. MISO stood for Military Intelligence: Special Operations. But what was the secret service doing with a teenage boy? How had Alex managed to get himself shot? And why had there been two armed policemen sitting outside his room for the first four days of his stay? Diana tried to push these thoughts out of her mind as she put the tray down. Maybe she should have stuck with the NHS.

"How are you feeling?" she asked.

"I'm fine, thanks."

"Looking forward to going home?"

"Yes."

Diana realized she was staring at Alex and turned her attention to the medicines. "Are you in any pain?" she asked. "Can I get you something to help you sleep?"

"No, I'm all right." Alex shook his head and for a moment something flickered in his eyes. The pain in his chest had slowly faded but he knew it would never leave him completely. He could feel it now, vague and distant, like a bad memory.

"Would you like me to come back later?"

"No, it's all right, thanks." He smiled. "I don't need anyone to tuck me in."

Diana blushed. "That's not what I meant," she said. "But if you need me, I'll be just down the hall. You can call me any time."

"I might do that."

The nurse picked up her tray and walked out of the room. She left behind the scent of her perfume – heather and spring flowers – in the air. Alex sniffed. It seemed to him that since his injury, his senses had become more acute.

He reached for his French book, then changed his mind. To hell with it, he thought. Irregular verbs could wait. It was his own future that concerned him more.

He looked around at the neat, softly lit room that tried hard to pretend it belonged to an expensive hotel rather than a hospital. There was an Ultra Slim HD TV mounted on the wall and, beside the bed a remote control that allowed patients to change channels, dim the lighting, open the curtains, adjust the air conditioning or even call a nurse. A window looked out over a wide north London street lined with trees. His room was on the second floor, one of about a dozen arranged in a ring around a bright and modern reception area. In the early days after his operation, there had been flowers everywhere, but Alex had asked for them to be taken away. They'd reminded him of a funeral parlour and he had decided he preferred being alive.

But there were still cards. He had received more than twenty and he'd been surprised how many people had heard that he'd been hurt – and how many had sent a card. There had been a dozen from school: one from the head; one from Miss Bedfordshire, the school secretary; and several from his friends. Tom Harris had sent him some photos taken on their trip to Venice and a note:

They told us it's appenderctis but I bet it isn't. Get well soon anyway.

Tom was the only person at Brookland who knew the truth about Alex.

Sabina Pleasure had somehow discovered he was in hospital and had sent him a card from San Francisco. She was enjoying life in America but missed England, she said. She was hoping to come over for Christmas. Jack Starbright had sent him the biggest card in the room and had followed it up with chocolates, magazines and energy drinks, visiting him twice a day. There was even a card from the prime minister's office – although it seemed the prime minister had been too busy to sign it.

And there had been cards from MI6. One from Mrs Jones, another from Alan Blunt (a printed message with a single word – BLUNT – signed in green ink as if it were a memorandum not a get well card). Alex had been surprised and pleased to receive a card from Wolf, the soldier he had met while training with the SAS. The postmark showed it had been mailed in Baghdad. But his favourite had been sent by Smithers. On the front was a teddy bear. There was no message inside, but when Alex opened the card, the teddy bear's eyes blinked and it began to talk.

"Alex – very sorry to hear you've been hurt." The bear was speaking with Smithers' voice. "Hope you get better soon, old chap. Just take it easy – I'm sure you deserve a rest. Oh, and by the way, this card will self-destruct in five seconds."

Sure enough, to the horror of the nurses, the card had immediately burst into flames.

As well as cards, there had been visitors. Mrs Jones had been the first.

Alex had only just come round after surgery when she appeared. He had never seen the deputy head of Special Operations looking quite so unsure of herself. She was wearing a charcoal-grey raincoat which hung open to reveal a dark suit underneath. Her hair was wet and raindrops glistened on her shoulders.

"I don't quite know what to say to you, Alex," she began. She hadn't asked him how he was. She would have already got that from the doctors. "What happened to you in Liverpool Street was an unforgivable lapse of security. Too many people know the location of our headquarters. We're going to stop using the main entrance. It's too dangerous."

Alex shifted uncomfortably in the bed but said nothing.

"Your condition is stable. I can't tell you how relieved I am personally. When I heard you'd been shot, I..." She stopped herself. Her black eyes looked down, taking in the tubes and wires attached to the boy lying in front of her, feeding into his arm, nose, mouth and stomach. "I know you can't talk now," she went on. "So I'll be brief.

"You are safe here. We've used St Dominic's before, and there are certain procedures being followed. There are guards outside your room. There'll be someone there twenty-four hours a day as long as necessary.

"The shooting in Liverpool Street was reported in the press but your name was kept out of it. Your age too. The sniper who fired at you had taken a position on the roof opposite. We're still investigating how he managed to get up there without being detected – and I'm afraid we've been unable to find him. But right now, your safety is our primary concern. We can talk to Scorpia. As you know, we've had dealings with them in the past. I'm sure I can persuade them to leave you alone. You destroyed their operation, Alex, and they punished you. But enough is enough."

She stopped. Alex's heart monitor pulsed softly in the dim light.

"Please try not to think too badly of us," she added. "After everything you've been through – Scorpia, your father... I will never forgive myself for what happened. I sometimes think it was wrong of us ever to get you involved in the first place. But we can talk about that another time."

Alex was too weak to reply. He watched as Mrs Jones got up and left, and he guessed that Scorpia must have decided to leave him alone, because a few days later the armed guards outside his room quietly disappeared.

And now, in just over twelve hours, he would be out of here too. Jack had already been planning the weeks ahead. She wanted to take him on holiday to Florida or perhaps the Caribbean. It was October and the summer was definitely over, leaves falling and cold breezes coming in with the night. Jack wanted Alex to rest and regain his strength in the sun – but secretly he wasn't so sure. He picked up the textbook again. He never thought he'd hear himself say this, but the truth was he just wanted to go back to school. He wanted to be ordinary again. Scorpia had sent him a simple, unforgettable message. Being a spy could get him killed. Irregular verbs were less dangerous.

There was a movement at the door and a boy looked in.

"Hi, Alex."

The boy had a strange accent – Eastern European, possibly Russian. He was fourteen, with

28

short blond hair and light blue eyes. His face was thin, his skin pale. He was wearing pyjamas and a large dressing gown which made him seem smaller than he was. He was staying in the room next door to Alex and really had been treated for appendicitis, with complications. His name was Paul Drevin – the surname was somehow familiar – but Alex didn't know anything more about him. The two of them had spoken briefly a few times. They were nearly the same age, and the only teenagers on the corridor.

Alex raised a hand in greeting. "Hi."

"I hear you're getting out of here tomorrow," Paul said.

"Yes. How about you?"

"Another day, worst luck." He hovered in the doorway. He seemed to want to come in, but at the same time something held him back. "I'll be glad to leave," he admitted. "I want to go home."

"Where *is* home?" Alex asked.

"I'm not sure." Paul was completely serious. "We live in London a lot of the time. But my father's always moving. Moscow, New York, the South of France ... he's been too busy even to come in and see me. And we have so many houses, I sometimes wonder which is my home."

"Where do you go to school?" Alex had picked up on the mention of Moscow and assumed that Paul must be Russian.

"I don't go to school; I have tutors." Paul

shrugged. "It's difficult. My life's sort of weird, because of my father. Because of everything. Anyway, I'm jealous of you getting out before me. Good luck."

"Thanks."

Paul hesitated a fraction longer, then left. Alex gazed thoughtfully at the empty doorway. Perhaps his father was some sort of politician or banker. On the few occasions they had spoken he'd got the impression that the other boy was friendless. He wondered how many kids were admitted into this hospital who had fathers willing to spend thousands to make them better, but who had no time to visit them while they were there.

It was nine o'clock. Alex flicked through the TV channels, but there was nothing on. He wished now that he had accepted the sleeping pill from the nurse. A little sip of water and he would have been out for the night. And out of the hospital the next day. Alex was looking forward to that more than anything. He needed to start his life again.

He watched half an hour of a comedy that didn't make him laugh. Then he switched off the television, turned off the light and curled up in the bed one last time. He rather wished Diana Meacher had come back to see him. Briefly he remembered the scent of her perfume. And then he was asleep.

But not for long.

The next thing Alex knew, it was half past twelve.

30

There was a clock beside the bed, its numerals glowing in the dark. He woke up reluctantly, trying to climb back down into the pit from which he had come. The truth was, it was difficult to sleep when he had done nothing to make him tired. All day he'd been lying there, breathing in the clean, conditioned atmosphere that at St Dominic's passed for air.

He lay in the semi-darkness, wondering what to do. Then he got up and slipped into his dressing gown. This was the worst thing about being in hospital. There was no way out, nowhere to go. Alex couldn't get used to it. Every night for a week, he'd woken up at about the same time, and finally he'd decided to break the rules and escape from the sterile box that was his room. He wanted to be outside. He needed the smell of London, the noise of the traffic, the feeling that he still belonged to the real world.

He put on a pair of slippers and went out. The lights had been dimmed, casting no more than a discreet glow outside his room. There was a computer screen gleaming behind the nurses' station but no sign of Diana Meacher or anyone else. Alex took a step forward. There are few places more silent than a hospital in the middle of the night and he felt almost afraid to move, as if he was breaking some sort of unwritten law between the healthy and the sick. But he knew he would just lie awake for hours if he stayed in bed. He had nothing to worry about. Mrs Jones was certain that Scorpia was no longer a threat. He was almost tempted to leave the hospital and catch the night bus home.

Of course, that was out of the question. He couldn't go that far. But he was still determined to reach the main reception with its sliding glass doors and – just beyond – a real street with people and cars and noise and dirt. By day, three receptionists answered the phones and dealt with enquiries. After eight o'clock there was just one. Alex had already met him – a cheerful Irishman called Conor Hackett. The two of them had quickly become friends.

Conor was sixty-five and had spent most of his life in Dublin. He'd taken this job to help support his nine grandchildren. After they'd talked a while, Alex had persuaded Conor to let him go outside, and he had spent a happy fifteen minutes on the pavement in front of the main entrance, watching the passing traffic and breathing in the night air. He would do the same again now. Maybe he could stretch it to half an hour. Conor would complain; he would threaten to call the nurse. But Alex was sure he would let him have his way.

He avoided the lift, afraid that the noise of the bell as it arrived would give him away. He walked down the stairs to the first floor, and continued along a corridor. From here he could look down on the polished floor of reception and the glass entrance doors. He could see Conor sitting behind his desk, reading a magazine. Even down here the lights were dimmed. It was as if the hospital wanted to remind visitors where they were the moment they came in.

Conor turned a page. Alex was about to walk down the last few stairs, when suddenly the front doors slid open.

Alex was both startled and a little embarrassed. He didn't want to be caught here in his dressing gown and pyjamas. At the same time, he wondered who could possibly be visiting St Dominic's at this time of night. He took a step back, disappearing into the shadows. Now he could watch everything that was happening, unobserved.

Four men came in. They were in their late twenties, and all looked fit. The leader was wearing a combat jacket and a Che Guevara T-shirt. The others were dressed in jeans, hooded sweatshirts and trainers. From where he was hiding, Alex couldn't make out their faces very clearly, but already he knew there was something strange about them. The way they moved was somehow too fast, too energetic. People move more cautiously when they come into a hospital. After all, nobody actually wants to be there.

"Hey – how are you doing?" the first man asked. The words cut through the gloom. He had a cheerful, cultivated voice.

"How can I help you?" the receptionist asked. He sounded as puzzled as Alex felt.

33

"We'd like to visit one of your patients," the man explained. "I wonder if you can tell us where he is."

"I'm very sorry." Alex couldn't see Conor's face, but he could imagine the smile in his voice. "You can't visit anyone now. It's almost one o'clock! You'll have to come back tomorrow."

"I don't think you understand."

Alex felt the first stirrings of nervousness. A note of menace had crept into the man's voice. And there was something sinister about the way the other three men were positioned. They were spread out between the receptionist and the main entrance. It was as if they didn't want him to leave. Or anyone else to enter.

"We want to see Paul Drevin."

Alex heard the name with a shiver of disbelief. The boy in the room next to his! Why would these men want to see him so late at night?

"What room is he in?" the man in the combat jacket asked.

Conor shook his head. "I can't give you that information," he protested. "Come back tomorrow and someone will be happy to help you then."

"We want to know *now*," the man insisted. He reached into his jacket and Alex felt the floor sway beneath him as the man produced a gun. It was equipped with a silencer. And it was pointing at the receptionist's head.

"What are you...?" Conor had gone rigid; his voice had risen to a high-pitched squeak. "I can't tell you!" he exclaimed. "What are you doing here? What do you want?"

"We want the room number of Paul Drevin. If you don't give it to me in the next three seconds, I will pull the trigger and the only part of this hospital you'll ever need again will be the morgue."

"Wait!"

"One..."

"I don't know where he is!"

"Two..."

Alex felt his chest hurting. He realized he was holding his breath.

"All right! All right! Let me find it for you."

The receptionist began to tap hurriedly at the keyboard hidden below the top of his desk. Alex heard the clatter of the keys.

"He's on the second floor! Room eight."

"Thank you," the man said, and shot him.

Alex heard the angry cough of the bullet as it was spat out by the silencer. He saw a black spray in front of the receptionist's forehead. Conor was thrown backwards, his hands raised briefly.

Nobody moved.

"Room eight. Second floor," one of the men muttered.

"I told you he was in room eight," the first man said.

"Then why did you ask?"

"I just wanted to be sure."

One of them sniggered.

"Let's go and get him," another said.

Alex was frozen to the spot. He could feel his wound throbbing angrily. This couldn't be happening, could it? But it was happening. He had seen it for himself.

The four men moved.

Alex turned and ran.

EMERGENCY TREATMENT

Alex took the stairs two at a time, a hundred different thoughts tumbling through his mind. Who were the four men and why were they here? What did they want with Paul? The name Drevin meant something to him, but this wasn't the time to work out what it was. What could he do to stop them?

He came to a fire alarm in a red box on the wall and stopped beside it. For a few, precious seconds his fist hovered over the glass. But he knew that setting off the alarm would do no good. For the moment, surprise was all he had on his side. The fire alarm would only tell the men that they had been seen, and then they would go about their work all the faster, killing or kidnapping the boy long before the police or fire brigade arrived.

Alex didn't want to confront the four men on his own. He was desperately tempted to call for help. But he knew it would come too late.

He continued up the stairs, one small piece of knowledge spurring him on. The men had shown themselves to be single-minded and ruthless. But they had already made one mistake.

When they had set off, they had been moving in the direction of the lift, and Alex knew something they didn't. The lifts at St Dominic's were the original bed lifts, almost twenty years old. They were designed to carry patients up from the operating theatres on the first floor and had to stop without even the slightest shudder. For this reason they were very, very slow. It would take Alex less than twenty seconds to reach the second floor; it would take the men almost two minutes. That gave him one minute and forty seconds to do something.

But what?

He burst through the doors and into the nurses' area in front of his room. There was still nobody around, which was strange. Perhaps the four men had created some sort of diversion. That would make sense. They could have got rid of the nurse with a single phone call and right now she could be anywhere in the hospital. Alex stood panting in the half-light, trying to get his brain to work. He could imagine the lift making its way inch by inch towards him.

He was painfully aware of the unevenness of the competition. The men were professional killers. Alex would have known that even if he hadn't seen them murder the night receptionist. It was obvious from their body language, the way they smiled, the conversation he'd overheard. Killing was second nature to them. Alex couldn't possibly fight them. He was unarmed. Worse, he was in pyjamas and slippers with a chest wound held together by stitches and bandages. He had never been more helpless. Once he was seen, he would be finished. He didn't stand a chance.

And yet he had to do something. He thought about the strange, lonely boy in the room next to his. Paul Drevin was only just fourteen – eight months younger than Alex. These men had come for him. Alex couldn't let them take him.

He looked at the open door of his own room – number nine. It was exactly opposite the lift, and was the first thing the men would see when they stepped out. Paul Drevin was asleep in the next room. His door was closed. Their names were visible in the half-light: ALEX RIDER and PAUL DREVIN. They were printed on plastic strips that fitted into a slot on each door. Underneath, also on strips, were the room numbers.

Suddenly, out of nowhere, a plan started to form in Alex's mind. Wondering if he had left himself enough time, he darted forward and snatched a teaspoon from a cup and saucer a nurse had left on the desk. Using the spoon handle, he prised his name and room number out of their slots, then did the same to the next door. It took another few seconds to snap the plastic strips back into place.

Now it was Alex Rider who was asleep in room nine. The door to room eight was open and Paul Drevin wasn't there.

Alex ran into his room, pulled open the cupboard and grabbed a shirt and a pair of jeans. He knew what he had done wasn't enough. If the men glanced at the doors more than briefly, they would see the trick that had been played, because the sequence was wrong: six, seven, *nine*, *eight*, ten. Alex had to make sure they didn't have time to examine anything.

He had to make them come after him.

He didn't dare get dressed in sight of the lift. He hurried out with the clothes – past the nurses' station, away from the two rooms. He came to a corridor leading off at ninety degrees. It ran about twenty metres to a pair of swing doors and another staircase. There was an open store cupboard on one side of the corridor and next to it a trolley with some sort of machine: low and flat with a series of buttons and a narrow, rectangular TV screen that looked like it had been squashed. Alex recognized the machine. There were also two oxygen cylinders. He could feel his heart pounding underneath the bandages. The silence in the hospital was unnerving. How much time had passed since Conor had been killed?

Swiftly he stripped off the pyjamas and pulled on his own clothes. It felt good to be dressed again after ten long days and nights. He was no longer a patient. He was beginning to get his life back.

The lift doors opened, breaking the silence with a metallic rattle. Alex watched the four men walk out. Quickly he summed them up. Two were black, two white. They moved as a single unit, as if they were used to working together. He gave them names based on their appearances. The man who had shot Conor was the leader. He had a broken nose that seemed to split his face like a crack in a mirror. Alex thought of him as Combat Jacket. The next was thin, with crumpled cheeks and orange-tinted glasses. Spectacles. The third was short and muscular, and obviously spent a serious amount of time at the gym. He had a heavy dull metal watch on his wrist, and that gave him his name: Steel Watch. The last man was unshaven, with straggly black hair. At some point he'd been to a bad dentist, who had left his mark very visibly. He would be Silver Tooth.

All four were moving quickly, impatient after the long wait in the lift. This was the moment of truth.

Combat Jacket registered the open door and the empty bed inside. He read the name. At that moment, Alex appeared, walking down the corridor as if he had just been to the toilet and was returning to his room. He stopped and gave a small gasp of surprise. The men looked at him. And immediately made the assumption that Alex had guessed they would. Even if they knew what their target

41

was supposed to look like, they couldn't see his face in the soft light. He was Paul Drevin. Who else could he be?

"Paul?" Combat Jacket spoke the single word.

Alex nodded.

"We're not going to hurt you. But you're going to have to come with us."

Alex took a step back.

Combat Jacket took out a gun. The same gun that he had used to kill the night receptionist.

Alex turned and fled.

As his bare feet pounded on the hospital carpet, he was afraid that he had left it too late, that he would feel the white heat of a bullet between his shoulder blades. But the corridor was right in front of him. With a feeling of relief, he threw himself round the corner. Now he was out of sight.

The four men were slow to react. This was the last thing they'd expected. Paul Drevin should have been sound asleep in bed. But he had seen them. He had run away. As one, they surged forward. Their movements seemed clumsy – they didn't want to make any noise – but they were still making fast progress. They reached the corridor and saw the swing doors ahead. One of the doors was still closing. The boy had obviously passed through seconds before. With Combat Jacket in the lead, they pressed on. None of them noticed the store cupboard on their left.

Combat Jacket pushed through the doors; Steel

Watch and Spectacles followed. Silver Tooth was left behind – and that was when Alex made his move.

Alex had run the full length of the corridor, flung open the doors, then doubled back to the store cupboard. That was where he was now. Moving on tiptoe, he slipped out. Now he was behind Silver Tooth. He was holding something in each of his hands, a circular disc, padded, trailing electric wires.

The machine he had seen on the trolley was a Lifepak 300 defibrillator, a standard piece of equipment in most British hospitals. Alex had seen defibrillators often enough in TV dramas to know what they did and how they worked. When a patient's heart stopped, the doctor would press the pads against their chest and use the electric charge to bring them back to life. Alex had connected up this defibrillator in the last seconds before the lift arrived. It was designed to be easy to use and ready in an instant; the batteries were always kept fully charged. Gritting his teeth, he slammed the pads against the neck of the man in front of him and pressed the buttons.

Silver Tooth screamed and leapt high in the air as the electric current coursed through him. He was unconscious before he hit the floor.

The doors swung open again: Spectacles had heard the scream. He came back, half crouching, running forward, a knife in his hand. His face was twisted in an ugly sneer of anger. Something had gone wrong. But how? Why hadn't the boy been asleep?

He didn't even make it halfway down the corridor. The full force of a ten-kilogram oxygen cylinder hit him right between the legs. His face went mauve and he dropped the knife. He tried to breathe, but oxygen was the one thing he couldn't find. He crumpled, eyes bulging.

Alex dropped the tank. It had taken all his strength to swing it, and he ran a hand across his chest, wondering if he had damaged himself. But the stitches seemed to have held.

Leaving the two unconscious men behind him, he ran back past his room and over to the main stairs. He heard the swing doors crash against the wall as the others came after him. At least he'd halved the opposition, even if it was going to be more difficult from now on. The remaining two men knew he was dangerous; they wouldn't let themselves be surprised again. Alex considered disappearing. There were dozens of places he could hide. But that wasn't the point. He forced himself to slow down. He had to lead them away from rooms eight and nine.

They saw him. He heard one of them swear – a single, taut whisper of pure hatred. That was good. The angrier they were, the more mistakes they would make. Alex ran down the stairs. He felt dizzy and for a moment he thought he was going to pass out. After spending so long in bed, his body wasn't ready for this. His left arm was hurting too.

The arm reminded him where he was going. The physio department was on the first floor. Alex had been there many times; it had been a necessary part of his treatment.

The bullet that had sliced through his artery had also done serious damage to his brachial plexus. This was a complicated network of spinal nerves leading into his left arm. The doctors had warned him that the arm would hurt; there would be stiffness and pins and needles – perhaps for the rest of his life. But once again Alex had youth on his side. After a few days of therapy, much of the pain had subsided. In that time, he had been put through a series of exercises – static resistance, stretching, reaction and speed work. By the end of the week, Alex had got to know the physio department better than any other department in the hospital. That was why he was heading there now.

He half stumbled through the doors and stood for a moment, catching his breath. On his left, there were two cubicles with beds where patients would lie while they were put through a series of exercises. A human skeleton – very realistic but in fact made of plastic – hung on a metal frame opposite. The corridor dog-legged, then continued past a series of doors and cupboards to another pair of swing doors at the far end. Alex knew exactly what he would find in the cupboards. One of the rooms leading off the corridor was a fully equipped gym with cycling machines, dumb-bells, heavy medicine balls and treadmills.

The cupboards contained more equipment, including chest expanders and rolls of elastic. Each day, the physiotherapist had cut off a length of elastic and given it to Alex to use in simple stretching exercises. These had been gentle at first but had become more strenuous, using thicker lengths of elastic, as he healed.

He opened the first cupboard. He had worked out what he was going to do. The question was the same as before. Had he left himself enough time?

Forty seconds later, the doors opened and Combat Jacket came in. He was breathing heavily. He was meant to be in command of this operation, and it had all gone horribly wrong. Two of his men were lying unconscious upstairs – one of them electrocuted. And what made it worse – what made it unbelievable – was that both had been taken out by a kid! They had been told it would be simple. Maybe that was why they had made so many mistakes. Well, he wasn't going to make any more.

He crept forward slowly, his fist curled around an ugly, square-nosed handgun. It was an FP9, a single-action pistol manufactured in Hungary, one of dozens coming in illegally from Eastern Europe. There were no lights on in this part of the hospital. The only illumination came from the moonlight streaming in through the windows. He looked to one side and saw the skeleton standing there like something out of a cheap fairground ride. The hollow eye sockets seemed to be staring at him. Warning him? The man looked away in disgust. He wasn't going to let it give him the creeps.

He glanced into the two cubicles. The curtains were drawn back and it was obvious the boy wasn't hiding there. Combat Jacket went past the skeleton and turned the corner. Now he found himself looking down the full length of the corridor. It was very dark but as his eyes adjusted, he made out a shape standing at the far end. He smiled. It was the boy! He seemed to be holding something against his chest. What was it? Some sort of ball. Well, this time he'd made a big mistake. He wasn't going to get a chance to throw it. If he so much as moved, Combat Jacket would shoot him in the leg and then drag him to the car.

"Drop it!" Combat Jacket commanded.

Alex Rider let go of the ball.

It was a medicine ball from the gym. It weighed five kilograms and for a second time, Alex had been afraid he would split his stitches. But what Combat Jacket hadn't seen was that Alex had also taken a length of elastic out of the cupboard. He had tied it across the corridor, from one door handle to another, and then stretched it all the way back with the medicine ball. The ball was now a missile in an oversized catapult, and when Alex released it, it shot the full length of the corridor as if fired from a cannon.

Combat Jacket was only faintly aware of the

great weight hurtling out of the shadows before it hit him square in the stomach, rocketing him off his feet. The gun flew out of his hand. The breath was punched out of his lungs. His shoulders hit the floor and he slid five metres before crashing into the wall. He just had time to tell himself that this wasn't Paul Drevin – that this was no ordinary fourteen-year-old boy – before he blacked out.

Steel Watch had just entered the physio department. He heard the crash and turned the corner in combat position, his own weapon ready to fire. He didn't understand what was happening, but he knew that he had lost the initiative. What should have been a simple snatch had gone horribly wrong. There was a figure sprawled on the floor in front of him, its neck twisted and face drained of colour. A large medicine ball lay near by.

Steel Watch blinked in disbelief. He saw one of the doors at the end of the corridor swing shut. That told him all he needed to know. He followed.

Twenty paces ahead of him, Alex was once more making his way downstairs. It seemed the only way to go. The stairs led him back to the ground floor, where it had all begun. The reception area was unnaturally silent apart from the soft hum of a refrigerated drinks dispenser. White light spilled over the rows of Coke and Fanta, throwing hard shadows across the floor. Three desks faced each other across the empty space. Alex knew there was a dead man behind one of them, but he couldn't bring himself to look. He could see the street on the other side of the glass doors. Should he make a break for it? Get outside and call for help? There was no time. He heard Steel Watch coming down the stairs and dived behind the nearest desk, searching for cover.

A moment later, Steel Watch arrived. Peering round from his hiding place, Alex could see the timepiece glinting on his wrist. It was a huge, chunky thing, the sort divers wear. The man had an unusually thick wrist. His entire body was overdeveloped, the various muscle groups almost fighting each other as he walked. Although he was the last survivor, he wasn't panicking. He was carrying a second FP9. He seemed to sense that Alex was near.

"I'm not going to hurt you!" he called out. He didn't sound convincing and must have known it, because a second later he snapped, "Come out with your hands up or I'll put a bullet in your knee."

Alex timed his move exactly, racing across the main reception. Something coughed twice and the carpet ripped itself apart in front of his feet. That was when he knew the rules had changed. Steel Watch had decided to take him dead or alive. And it looked like he'd prefer dead. But Alex was already out of sight. He had found another corridor with a sign reading RADIOLOGY – and he knew exactly where he was going. He had come here twice at the start of his stay in the hospital.

There was a locked door ahead of him – but Alex had watched the code being entered only a few days before. As fast as he could, he pressed the four-digit number, willing himself not to make a mistake. He pushed and the door opened. This part of the hospital was deserted at night but he knew the machines on the other side never slept. They were kept activated around the clock in case they were needed. And they had never been needed more than now.

Alex could hear Steel Watch coming up behind him, but he forced himself to stay calm. There was another lock to deal with, this one tripped by a switch concealed under one of the nurses' desks. Alex breathed a silent prayer of thanks to the hospital orderly who had made a joke about it as he had wheeled him in. There was a large, heavy door ahead of him. It was covered with warning signs beneath a single word:

MAGNETOM

Alex knew what the warnings said. The orderly had told him. He opened the door and went in.

There was a narrow, padded bench in front of him. It led to a large machine that reminded him of a tumble drier, a space capsule and a giant doughnut all rolled into one. There was a hole in the middle of it, the inner rim rotating slowly. The bench was designed so that it could be raised and passed slowly through the hole. Alex had been placed on the bench when he first came to St Dominic's, and the doctor had told him exactly what it did.

It was an MRI machine. The letters stood for magnetic resonance imaging. As Alex had passed through the hole, a scanner had taken a three-dimensional image of his body, checking the muscle damage in his chest, arm and shoulder. He remembered what the doctor had told him. He needed that knowledge now.

There was a movement at the door. Steel Watch had followed him in.

"Don't move," Steel Watch ordered. He was holding his gun at chest height. The silencer was pointing at Alex's head.

Alex let his shoulders slump. "Looks like I went the wrong way," he said.

"Well, now you're coming with me, you little toe-rag," the man replied. He ran his tongue over his lip. "The others ... maybe they didn't want to hurt you. But if you try anything, I'll put a bullet in you."

"I can't move."

"What?"

"I'm hurt..."

Steel Watch stared at Alex, trying to see what was wrong. He took a step forward. And that was when it happened.

The gun was torn out of his grip.

It was gone so fast that he didn't understand what was happening. It was as if a pair of invisible hands had simply ripped his weapon away. It was whisked into the darkness, nothing more than a blur. Steel Watch cried out in pain. The gun had dislocated two of his fingers, almost tearing them right off. There was a loud clang as it hit the machine and stayed there, as if glued to the surface.

An MRI uses an incredibly powerful magnetic field to scan soft tissue. The strength of this machine was 1.5 Tesla and the notices on the door had warned anyone approaching the room to remove all items made of metal. An MRI can pull a set of keys out of a pocket; it can wipe a credit card clean at twenty paces. Steel Watch had felt its enormous power but he still hadn't understood. He was about to find out.

Alex Rider had adopted the karate stance known as *zenkutsu dachi*, feet apart and hands raised. Every fibre of his being was concentrated on the man in front of him. It was a challenge to Steel Watch to take him on with his own bare hands, and Steel Watch couldn't resist. He took a step forward.

And screamed as his heavy steel watch entered the magnetic field. Alex watched in astonishment as what is known as the missile effect took place. The man was lifted off his feet and hurled through the air, dragged by the watch on his wrist. There was a horrible thud as he crashed into the MRI machine. He had landed awkwardly, his arm and head tangled together. He stayed where he was, half standing, half lying, his legs trailing uselessly behind him.

It was over. Four men had entered the hospital and every one of them was either unconscious or worse. Alex was still half convinced that any second he would wake up in bed. Maybe he had been given too many painkillers. Surely the whole thing was just some sort of ghastly medicated dream.

But it wasn't. Alex went back to reception and there was Conor, sprawled behind his desk, a single bullet wound in his head. Alex knew he had to call the police. He was amazed that he hadn't seen one single nurse during the entire ordeal. He leant over the desk, reaching for the phone. A cool night breeze brushed across his neck.

That should have warned him.

Four men had come into the hospital but five had been assigned to the job. There was another man: the driver. And if the main doors hadn't just opened, there wouldn't have been a breeze.

Too late Alex realized what that meant. He straightened up as fast as he could, but that wasn't fast enough. He heard nothing. He didn't even feel the blow to the back of his head.

He crumpled to the floor and lay still.

KASPAR

You're in pain. That's all you know. Your head is pounding and your heart is throbbing and you wonder if someone has managed to tie a knot in your neck.

It was a feeling that Alex Rider knew all too well. He had been knocked out by Mr Grin when he was at the Stormbreaker assembly plant, by the vicious Mrs Stellenbosch at the Academy of Point Blanc, and by Nile at the Widow's Palace in Venice. Even Alan Blunt had got one of his men to fire a tranquillizer dart into him when he had first infiltrated the headquarters of MI6.

And it was no different this time, the slow climb back from nothing to the world of air and light. Alex became aware that he was lying down, his cheek pressed against the dusty wooden floor. There was an unpleasant taste in his mouth. With an effort he opened his eyes and then closed them

again as the light from a naked bulb dangling overhead burned into them. He waited, then opened
them a second time. Slowly he straightened his
legs and stretched his arms and thought exactly
what he thought every time it happened.

You're still alive. You're a prisoner. But for some
reason they haven't killed you yet.

Alex dragged himself into a sitting position and
looked around him. He was in a room that was completely bare: no carpet, no curtains, no furniture,
no decoration. Nothing. There was a wooden door,
presumably locked, and a single window. He was
surprised to see that it wasn't barred, but when he
staggered over to it, he understood why.

He was high up, seven or eight storeys. Dawn was
only just breaking and it was hard to see through the
dirty glass, but he guessed he'd been unconscious for
a few hours and that he was still in London. It looked
like he was being held in an abandoned tower block.
There was another block opposite and, looking up,
Alex could just see a huge banner strung between
two wires running from the top of one building to
the other. The first words were outside his field of
vision but he could make out the rest:

TOWERS SOON TO BE AN EXCITING NEW DEVELOPMENT FOR EAST LONDON.

He went over to the door and tried it just in case.
It didn't move.

His left arm was aching badly and he massaged it, wondering how much damage he had done to himself. This was meant to be his last night in the hospital! How could he have allowed himself to get involved with a gang of murderers who had broken in...?

What for?

Alex rested his shoulders against a wall and slid back down to the floor, cradling his arm. He was still barefooted and he shivered. His single shirt wasn't enough to protect him against the chill of the early morning. Sitting there, he played back the events that had brought him here.

Four men had come to St Dominic's, but they hadn't been interested in him. They had asked for the boy in the room next door: Paul Drevin. Suddenly Alex remembered where he had heard the name. He'd seen it in the newspapers – but not Paul. Nikolei. That was it. Nikolei Drevin was some sort of Russian multibillionaire. Well, that made sense. The men must have wanted his son for the most obvious reason. Money. But they had accidentally kidnapped him instead.

What would they do when they found out? Alex tried to put the thought out of his mind. He had seen how they'd dealt with Conor, the night receptionist. Somehow he didn't think they'd apologize and offer him the taxi fare home.

But there was nothing he could do. He sat where he was, slumped against the wall, watching the sky turn from grey to red to a dull sort of blue.

He must have dozed off, because the next thing he knew, the door had opened and Spectacles was standing over him, an expression of pure hatred on his face. Alex wasn't surprised. The last time they'd met, Alex had slammed a ten-kilogram oxygen tank into his groin. If there was any surprise, it was that just a few hours later the man had found the strength to stand.

Spectacles was holding a gun. Alex looked into the man's eyes. They glinted orange behind the tinted glass and gazed at him with undisguised venom. "Get up!" he snapped. "You're to come with me."

"Whatever you say." Alex got slowly to his feet. "Is it my imagination," he asked, "or is your voice a little higher than it used to be?"

The hand with the gun twitched. "This way," Spectacles muttered.

Alex followed him out into a corridor that was as dilapidated as the room where he had been confined. The walls were damp and peeling. Many of the ceiling tiles were missing, revealing great gaps filled with a tangle of wires and pipes. There were doors every ten or fifteen metres, some of them hanging off their hinges. Once, they would have opened into people's flats. But it was obvious that – apart from rats and cockroaches – nobody had lived here for years.

Combat Jacket was waiting for them outside.

He had recovered from his encounter with the medicine ball but there was an ugly bruise on the side of his head where he had hit the wall. The two of them marched Alex down the corridor to a door at the end.

"In!" Spectacles said.

Alex pushed open the door and went through.

He found himself in a large, open space with litter strewn across the floor and graffiti everywhere. There were windows on two sides, some of them covered by broken blinds. Alex guessed he was inside one of the flats, although the partition walls had been smashed through to make a single area. He could see an abandoned bath in one corner. In the middle, there was a table and two chairs. A man was sitting there, waiting for him. Spectacles prodded his gun into Alex's back. Alex stepped forward and sat down.

With a shiver, he examined the man sitting opposite him. He was dressed in what might once have been a uniform but the jacket was torn and missing buttons. The man must have been about thirty years old but it was impossible to be sure. His face and head had been tattooed all over. Alex saw the United States of America reaching down one cheek, Europe on the other. His nose and the skin above his lips were blue, the colour of the Atlantic Ocean. Brazil and West Africa touched the corners of his mouth. If the man turned round, Alex knew he would see Russia and China. He had never seen anything quite so strange – or so revolting – in his life.

With difficulty, Alex tore his eyes away and looked around. Combat Jacket and Spectacles were standing on either side of the doorway. Silver Tooth was lurking in a corner. Alex hadn't noticed him in the shadows, but now he stepped into the light and Alex saw that his neck was swollen, two angry red marks burned into the skin. There was no sign of Steel Watch. Perhaps they'd been unable to peel him off the Magnetom.

The man with the tattoos spoke. "You have caused us a great deal of annoyance," he said. "In truth, you should be dead."

Alex was silent. He wasn't sure yet what to say.

"My name is Kaspar," the man continued.

Alex shrugged but said nothing.

The man continued to examine him. "Why were you out of your room last night?"

"I needed some air."

"It would have been better if you had simply opened the window," Kaspar said. When he spoke, whole continents moved. It occurred to Alex that if he sneezed it would set off a global earthquake. "Do you know who I am?" he asked.

"No," Alex replied. "But it would be useful to have you around in a geography exam."

"I wouldn't have thought you were in any position to make jokes." Kaspar's voice was flat and unemotional. He gestured at the other men. "You have caused my colleagues a great deal of pain and inconvenience. They would like me to kill you. Perhaps I will."

"What do you want me for?" Alex demanded.

"I will tell you." Kaspar ran a finger down the side of his face. It travelled from Norway to Algeria. "I can see that you are surprised by my appearance. You may think it extreme. But these markings represent who I am and what I believe in. We are all part of this world. I have made the world part of me."

He paused.

"I am what you might call a freedom fighter. But the freedom I believe in is a planet free of the exploitation and pollution caused by rich businessmen and multinationals who would destroy all life simply to enrich themselves. We have global warming. The ozone layer has been decimated. Our precious resources are fast running out. But still these fat cats continue lining their pockets today with no thought or care for tomorrow. Your father is such a man."

"My father? You've got it all wrong—"

The man moved incredibly quickly. He stood up and lashed out, hitting the side of Alex's head with the back of his hand. Alex snapped back, more startled than hurt. "Don't interrupt!" Kaspar commanded. "Your father made his fortune from oil. His pipelines have scarred three continents. And now, not content with damaging the earth, he is turning his attention to outer space. Four species of wild birds have been made extinct by the launch of his rockets from the Caribbean. Apes and chimpanzees have been the unwilling victims of his test flights. He is an enemy of mankind and has therefore become a legitimate target of Force Three."

Kaspar sat down again.

"There are those who think of us as criminals," he went on. "But it is your father who is the real criminal, and he has forced us to act the way we do. Now we have decided to make him pay. He will give us one million pounds for your safe return. This money will be used to continue our struggle to protect the planet. If he refuses, he will never see you again.

"That is why you were taken from St Dominic's last night. You will remain with us until the ransom has been paid. I do not personally wish to harm you, Paul, but we have to prove to your father that we have you. We must send him a message that he cannot ignore. And I'm afraid that will demand a small sacrifice from you."

Alex tried to speak but his head was reeling. It was all happening too fast. Before he could react, his right arm was seized from behind. Combat Jacket had crept up on him while Kaspar had been talking. Alex tried to resist, but the man was too strong. The cuff of his shirt was ripped open and the sleeve pulled back. Then his hand was forced down on the table and his fingers spread out one by one. There was nothing he could do. Combat

Jacket was holding him so tightly, his fingers were turning white. Silver Tooth approached from the other side. He had taken out his knife. He handed it to Kaspar.

"We could send your father a photograph," Kaspar explained. "But what would that achieve? He will know by now that you have been taken by force. There are stronger ways of making our demands known, ways that he may find more persuasive." He lifted the knife close to his chin, as if about to shave. The blade was fifteen centimetres long with a serrated edge. He examined his reflection in the steel. "We could send him a lock of your hair. He would, I'm sure, recognize it as yours. But then, he might take it as a sign of weakness – of compassion – on our part.

"And so I apologize, Paul Drevin. It gives me no pleasure to hurt a child, even a wealthy, spoilt child such as yourself. But what I intend to send your father is a finger from your right hand..."

Automatically Alex tried to pull back. But Combat Jacket had been expecting it. His full weight pressed down on Alex's hand. His fingers were splayed, helpless, on the table.

"The pain will be great. But there are children all over the world who have only ever known pain and starvation, while boys like you languish in the playground of the rich. Do you play the piano, Paul? I hope not. It will not be so easy after today."

He reached out and grabbed Alex's little finger.

That was the one he had chosen. The knife began its journey down.

"I'm not Paul Drevin!" Alex spat out the words urgently. His eyes had widened. He could feel the blood draining from his face. The knife was still moving. "You've made a mistake!" he insisted. "My name is Alex Rider. I was in room nine. I don't know anything about Paul Drevin."

The knife stopped. It was millimetres above his little finger.

"Do it!" Combat Jacket hissed.

"I was awake last night," Alex insisted. The words came tumbling out. "I was coming back from the toilet. I saw your men outside my room. One of them pulled out a gun, and then they began chasing me. I didn't know what was happening. I had to defend myself..."

"He's lying," Combat Jacket snarled. "I asked him his name." He turned to Spectacles. "Tell him."

"That's right," Spectacles agreed. "We saw his room. Room eight. It was empty. Then he appeared. We called out his name and he answered."

Kaspar tightened his grip on the knife. He had made up his mind.

"I was in room nine, not room eight!" Alex was shouting now. His head was swimming. He could already see the knife cutting through flesh and bone. He could imagine the pain. Then suddenly he had a thought. "What do you think I was in hospital for?" he demanded.

"We *know* what you were there for," Kaspar replied. "Appendicitis."

"Appendicitis. Right. Then look at my bandages. They're nowhere near my appendix."

There was a long pause. Alex could feel Combat Jacket still pressing down hard, longing for the cutting to begin. But Kaspar was uncertain. "Open his shirt," he ordered.

Nobody moved.

"Do it!"

Combat Jacket was still holding Alex as tightly as ever but now Silver Tooth stepped forward. He reached out and grabbed hold of Alex's shirt, tearing the top two buttons. Kaspar stared at the bandages crossing over his chest. Alex could feel his heart straining beneath them.

"What is this?" Kaspar demanded.

"I had a chest wound."

"What sort of chest wound?"

"An accident on my bike." It was the one lie Alex had told. He couldn't tell them what had really happened. He didn't want them to know who he was. "I met Paul Drevin," he admitted. "He's the same age as me. But he doesn't look anything like me. Just make a phone call. You can find out easily enough." He took a deep breath. "You can cut off all my fingers if you want, but his father isn't going to pay you a penny. He doesn't even know I exist!"

There was another silence.

"He's lying!" Combat Jacket insisted.

But Kaspar was already working it out for himself. He had heard Alex speak. Paul Drevin had a faint Russian accent. This boy had obviously lived in England all his life. Kaspar swore and stabbed down with the knife. The blade buried itself in the table less than a centimetre from Alex's hand. The hilt quivered as he released it.

Alex saw the disappointment in the faces of Spectacles and Silver Tooth. But Kaspar had made his decision.

"Let go of him."

Combat Jacket held him tightly for a moment longer, then released his arm and stood back, muttering something ugly under his breath. Alex snatched back his hand. His right arm was hurting as much as his left one. He wondered if Kaspar would send him back to the hospital. By the time he got out of here, he would need it.

But it wasn't over yet.

Spectacles and Silver Tooth were waiting to escort him out, but Kaspar gestured for them to wait. He was examining Alex a second time, reassessing him. It was impossible to see behind the markings on his face, to know what was going on in his mind. "If it turns out that you are who you say you are," he began, "if you really are not Paul Drevin, then you are of no use to us. We can kill you in any way that we please. And I think it will please my men to kill you very slowly indeed.

So perhaps, my friend, it would have been better for you if there had been no mistake. Perhaps the loss of one finger might have been the easier way."

Silver Tooth was grinning. Spectacles nodded gravely.

"Take him back to his room," Kaspar commanded. "I will make the necessary enquiries. And then we'll meet again."

FIRE ESCAPE

It was late afternoon when the door opened and Combat Jacket came in. Alex guessed that he had been in the room for eight hours. He had been allowed out once to use a chemical toilet, and at around midday he had been given a sandwich and a drink by an unsmiling Spectacles. The sandwich had been two days past its sell-by date and still in the plastic wrapping, bought from a garage. But Alex wolfed it down hungrily.

Combat Jacket had been sent to fetch him. He led Alex back down the corridor to the flat where the interrogation had taken place, his face with its ugly, broken nose giving nothing away. There was something about the whole set-up that Alex didn't understand. Kaspar had told him they were freedom fighters – eco-warriors or whatever. They were certainly fanatics. The tattoos were ample proof of that. But the way they were treating him, the threats, the demands for money, seemed to belong to a different world. They talked about pollution and the ozone layer; but they acted like thugs and common criminals. They had killed the night receptionist for no good reason. They seemed to have no regard at all for human life.

By now, Alex guessed, they must know the truth. So what were they going to do with him? He remembered what Kaspar had said and clamped down on his imagination. Instead, he searched for a way to break out of here. It wasn't going to be easy. The four men had already tested him once. They knew what he was capable of. They weren't going to give him a second chance.

Kaspar was waiting for him. There was a newspaper on the table in front of him but no sign of the knife. Spectacles and Silver Tooth were standing behind him. As Alex sat down, Kaspar turned the newspaper round. It was the *Evening Standard* and the front-page headline told the whole story in just three words.

Wrong boy kidnapped

Nobody was talking, so Alex quickly read the article. There was a photograph of St Dominic's Hospital but no picture of him or Paul Drevin. That didn't surprise him. He remembered reading somewhere that Paul's father – Nikolei Drevin – had managed to get an embargo on any photos of his family being published, claiming it was too much of a security risk. And, of course, MI6 would have prevented any picture of Alex being used. He didn't even get a mention by name.

A security guard was murdered in the small hours of the morning during a ruthless attack on a north London hospital. It seems almost certain that the intended target of the gang was fourteen-year-old Paul Drevin, son of one of the world's richest men, Russian businessman Nikolei Drevin. Drevin made the headlines earlier this year when he bought Stratford East Football Club. He is also the guiding light behind the hundred billion pound Ark Angel project – the first hotel in space.

In an astonishing development, police have confirmed that the gang managed to kidnap the wrong boy. This other boy, who has not been named, was discovered to be missing from his room following major surgery. Speaking from the hospital, Dr Roger Hayward made an urgent plea for the boy's fast return. His condition is said to be stable but serious.

Alex looked up. Kaspar seemed to be waiting for him to speak. "I told you," he said. "So why don't you let me go? I've got nothing to do with this. I was just next door."

"You got involved on purpose," Kaspar said.

"No." Alex denied it but his mouth was dry.

"You switched room numbers. You answered to the name of Paul Drevin. You crippled one of my men and injured the others."

Alex said nothing, waiting for the axe to fall.

"I don't understand why you chose to become involved," Kaspar went on. "I don't know who you are. But you made your decision. You chose to become an enemy of Force Three and so you must pay."

"I didn't choose anything."

"I'm not going to argue with you. I am fighting a war and in any war there are casualties – innocent victims who just happen to get in the way. If it makes it any easier, think of yourself as one of them." Kaspar sighed but there was no sadness in the map of his face. "Goodbye, Alex Rider. It was a pity that we had to meet. It has cost me a million pounds in ransom money. It will cost you rather more..."

Before Alex could react, he was grabbed from behind and dragged to his feet. He didn't speak as he was forced back out of the room and down the corridor. This time he was thrown into another room, smaller than his previous cell. Alex just had time to make out a chair, a barred window and four bare walls before he was shoved hard in the back and sent sprawling to the floor.

Combat Jacket stood over him. "I wish he'd let me have a little time with you," he rasped. "If I had my way, we'd do this differently—"

"Move it!" The voice came from outside. One of the other men was waiting.

Combat Jacket spat at Alex and walked out. The door closed and almost at once Alex heard the unmistakable sound of hammering. He shook his head in disbelief. They weren't just locking him in. They were nailing the door to the frame.

Once again, he examined his surroundings. He wondered why they had chosen this particular room. The bars on the window made no real difference. Even if the window had been wide open, he was at least seven storeys up. He wouldn't have been able to climb out. And what exactly were they proposing to do? They obviously weren't planning to come back and get him. Were they simply going to leave him here to starve to death?

The answer came about an hour later. The sun was beginning to set and lights were coming on in buildings all over east London. Alex was becoming increasingly anxious. He was on his own, high up in a derelict tower block. He had a feeling that Kaspar and the others had gone; he could hear nothing at all on the other side of the door. The silence was unnerving. He knew that MI6 would be doing everything they could, searching the city for him, but what hope did they have of finding him here? He couldn't open the window. The room was empty. There was no way he could attract anyone's attention. For once he really did seem to be completely helpless.

And then he smelled it. Seeping through the floorboards, coming from somewhere deep in the heart of the building.

Burning.

They had set fire to the tower block. Alex knew it even before he saw the first grey wisps of smoke creeping under the door. They had doused the place with petrol, set it alight and left him nailed inside what would soon be the world's biggest funeral pyre. For a moment he felt panic – black and irresistible – as it engulfed him. More smoke was curling under the door. Alex sprang to his feet and backed over to the window, wondering if there was some way he could knock out the glass. But that wouldn't help him. He forced himself to slow down, to think. He wasn't going to let them kill him. Only eleven days ago, a paid assassin had fired a .22 calibre bullet at his heart. But he was still alive. He wasn't easy to kill.

There were just two ways out of the room: the door and the window. Both of those were obviously hopeless. But what about the walls? They were made of hardboard and plaster. In the flat where he had been interrogated, they had been knocked through. Maybe he could do the same here. Experimentally he ran his hands over them, pushing and probing, searching for any weak spots. His throat was sore and his eyes were beginning to water. More and more smoke was pouring in. He stood back, then lashed out in a karate kick, his foot smashing into the centre of the wall. Pain shot up his leg and through his body. The wall didn't even crack.

That just left the ceiling. Alex remembered the corridor outside. It had been missing some of its ceiling tiles and he had seen a gap underneath the pipes and wires that ran above. The ceiling in this room was covered with the same tiles.

And they had left him a chair.

He dragged it over to the corner nearest the door and stood on it. The floor had almost disappeared beneath a swirling carpet of smoke. It seemed to be reaching up as if it wanted to grab hold and devour him. Alex checked his balance, then punched upwards with the heel of his hand. The tiles were made of some sort of fibreboard and broke easily. He punched again, then tore at the edges of the hole he had made. Dirt and debris showered down, almost blinding him. But when he next looked up he saw that there was a space above him. If he could reach, he could haul himself up, over the door and jump down the other side.

He ripped out more tiles until the hole was wide enough to squeeze through. He could hear something a few floors below him – a faint crackling. The sound made his skin crawl. It meant that the fire was getting close. He forced himself to concentrate on what he was doing. The chair was wobbling underneath him. If he fell and twisted an ankle, he was finished.

At last he was ready. He tensed himself, then jumped. He felt the chair topple and crash to the floor – but he had done it! His hands had caught hold of an old water pipe and now he was dangling just below the ceiling, his arms disappearing into the space above. Once again he was all too aware of the stitches in his chest and wondered briefly if they would hold. God! The physio people had told him he ought to keep up his stretching exercises, but he doubted they'd had this in mind.

Gritting his teeth, Alex summoned all his strength to pull himself up into the cavity. His face passed through a cobweb and he grimaced as the fine strands laced themselves over his nose and mouth. His stomach touched the edge of the hole. He was half in and half out of the room. The crawl space was in front of him. The wall with the door was underneath him. Dozens of wires and insulated pipes ran inches above his head, stretching into the distance. Dust stung his eyes. What now?

Alex dragged himself along the pipe, bringing his feet up into the ceiling recess. He kicked down with his heels. More ceiling tiles fell loose and he saw the corridor below. There was a drop of about four metres. Awkwardly he swung himself forward, then let his legs and torso hang. Finally he let go. He dropped down, landing in a crouch. He was in the corridor, on the other side of the locked door. With a sigh of relief, he straightened up. He was out of the room but he was at least seven floors up in an abandoned building that had been set on fire. He wasn't safe yet.

The crackling of the flames was louder out in the corridor. The block of flats had seemed damp and musty to Alex but it was going up like a torch. He could feel the heat in the air. The end of the corridor – where he had been interrogated – was already shimmering in the heat haze. Where was the fire brigade? Surely someone must have seen what was happening. Alex noticed a fire alarm set in the wall, but the glass was already broken and the alarm button was missing. He would have to get out of here on his own.

Which way? He only had two choices – left or right – and he decided to head away from the interrogation room. He hadn't seen a staircase when he had been taken there to meet Kaspar, but there might be one in the other direction. Smoke trickled up through the floorboards. It hung eerily in the doorways. Soon it would be impossible to see. Very soon it would be impossible to breathe.

He sprinted past the first room where he had been held and continued down the corridor, passing a set of lift doors. He didn't even think about trying the lift. Nothing in the building worked and the doors were welded shut. But next to the lift he found what he was looking for: a staircase leading up and down. The steps were made of concrete, zigzagging round behind the lift shaft. He rested his hand briefly on the metal stair rail.

It was hot. The fire was near.

But he had no choice. He began to run down, his bare feet slapping against the cement. He would just have to hope he didn't come across any broken glass. There were twenty-five steps between each floor; he counted them without meaning to. He turned a corner and saw a door leading into a smoke-filled corridor. Definitely no way out there.

The further down he went, the worse it got. Twenty-five more steps and he came to another door. The corridor on the other side was well alight. There were brilliant red and orange flames, tearing into the walls, leaping up through the floor, devouring everything in their path. Alex was shocked by their speed and elemental strength. He had to put up a hand to protect himself, to stop his cheeks from burning.

He continued down. Force Three had started the blaze on the ground floor, allowing the air to carry the flames upwards. As Alex reached the third floor and began the next flight of steps down, he could barely breathe. The smoke was smothering him. He wished he'd thought to soak his shirt in water, to cover his eyes and mouth. But where would he have found water in the building anyway? Another twenty-five steps. Then another. Alex was choking. He could feel the sweat dripping down his sides. It was like being inside a giant oven. How much further?

He saw daylight. A door leading out onto the street.

And that was when Combat Jacket appeared, a nightmare creature, stepping out of nowhere as if in slow motion, his gun raised in front of him. Alex saw the muzzle flash and threw himself backwards as a bullet shot past centimetres above him. He landed awkwardly on the stairs and he was already rolling as a second bullet spat into the concrete, sending fragments of cement flying into the side of his face. Somehow he scrambled to his feet and began to climb up again. Combat Jacket fired twice more but for a brief moment, the smoke was on Alex's side, and the bullets missed. Alex turned a corner. He didn't stop until he was back on the first floor.

He felt sick – a mixture of fury and despair. He'd almost made it. What was Combat Jacket doing there, waiting for him? Had he guessed that Alex might somehow manage to escape? It made no sense. But he couldn't think about it now. He was still trapped inside a burning building and he was rapidly running out of options. It was getting harder and harder to breathe. He looked along the corridor. It was a furnace. He couldn't go that way. He couldn't go down. That only left up.

Wearily, he started to climb. He made it to the second floor with just seconds to spare. As he continued up, there was a sudden rush of flames and a crash as part of the ceiling collapsed. Burning wood, metal and glass cascaded down. The fire had reached the stairs: now the way down was permanently blocked. He would have to try to make it to the roof. Perhaps he would be lucky. The police and fire brigade would be on the way. There might be helicopters.

Alex kept climbing. His hands were black; his face was streaked with tears. But he didn't stop. At the very worst, he would die in the open air. He wasn't going to let the fire finish him here.

He was no longer counting the steps. His legs were aching and the bandages around his chest had come loose. He ran past the eighth floor with a growing sense of despair. This was where he had begun. Forcing himself on, he continued to climb, past the ninth, the tenth ... eleventh ... twelfth... He was aware of the flames chasing him, filling the stairwell, licking at his heels. It was as if the fire knew he was there and was afraid of losing him. At last he came to a solid door with a metal push mechanism. He slammed his palms against it, terrified it would be locked. But the door swung open. The cool evening air rushed to greet him. The sun had set but the sky was a brilliant red, the same colour as the fire that would be with him all too soon.

Alex was close to exhaustion. He had barely eaten all day. He was meant to be in bed. He almost wanted to cry but instead he swore, once, shouting out the ugly word. Then he wiped a grimy sleeve across his face and looked around.

He was on the roof, fifteen storeys up. He could

see a water tank in front of him and a brick building that housed the cables for the lifts. Well, there were no working lifts and there was probably no water either, so neither of them would help. At some stage builders must have carried out some work up here. They had left a few lengths of scaffolding and plastic piping as well as a cement mixer and two steel buckets, both half filled with cement that had long ago dried and solidified. Alex ran to the edge of the roof, searching for a fire escape down. He could feel the tarmac against the soles of his feet. It was already hot. Soon it would begin to melt.

There was no fire escape. There was no way down. He could see the street far below. No cars. No pedestrians. He was in some sort of industrial district in east London. The whole area looked like it was cordoned off, waiting for the money that would make redevelopment possible. The building opposite was identical to this one, similarly condemned. It stood less than fifty metres away, connected by the banner that Alex had seen when he woke up.

HORNCHURCH TOWERS SOON TO BE AN EXCITING NEW DEVELOPMENT FOR EAST LONDON.

If he had come here in a year's time, he might have found himself standing on the balcony of a fabulous penthouse flat. Alex took in the view. He could see the River Thames in front of him. The O2 arena sat on a spur of land with the water bending round it.

A plane dipped out of the sky, making for City Airport, which he could see over his shoulder. Alex raised his arm, waving for attention, but he knew at once that it was no good. The plane was too high up. It was already too dark. And the smoke was too thick.

He hurried back to the door. He would have to head down again and hope that the upper corridors were still passable. Maybe he could try the other side of the building. He pulled the door open carefully. It seemed impossible that Combat Jacket would have followed him all the way up, but he wasn't taking any chances. But as the door swung wide, he realized that Combat Jacket was the least of his problems.

A fist of flame punched at him. The stairs had become an inferno.

At the same moment, there was an explosion and Alex was hurled backwards by a thousand fragments of burning, splintered wood which had been blasted up from below. He landed painfully on his back, and when he next looked up he saw that the door itself was now on fire. It was the only way off the roof.

He was trapped.

Alex stood up. The tarmac was definitely getting hotter. He could no longer stay too long on one foot. Black smoke was pouring out of the stairwell, billowing into the sky. Now he heard the sound he had been hoping for – the wail of sirens. But he knew that by the time they got to him, it would be too late. There was another explosion below him. The windows were beginning to shatter, unable to take the heat. No way down. What could he do?

The banner.

It was twenty metres long, about a hundred metres above the ground, a lifeline between this building and the next. The advertisement for Hornchurch Towers was suspended between two steel cables; the top cable was level with the roof, bolted into the brickwork. Alex ran over to it. Could he stand on the lower cable and hold onto the higher one? It would be like a swing bridge in the jungle. He could slowly inch his way across to the other side and safety.

But the cables were too far apart – and the material was flapping in the wind. It would knock him off before he was even halfway.

Could he somehow crawl across on his hands and knees?

No. The cable was about two centimetres thick. It wasn't wide enough to support him. He would lose his balance and fall. That was certain.

So how?

The answer came to him in an instant. Everything he needed was there in front of him. But it only worked when he put it all together. Could he do it?

Another window shattered. Behind him, the exit had disappeared in a whirlwind of flames and smoke. He was standing on a giant hot plate and it was becoming more unbearable with every passing second. Alex could see the fire engines, the size of toys, speeding along about half a mile away. He had to try. There was no other way.

He snatched up one of the lengths of plastic piping, weighing it in his hands. It was about six metres long and light enough for him to carry without feeling any strain. He had to make it heavier. Moving more quickly, he examined the steel buckets. They were half full of hardened cement, and weighed about the same. Somehow he had to attach them to the piping. But there was no rope. He choked and wiped sweat and tears from his eyes. What could he use? Then he looked down and saw the bandages flapping around his chest. He grabbed an end and began to tear them off.

Sixty seconds later he was ready.

It was Ian Rider he had to thank, of course. A visit to a circus in Vienna six years ago when Alex was only eight. It had been his birthday. And he still remembered his favourite act. The tightrope walkers.

"Funambulism," Ian Rider said.

"What's that?"

"It's Latin, Alex. Funis *means rope. And* ambulare *is to walk. Funambulism is the art of tightrope walking."*

"Is it difficult?"

"Well, it's a lot easier than it looks. Not many

people realize it, but there's a trick involved..."

Alex lifted the plastic pole, the middle pressed against his chest, about three metres stretching out each side. There was a heavy steel bucket attached to each end, tied in place with a torn bandage. Every second he waited he could feel the heat increasing. His soles were already blistering and he knew he couldn't wait any more. He walked to the edge of the roof. The metal cable running above the advertisement stretched out into the distance. Suddenly the other tower block seemed a very long way away. He tried not to look down. He knew that would make it impossible for him even to begin.

This was how it was meant to work. This was what Ian Rider had explained.

The wire acts as an axis. If you try to walk across the wire, you will fall the moment that your centre of mass is not directly above it. One wobble and gravity will do the rest.

But a long pole increases what is called the rotational inertia of the tightrope artist. It makes it more difficult to fall. And if you add enough weight to each end, you will actually shift your centre of gravity *below* the wire. This was what Alex had done with the two buckets. Provided he didn't drop the pole, he would find it almost impossible to lose his balance. He had seen toys that worked on the same principle. It should be easy.

At least, that was the theory.

Alex took a step. He had one foot on the very edge of the brickwork and one foot on the metal cable. All he had to do was lean forward, transferring his weight from one foot to the other, and he would be walking the tightrope. If the laws of physics worked, he would make it across. If they didn't, he would die. It was as simple as that.

He took a deep breath and launched himself off the building.

He could feel the pole flexing as the buckets hung down, one on each side. For a terrifying moment the world seemed to lurch sideways and he was certain he was about to fall. But he forced himself not to panic. He clutched the pole more tightly against his chest and focused on the cable ahead of him. Briefly he closed his eyes, willing himself not to fight for balance, to let the laws of physics guide him.

And it worked. He wasn't falling. He could feel the cable cutting into his feet but miraculously he was stable. Now – how many steps to the other side? The flames were warming his back. It was time to move.

One step after another, he made his way across. He wanted to look down. Every nerve in his body was screaming at him to do just that, and his neck and spine were rigid with tension. But that was the one thing he must not do. He tried to imagine that he was back on the sports field at Brookland School. He had walked along the painted white lines often enough. This was exactly the same –

just a bit higher up.

He was about halfway across when things began to go wrong. And they went wrong spectacularly.

First, the police and fire engines arrived. Alex heard the screams of the sirens directly beneath him and, before he could stop himself, he looked down. It was a mistake. He was no longer walking across a sports field. He was standing on a wire, insanely far above the ground. He saw people in uniform pointing up at him and shouting; he could just about hear their voices. One of the fire trucks was extending its ladder towards him but he doubted it would reach him in time.

The whole world began to spin. He felt a rush of panic that seemed to dissolve every muscle in his body and left him so weak that he thought he would faint. At the same time, the wind rose and the banner began to flutter like the sail of a yacht, the cable swaying from side to side. Alex knew that only the weights on the ends of the pole were keeping him upright. He was paralysed. There was nothing he could do.

And that was when the rooftop exploded. The flames had finally broken free. A fireball burst through the tarmac. The police and firemen dived for cover as bricks and pieces of metal rained down. The whole tower block was close to collapse. Alex felt a vibration travel up through his body and realized with horror that the metal stanchion holding the top cable was about to come loose.

He couldn't wait for the firemen to reach him. He had perhaps seconds left.

The shock of the explosion broke his paralysis. Alex ran, pushing against the pole like a sprinter breaking through the finishing line. The buckets swung madly, held fast by the bandages. Another explosion, louder this time. He didn't dare look round.

The other building was getting nearer but it still wasn't near enough. His arms were aching, barely able to hold the heavy weight. The cable was cutting into his feet. He was being battered by the wind. He wasn't going to make it.

And then the cable snapped.

Alex heard a sound like a crack of a whip and knew that his lifeline had been severed. With a cry, he dropped the pole and threw himself forward, reaching out for the roof just a few metres away. The cable and the banner crumpled under his feet. His hands missed the edge of the building and he began to plunge down. But now he was tangled up with the banner; it was folding itself around him. Alex grabbed hold of the material and gasped as he crashed into the wall. His feet were dangling in space. The cable was unravelling beneath him. But it was still attached to the rooftop just a few metres above his head. Alex waited until he was sure nothing else was moving. Then, painfully, he began to pull himself up.

Two of the firemen had managed to reach the

roof. They were standing there, watching as the building opposite completed its spectacular collapse. They heard a noise and looked down. A boy had just crawled up over the edge, right by their feet. His shirt was in rags, and a few tattered bandages trailed from his chest. His face and hands were covered in soot. His hair was black with sweat.

"What the...?" They grabbed hold of him and pulled him to safety.

Alex sat down heavily. He gazed at the remains of the building where he had been held prisoner. There was very little of it left. Sparks leapt into the darkening sky.

"Nice night for a walk," he said, and passed out.

R & R

Jack Starbright made the best scrambled eggs in the world. The secret, she said, was to use only free-range eggs, mix them with unsalted butter and a little milk – and then get the whole thing over with as quickly as possible. She didn't enjoy cooking and only used recipes that could be prepared in less than ten minutes. This breakfast, for example, would go from fridge to table in exactly eight and a half.

She heaped the eggs onto two plates, added grilled bacon, tomatoes and toast, and carried them over to the kitchen table where Alex Rider was waiting. It was eleven o'clock in the morning and the two of them were back in the house in Chelsea where Alex had once lived with his uncle. Jack had first come there as a student, paying for her room by looking after Alex while Ian Rider was away. Gradually she had become a sort of housekeeper.

Now she was Alex's legal guardian and also his best friend.

Alex was wearing tracksuit trousers and a loose T-shirt; his hair was still wet from the shower. Two days had passed since his confrontation with Force Three and he was already looking a lot like his old self – although Jack noticed that he was still massaging his left arm. She put the plates down and poured two mugs of tea. Neither of them spoke.

Alex had been taken straight back to hospital after his dramatic escape. None of the firemen could believe what they had seen, and assumed they had been sent to rescue someone who had trained at the circus. Once again, MI6 had been forced to clamp down on the press reports. Photographs of Alex on the wire had appeared in newspapers all over the world, but he had been too far away to be recognized and his name was kept out of it. An ambulance had rushed him away before any journalists arrived, and by ten o'clock that night he was back in his old bed at St Dominic's. He fell asleep at once.

The next morning, he was woken by the nurse – Diana Meacher – coming into his room.

"How are you feeling?" she asked.

"Tired," Alex replied.

"Was that really you on the roof? I saw it on the news last night." She went over to the window and raised the blinds. "Everyone's talking about it – although we've all been told we're not allowed to." She came back to the bed and slipped a thermometer into his mouth. "And those men who broke in! We all know what you did and we think you're incredibly brave."

"'Ank you," Alex said with difficulty.

"I'd watch out, though, if I were you. Dr Hayward's hopping mad. He says he didn't spend hours operating on you just for you to get nearly killed a second time. He'll be here shortly." She removed the thermometer and examined it. "Your temperature's normal, though I'd say it's the only thing about you that is!"

Later that morning, Dr Hayward came in and he certainly seemed less than cheerful. He gave Alex a thorough check-up, starting with his blood pressure and pulse rate and moving on to examine his wound. He barely spoke a word as he did it.

"It's lucky that you keep yourself fit," he remarked at last. He looked and spoke like a long-suffering headmaster. "All those shenanigans could have caused you serious damage, but it looks as if your stitches have held and you're generally in one piece."

"When can I go home?"

"We'll just keep you here until the end of the day. I'm afraid the people you work for want to speak to you."

"I don't work for anyone," Alex said.

"Well ... you know who I mean. Anyway, there's always a chance your system will react against the beating you've given it. So I want you to stay in bed today and I'll come in and have another look at you after tea."

He stood up. "And one last thing, Alex. I'm going to prescribe you at least two weeks' rest and recuperation. I absolutely insist on it."

"Can I go back to school?"

"I'm afraid not. Just over a week ago you were having major surgery. I know you've made an amazing recovery but there are still all sorts of risks – infection and all the rest of it. Two weeks' holiday, Alex. And no arguments!"

Dr Hayward departed and Alex was left on his own. To kill some time, he went for a walk down the corridor, past room eight. It was empty. Nobody had mentioned Paul Drevin and it seemed that the other boy had gone.

There is nothing worse than being in hospital when you don't feel you need to be there, and by eleven o'clock Alex was in a bad mood. Jack rang and he told her not to come in; he would see her when she came to collect him. His next visitor arrived just before lunch. It wasn't the person he had expected.

He had realized that MI6 would want to know what had happened at Hornchurch Towers and that they would send someone to debrief him. He had expected Mrs Jones. But instead it was John

Crawley who arrived, dressed in a nasty blue blazer with a crest on the pocket, and holding a box of Roses chocolates. Crawley had once claimed to be a personnel manager, and Alex still wasn't quite sure what he did at MI6. He was in his late thirties with thinning hair and a rather worried-looking face. He looked like the sort of man who counted paperclips and kept his pencils in a special drawer.

He sat down by the bed. "Got you these," he said, handing over the chocolates.

"Thank you, Mr Crawley." Now that he was closer, Alex could see that the badge on the jacket belonged to Royal Tunbridge Wells Golf and Croquet Club.

"Mrs Jones apologized for not coming herself. She's in Berlin. She asked me to find out what's been going on. The police wanted to talk to you too, but I've had a word with them and they won't be bothering you. How are you feeling, by the way? We were all very shocked by what happened. I had a run-in with Scorpia about ten years ago and it nearly did for me. Anyway, let's get back to Force Three. What exactly happened?"

Crawley took out a miniature recording device and laid it on the bed. Quickly, Alex took him through the events, starting with the moment the four men had walked into the hospital. It occurred to him that Crawley had let slip a little clue about his past. He too had fought against Scorpia. Had he once been a field agent himself? Alex described the fight in the hospital, his meeting with Kaspar in the derelict flat, the ransom demand and his escape from the fire. Crawley blinked several times as Alex spoke but didn't interrupt.

"Well, that's quite an adventure," he commented, when Alex had finished. "I remember when you and I first met. I could see straight away you were something special. I knew your father. I wasn't allowed to tell you that before. I worked with him a couple of times."

"In the field?"

"Yes. That was before..." Crawley ran a hand through his hair. "Well, I got hurt and had to stop. But you're just like him. Remarkable. Anyway, I have a few questions and then I'll leave you in peace." He had turned the recorder off; now he switched it back on. "The man who interrogated you. You say he called himself Kaspar. Can you describe him?"

"That's easy, Mr Crawley. He hasn't got the sort of face you'd forget."

"Tattoos?"

"Yes." Alex described the man who had come so close to removing his little finger.

"And he definitely told you that he represented Force Three."

"Yes. He talked a lot about global warming and that sort of thing."

"I would have said he rather added to it by setting fire to the building."

"I thought so too."

"What else can you tell me about him? Did he speak with an accent?"

Alex thought back. "I don't think he was English. He might have had a slight French accent. I'm not sure."

Crawley nodded. "Just one more question. The other three men in the tower block. You call them Combat Jacket, Spectacles and Silver Tooth. Did you hear any names?"

"No. I'm afraid not."

"Thank you, Alex." Crawley pressed a button on the recorder. There was a click as it stopped turning.

"So who is Kaspar? Who are Force Three? What was it all about?"

"It's a long story."

"I'm not going anywhere."

"Well," Crawley began. "Let's start with Nikolei Drevin. I suppose you know who he is."

"I've heard of him. He's a Russian multimillionaire."

"Born in Russia, yes. But he's more of a multibillionaire, as a matter of fact. An absolutely wonderful man. He lives in England a lot of the time, and he's made it clear that he likes to think of himself as English."

"He bought a football club."

"Stratford East. That's right. Nobody had ever heard of them but he's forked out for some of the best players in the world and now they're in the Premiership. He has a huge place in Oxfordshire, a penthouse near Tower Bridge and houses all over the world. He even has his own island out in the Caribbean. Flamingo Bay. That's where the launches take place."

"Ark Angel," Alex said.

"Ark Angel is the name of the space hotel that he's building. It's being put together piece by piece, and he has to send rockets up every now and then with the next component. You may not know this, Alex, but the British government are partners in the project and it means a great deal to them. The first hotel in space and it'll be flying a British flag! Ten years from now, commercial space travel will be a reality. In fact, it already is. An American businessman has already gone into outer space. Paid twenty million dollars for the privilege. Once Ark Angel is up and running, more will follow. The most powerful and influential people in the world will be queuing up for tickets, and we'll be the ones supplying them."

"Kaspar mentioned outer space," Alex said. "He didn't seem too happy about the idea."

"Kaspar is a fanatic," Crawley replied. "It's true that a few wild birds got wiped out on Flamingo Bay when the launch pad was set up. As a matter of fact, there aren't any flamingos there any more. Friends of the Earth and the World Wildlife Fund got a bit upset about it, but you don't see them going around murdering people. Force Three's a different matter."

"What do you know about them?"

Crawley scowled. "Not a lot. Before this year, nobody had ever heard of them. Then a woman in Germany wrote an article about them in *Der Spiegel* and a few days later she was shot in the street. The same thing happened in London just over a week ago. A chap by the name of Max Webber denounced them at a conference on international security and got blown up as a result. We're looking into both deaths right now – that's why Mrs Jones is in Berlin. Force Three seems to be something quite new. Eco-terrorists ... I suppose that's what you'd call them. It's all very alarming."

"What about Kaspar?"

"Apart from what you've told us, we hardly know anything about him."

"Well, he should be easy enough to catch." It was something that had puzzled Alex from the start. The tattoos. "With a face like his, you'll be able to spot him a mile away."

"At least we know what we're looking for. As for Drevin, he can take care of himself, I imagine. He's got plenty of security out on Flamingo Bay. Our real worry is that Force Three might have a crack at Ark Angel. They've already blown up a car manufacturing plant, a research centre and quite a few other installations. Of course, they'll have their work cut out. After all, Ark Angel is three hundred miles up in outer space. But none of this is any concern of yours."

Crawley stood up. "You did a superb job, Alex," he said. "I'm sure Drevin is enormously grateful. I wouldn't be surprised if a large cheque didn't turn up in the post. At the very least, you might get a couple of tickets to see Stratford East play."

"I don't want a cheque," Alex said. "I just want to go home."

"I hear the doctor says you can leave this evening." Crawley slid the recorder into his pocket. "I've stayed long enough," he said. "Very good to see you, Alex. I'm sure we'll meet again."

I'm sure we'll meet again.

Alex remembered the words now as he ate his scrambled eggs. Did Crawley really think he would ever work for MI6 again? If so he was very much mistaken. The strange thing was, he could think of dozens of boys at Brookland School who probably dreamt about being a spy. They'd imagine it would be fun. Alex had discovered the unpleasant reality. He'd been hurt, threatened, manipulated, shot at, beaten up and almost killed. He'd found himself in a world where he couldn't believe anybody and where nothing was quite what it seemed. And he'd had enough. In two years he would be taking his GCSEs. From now on he was going to keep his head down, and the next time four terrorist kidnappers broke into a hospital he'd simply turn over and go back to sleep!

Jack Starbright had almost finished eating and Alex realized she hadn't said a word since she had sat down. She'd been very quiet when she picked him up from hospital too.

"Jack, are you angry with me?" he asked.

"No," she said. But the single word told him the exact opposite.

Alex put down his knife and fork. "I'm sorry."

Jack sighed. "I don't know what to say to you, Alex," she said. "I'm not sure I can look after you any more."

"Are you going back to America?"

"No! I don't know." She looked at him sadly. "You have no idea what it's been like for me recently. First you tell me you're going on vacation in Venice. The next thing I know, you've got caught up with some international band of criminals and then you get shot. How do you think I felt when they told me? But somehow you pull through and you're in hospital, and any other kid would just stay there and get better. But not you! You have to take on a gang of kidnappers and nearly get killed all over again."

"It wasn't my fault," Alex protested. "It just happened."

"I know. That's what I tell myself. But the fact is, I feel completely useless." She fell silent. "And I don't want to be sitting here next time when they tell me you didn't make it. I couldn't bear that."

Alex went over to her. "There isn't going to be a next time," he said. "And you're not useless, Jack. I don't know what I'd do without you. There's no one else to look after me. And it's not just that. I sometimes think you're the only person who really knows me. I only feel normal when I'm with you."

Jack stood up and gave him a hug. "Just my luck," she said ruefully. "All the fourteen-year-olds in the world, and I end up looking after you."

The phone rang in the hall.

"I'll get it," she said.

Alex took the plates over to the dishwasher and began to stack them. About two minutes later, Jack came back in. There was an odd look on her face.

"Who was it?" he asked.

"It was for you. I don't believe it! That was Nikolei Drevin."

"He rang himself?"

"Yes. He's invited you to have tea with him this afternoon. He's giving a press conference at the Waterfront Hotel and he wanted to know if you'd come along and meet him afterwards."

"What did you say?"

"Well, I told him I'd ask you and he said he'd send a car." She shrugged. "I guess he expected you to say yes."

Alex thought for a moment. Mr Crawley had said that Drevin would probably get in touch. "Do you think I should go?"

Jack sighed. "I don't know. I suppose he wants to thank you. After all, you saved him one million pounds. And you stopped his son getting hurt."

Alex remembered Paul Drevin. He wondered if the other boy would be at the hotel.

"I could call him back and say you're too tired," Jack added.

For a moment, Alex was tempted. The last time he'd met a multimillionaire, it had been Damian Cray – and the experience had nearly killed him. On the other hand, this was different. Drevin was a target. It was the man called Kaspar who was the enemy. And it was fair enough that Drevin should want to meet him after what had happened. Alex felt awkward about saying no.

Sometimes it's the tiniest things that can mean the difference between life and death. A few centimetres of kerb had saved Alex when he stepped off the pavement on Liverpool Street just as a sniper fired at him. Now two words were going to drag him back into the world he thought he'd left behind.

"Let's go."

AT THE WATERFRONT

The Waterfront Hotel was brand new – a silver and glass tower rising above the Thames at St Katharine's Dock. Looking up the river, Alex could see Tower Bridge with HMS *Belfast* moored near by. He didn't look the other way. He was only a few miles from where he'd been held prisoner. He didn't need any reminder of that.

Behind him, Jack Starbright stepped out of the ordinary London taxi that had brought them here. At first she had been a little disgruntled. "So what happened to the Rolls-Royce?" she wondered out loud. But in the end she agreed that Drevin had made the right decision. The last thing either of them wanted was to make a grand entrance.

They walked into a foyer where everything seemed to be white or made of glass. A young woman was waiting there to greet them.

"Hi," she said. "You must be Alex Rider and

Jack Starbright. Mr Drevin asked me to look out for you." She spoke with an American accent. "My name's Tamara Knight. I'm Mr Drevin's personal assistant."

Alex cast an eye over her as they shook hands. Tamara Knight was twenty-five, although she looked much younger. She was not much taller than he was, with light brown hair tied back, and attractive blue eyes. Alex felt that the formal business suit and brightly polished leather shoes didn't suit her. He also wished she'd smile a bit more. She didn't look at all pleased to see him.

"Mr Drevin is still tied up with his press conference," she explained as she led them across the central atrium of the hotel. Silver and glass lifts rose and fell around them, travelling silently on hidden cables. A group of Japanese businessmen walked across the marble floor. "He said you were welcome to look in if you wanted to. Or you can wait for him in his private suite."

"I'd like to know what a suite costs here," Jack muttered.

Tamara Knight smiled coldly. "It doesn't cost Mr Drevin anything. He owns the hotel."

"Let's take a look at the press conference," Alex said.

"Of course. He's talking about Ark Angel. I'm sure you'll find it interesting."

She led them up a wide flight of stairs and along a corridor until they came to a pair of smoked glass doors. Two large men in suits were guarding this entrance. "We'll slip in at the back," Tamara whispered. "Just take a seat. Nobody will notice you."

She nodded and one of the men opened the doors.

Alex went through and found himself in a wide, imposing room with large windows giving a panoramic view of the river. There were about a hundred journalists sitting in rows facing a long table on a platform. The words ARK ANGEL had been spelled out in solid steel letters, each one two metres high, and there were photographs of the earth, taken from space, suspended on thin wires. Three people were seated behind the table. One was the minister for science and innovation. The other looked like some sort of civil servant. Alex didn't recognize him. The man in the middle was Nikolei Drevin.

Drevin was unimpressive. That was Alex's first thought. If he'd bumped into him in the street he might have mistaken him for a bank manager or an accountant. Drevin was a serious-looking man in his forties with watery, grey eyes and hair that had once been fair but was now fading to grey. He had bad skin; there was a rash around his chin and neck as if he'd had trouble shaving. All his clothes – his suit, his shirt with its buttoned-down collar, the plain silk tie – looked brand new and expensive. But they did nothing for him. He wore them with as much style as a mannequin in a shop window. Alex noticed a gold watch on one hand. There was a ring made of platinum or white gold on the other.

Drevin seemed dwarfed by his surroundings. He was physically smaller than the two men who were sharing the platform with him. The minister had been answering a question when Alex came in. Drevin was fidgeting nervously, twisting the ring on his finger. Tamara gestured to a seat and Alex sat down. The minister finished talking and the other man looked around for another question.

One of the journalists raised a hand. "I understand that Ark Angel is now two months behind schedule and two billion dollars over budget," he said. "I'd like to ask Mr Drevin if he now regrets getting involved."

"You are mistaken," Drevin replied, and at once Alex could hear the accent in his voice. It was more pronounced than his son's had been. He spoke slowly, accentuating each word. "Ark Angel is actually two billion *pounds* over budget. This is a British project, you must remember." There was a murmur of laughter around the room. Drevin shrugged. "Some difficulties were to be expected," he went on. "This is the most ambitious building project of the twenty-first century. A fully functioning hotel in space! But do I regret it? Of course not. What we are talking about is the beginning of space tourism, the greatest adventure of our lifetime. A hundred years from now, it will not only be possible to travel to the edge of the universe, it will be cheap! Maybe one day your great-grand-children will walk on the moon. And they will remember that it all began with Ark Angel. It all began here."

Another hand went up. "How is your son? Does it concern you that the people who tried to kidnap him are still at large?"

Jack nudged Alex. They had arrived at the right time.

"I do not normally speak about my family," Drevin replied. "But I will say this. These people – Force Three – claim they are fighting for the environment. It is true that the wildlife on Flamingo Bay was disturbed when we launched our first rockets, and I very much regret that. But I have only contempt for these people. They tried to extort money from me. They are common criminals and I have every confidence that the British or European police will soon bring them to justice."

"Absolutely!" agreed the minister.

"We have time for just one more question," the second man said.

A bearded man sitting in the front row raised a nicotine-stained finger. "I have a question," he said. "I've heard rumours that the federal govern-ment of the United States is currently investigating Mr Drevin. Apparently they're looking into certain financial irregularities. Is there any truth in that?"

"Mr Drevin is not here to answer questions about

his personal affairs." The civil servant scowled and the minister nodded.

Drevin cut in. "It's all right." He didn't seem concerned. He looked the journalist straight in the eye. "I am a businessman," he said. "I am, you might agree, a fairly successful businessman." That produced a few smiles. Everyone in the room was aware that they were being addressed by one of the richest people in the world. "It is absolutely true that the CIA are looking into my affairs. It would be surprising if they weren't. It's their job. But..." – he spread his hands – "I have nothing to hide; indeed, I am willing to offer them my full cooperation." He paused. "It is possible that they will find some irregularities. I went out to lunch last week and forgot to keep the receipt. If they decide to prosecute me because of it, I'll make sure you're the first to know."

This time there was real laughter and even a scattering of applause. The man with the beard blushed and buried himself in his notebook. The other journalists stood up and began to file out. The press conference was over.

"He's such a brilliant speaker," Tamara Knight said, and Alex couldn't doubt the enthusiasm in her voice. She led Alex and Jack back the way they'd come, then across the atrium and over to one of the lifts. Once inside, she produced a key. The building had twenty-five storeys; the key activated the button for the top floor.

The doors closed and they were whisked upwards at speed. Alex felt his stomach sink as the atrium disappeared beneath them. Twenty floors up, the lift entered a solid shaft and the view was blocked. Another few seconds and they slowed down. The lift stopped and the doors slid open.

They had arrived.

They were in a huge room with windows on two sides giving breathtaking views over St Katharine's Dock, the yachts and cruisers resting at their moorings far below. Tower Bridge was close by. It looked unreal, a toy replica, sitting in the afternoon sun. Alex looked around him. The room was simply but expensively furnished with three Persian rugs spread over light wood floorboards. The furniture was modern. On one side stood a dining-room table with a dozen leather chairs. A corridor ran past a black Bechstein grand piano to a closed door at the end. There was a sunken area in the middle of the room with three oversized sofas and a glass coffee table. Tea – sandwiches and biscuits – had already been served.

"Quite a place!" Jack said.

"This is where Mr Drevin stays when he's in London." Tamara Knight pointed out of one window. "You see the boat third from the left? The *Crimean Star*. That belongs to him too."

Jack gasped. The vessel was gleaming white, the size of a small ocean liner. "Have you been on board?" she asked.

"Certainly not. My work with Mr Drevin doesn't allow me to enter his private quarters," she explained primly.

Just then the door at the end of the corridor opened and Nikolei Drevin came in. It occurred to Alex that there must be a second lift, bringing him up to another part of the penthouse. He was alone, hands clasped in front of him, his fingers tugging at the ring. "Thank you very much, Miss Knight," he said. "You can leave us now."

"Yes, Mr Drevin."

"Have you made the arrangements for Saturday?"

"I've left the file on your desk, Mr Drevin."

"Good. I'll talk with you later."

Tamara Knight nodded at Alex. "It was good to meet you," she said – but without a lot of enthusiasm. Then she turned and walked back into the lift. The doors closed and she was gone.

For the first time, Nikolei Drevin seemed to relax. He walked up to Alex and rested a hand on each shoulder, and for a second Alex wondered if he was going to kiss him. Instead Drevin held him firmly in what was almost an embrace. "You're Alex Rider," he said. "I am very, very happy to meet you." He let Alex go and turned to Jack. "Miss Starbright." He shook hands with her. "I am so glad you were able to come. Please, will you sit down?" He led them to the sofas and picked up the teapot. "Tea?" he asked.

"Thank you."

Nobody spoke while he poured. At last he sat back and studied his two guests. "I cannot tell you how grateful I am, Alex," he said. "Although I hope you will permit me to try. You quite possibly saved my son's life. Certainly you saved him from a terrible ordeal. I am very much in your debt."

"How is he?" Alex asked.

"Paul is well, thank you. Please, help yourself..."

Jack took a sandwich but Alex wasn't hungry. He was feeling a little uncomfortable being this close to Drevin. The man was only a few inches taller than he was, and still seemed very ordinary. And yet he radiated power. It was the same with all the rich people Alex had met. Their money, the billions of pounds in their bank accounts, spoke before they did.

"I should be asking how *you* are, Alex," Drevin went on. "I understand you were recovering from a chest injury. A bike accident?"

"Yes." Alex hated lying but that was the story that had been agreed.

"Alex is very accident-prone," Jack muttered, holding up her sandwich.

"Well, it was very lucky for me that you should end up in the room next to Paul. I still find it hard to believe that you acted the way you did. But let me get straight to the point. I am sure you know who I am. I don't seek attention, but the papers like to write about me, especially when my team loses. I am a very wealthy man. If there is anything that you want in the world, Alex, I can give it to you. I don't say this as a boast. I mean it. You have done me a great service and I would like to repay you."

Alex thought for a moment. "There's nothing I really want, thank you," he said. "I'm glad I was able to help your son. But it just sort of happened. I don't need any reward."

Drevin nodded. "I had a feeling you might say that, and I'm afraid I can't accept it as an answer. So I would like to make a proposition." He paused. "I spoke to your doctor this morning. Dr Hayward. You might like to know that I have made a donation of two million pounds on your behalf towards a new cardiology wing at St Dominic's."

"That's very kind of you," Alex said. "So long as they don't name it after me."

Drevin smiled. "Don't worry! Dr Hayward tells me that you must not return to school for a couple of weeks. What I would like to propose is that you come and stay with me, as my guest. I'd be very glad to look after you while you recuperate. I employ a full-time medical staff, so you will be in safe hands if any complications should arise. More to the point, my chef is world class. Everything you want will be given to you. Miss Starbright is also very welcome."

"I'm not sure—" Alex began.

"Please, Alex!" Drevin interrupted. "There's something I haven't mentioned. My son, Paul. He's almost your age and he told me that you spoke together a few times in hospital. I know he would welcome your company. Paul doesn't meet many other boys – that's largely my fault. I'm afraid for him. There's always the danger that someone will try to get at me through him. What happened at St Dominic's is proof of that. He met you and liked you, and it would be good for him to have someone else around for a while. You'd be doing me a favour if you agreed to come."

He paused. Alex felt the grey eyes examining him.

"I want to offer you two weeks with more luxury than you have ever known in your life. We'll start here in England. I can't leave until the weekend; I have business and, more importantly, we're playing Chelsea on Saturday and I can't miss that. After that I'm flying to New York. I have an apartment there, and again there is some business I have to take care of. You see? Paul is always on his own."

He put down his cup and leant forward. Although his tone hadn't changed, Alex could sense his energy and excitement.

"But in just over a week's time, there's something you really can't miss. We have a launch at Flamingo Bay. Have you ever seen a rocket being fired? It's an unforgettable experience. If the weather's right, it'll blast off at exactly nine o'clock local time on Wednesday morning. It'll be carrying the observation module for Ark Angel. It's taken us three years to build. It will be the very heart of Ark Angel; the communications centre, a window like no other window in the world. Paul will, of course, be there, and I want you to be there with him. I have a house on the island and the beaches are spectacular. After the launch, you can stay for as long as you like."

Alex said nothing. He wanted to go. He had never seen a rocket launch and it sounded like the sort of adventure he could actually enjoy – without anyone trying to kill him. And yet...

Drevin seemed to sense his uncertainty. "I'm sure Dr Hayward would agree that a bit of Caribbean sun would do you good," he said. "Please! Don't refuse me. I have to tell you, I've already made up my mind and I'm the sort of person who is used to getting his own way."

Alex turned to Jack. He still wasn't sure. And he was vaguely aware that something was bothering him. It was something Drevin had said. It didn't add up. "What do you think?" he asked.

Jack's eyes were gleaming. She had obviously been impressed by Drevin, the penthouse, the *Crimean Star*. "I think it's a great idea," she said. "A couple of weeks in the sun are exactly what you need. And I'm sure Mr Drevin will look after you."

"You have my word."

Alex nodded. "OK then. Thank you." He took a sandwich. "But I think I should warn you: I'm a Chelsea supporter."

Drevin smiled. "That's all right. Nobody's perfect. I'll send a driver to collect you – shall we say the day after tomorrow? He'll drive you down to Neverglade – that's my house in Oxfordshire. Paul is there now. I must call him and let him know you're coming." He glanced at his watch. "And now, if you'll forgive me, I must leave you. I have a meeting at the Bank of England."

"Is that where you have your account?" Jack asked.

"One of them." He stood up. "Miss Knight will show you out when you have finished – and she'll also arrange a car to take you home. Thank you again, Alex. I know you're not going to regret this."

Another twist of the ring. Alex had noticed that his hands were never still. Drevin left the way he had come in.

There was a long silence.

"Wow!" Jack exclaimed.

"Flamingo Bay..." Alex murmured.

"It's exactly what the doctor ordered, Alex." She helped herself to another sandwich. "It couldn't have come at a better time."

"Sure..."

But Alex *wasn't* sure. What was it that was bothering him?

Yes. That was it.

Paul Drevin was a target. That was what Drevin had said. He was always in danger.

So why had he been on his own? That night at the hospital, four men had broken in to kidnap him. They had known he was there.

But there hadn't been a single guard in sight.

THE LAP OF LUXURY

"Welcome to Neverglade," Paul Drevin said.

Alex stepped out of the luxury car that had brought him here and looked around. He had seen wealth before. He had once gone undercover as the son of a supermarket magnate, which had meant spending a week in a mansion in Lancashire. But this place was something else again.

His first sight of Drevin's country estate had been a pretty but very ordinary gatehouse on a country lane about twenty miles north of Oxford. But even here, Alex had noticed the high walls and woodland surrounding the estate, and the CCTV cameras rotating discreetly between the trees. The driveway must have been a mile long, emerging from the woods into fields so perfectly mown it was hard to believe they were made of grass. On one side was a lake with two jet skis and a Lapwing wooden sailing boat moored beside a jetty. On the other, partly hidden in a slight dip, a miniature racing circuit twisted and turned, with its own grandstand for spectators. Four of the most beautiful horses Alex had ever seen were grazing in a paddock. The sun was shining. It was as if the summer had returned.

And there was Neverglade. It wasn't a house but a fourteenth-century castle – with its own moat, battlements, towers and outlying church. It was built of grey stone, with dark green ivy spreading diagonally across the face. Alex caught his breath as they drove towards it and crossed the drawbridge. The castle didn't seem real. It was like something out of a picture book. And why had it been built here of all places? He wondered why he had never heard or seen pictures of it before.

Alex wished now that Jack Starbright had decided to come.

She had seemed uneasy and deep in thought in the taxi home from the Waterfront, but it was only later in the evening that she announced her decision.

"I'd love to come with you, Alex," she said. "And I'd love to watch this rocket being launched. But I can't. I haven't seen my mum and dad for nearly a year, and I need to go back home to Washington DC. It's their wedding anniversary next week, and this would be a good opportunity to take a vacation. You're safe, and you're going to be well looked after. Anyway, you've got Paul Drevin. He's

116

your age and you won't want me hanging around. So go and enjoy yourself. And just you make sure you don't get into any more trouble. Rest and recuperation. That's what the doctor said."

This time Nikolei Drevin had sent a uniformed chauffeur to pick Alex up – and he had arrived in a Rolls-Royce, a pale blue Corniche with a retracting hood. They had cruised out of London and up the M40, the 6.75 litre V8 engine effortlessly gliding past all the other traffic as if the roads had been built exclusively for its use. Now the car disappeared round the side of the house as Paul Drevin came out to greet him.

The last time Alex had seen the other boy, he had been wearing a dressing gown and pyjamas. Now he was dressed in jeans and a loose-fitting jersey. He looked a lot healthier than he had in hospital – but there was more to it than that. He was more confident. This was his home, his territory, and one day he would inherit it. Alex had to remind himself that this boy was probably a multimillionaire himself. His weekly pocket money probably arrived in a security van. Suddenly Alex wondered if coming here had been a good idea.

"Quite a place," he said as they walked towards the front door, their feet crunching on the gravel.

"My father had it built here. The castle used to be somewhere in Scotland. It was falling down so he bought it and shipped it here, piece by piece, and then put it back together again. Come on, I'll show you your room."

Alex followed Paul into an entrance hall with flagstones, tapestries and a fireplace big enough to burn a bus. As they climbed up a majestic staircase, they passed paintings by Picasso, Warhol, Hockney and Lucian Freud. Nikolei Drevin obviously liked modern art.

"What you did at the hospital was amazing," Paul said. "Did you really mean to take my place?"

"Well, it just sort of happened..."

"If those men had kidnapped me, they were going to cut my finger off!" Paul shuddered and Alex wondered how he knew about that. The exact details of what had happened at Hornchurch Towers hadn't been in the papers. But he assumed that for a man like Drevin, even the most classified information wouldn't be hard to get. "They nearly killed you because of me," Paul went on. "I don't know what to say."

"There's no need to say anything."

"I'm glad you agreed to come."

Alex shrugged. "Your dad made it difficult for me to refuse."

"Yes. He's like that." They had reached the top of the stairs. Paul took out an inhaler and puffed at it twice. "I have asthma," he explained.

"That's bad luck."

"This way..." They walked down a corridor with ornate wooden doors at intervals on either side.

118

"There are thirty bedrooms," Paul told him. "I don't know why we need so many. They're never full. I've put you next to me. If you want anything, just pick up the phone. It's like living in a hotel, except you don't have to pay."

They came to an open door and went into a bedroom with windows looking out over the lake. The chauffeur must have come in through another entrance; Alex's luggage was on the bed. The room was modern. Alex took in the plasma screen TV, the console with various games and music systems, the phone with about a dozen buttons for the different services it provided, the back shelves stacked with bestsellers, all brand new by the look of them. He glanced inside the bathroom with its huge bath, power shower and sauna. Drevin had promised him a luxurious life-style and he had certainly been true to his word.

"What do you want to do?" Paul asked.

"You tell me."

"Well, we can go horse-riding if you like. We've got two swimming pools: indoor and out. Later we can watch a film. There's a cinema and Dad gets all the new releases. We can play tennis or golf, or go clay pigeon shooting. You saw the lake; we can go jet-skiing or sailing or fishing or whatever. I suppose I'd better start by showing you around. That'll take most of the day, and Dad's having dinner with us tonight. It's up to you."

Alex didn't know what to say. "I don't mind."

"Well, I'll show you the house and then we can grab a couple of quad bikes and I'll take you round the grounds. There are about two hundred acres. Are you hungry?"

"No. I'm fine."

"Then let's go."

"Right." Alex tried to sound enthusiastic, but somehow he couldn't.

Paul had picked up on this. "I guess this must be very weird for you," he said. "You don't know me and you probably don't even like me. Not a lot of people do. They think I'm a rich, spoilt brat and if they come here at all it's only because of all the free stuff. My father invited you because he wanted to thank you for what you did at the hospital. But it was more than that. He's hoping we're going to be friends and it's the one thing he can't actually buy. Friendship. But I'll understand if you want to take your bags and get the hell out of here. Sometimes I feel the same."

Alex thought for a moment. "No," he said. "I'm glad to be here. I can't go back to school and I'm meant to be resting for the next couple of weeks, and to be honest, I've got nowhere else to go. So if your dad wants to treat me like a multimillionaire, I'm not going to complain."

"OK." Paul looked relieved. "We're going to New York on Sunday and that'll be cool. And then there's Flamingo Bay. Have you tried kite-surfing?"

Alex shook his head.

"I can show you how to do it. We're on the Atlantic side so we get huge waves." Paul had suddenly become more animated and Alex found himself warming to him. "Let's start in the cinema," he said. "We can work our way down..."

Two hours later, they still hadn't finished. Alex had seen more wealth than he could possibly imagine. This wasn't how the other half lived. There were probably only a handful of people in the world with the resources of Nikolei Drevin. Anything he wanted he could have – from the medieval suit of armour outside the dining room to the two Polaris MSX jet skis out on the lake. He had also learnt a little more about Paul's background. He was an only child. His parents had divorced when he was six and his mother was now living in America. He saw her a couple of times a year, but she and his father never spoke. When Paul was younger he had gone to an ordinary school, but in the end there had been too many security problems and now he was being educated by private tutors. Part of the house had been converted into a school. Alex had seen it and felt sad. There were books and blackboards, desks and computers. But no schoolchildren. No shouting. No real life.

At five o'clock he went back to his room and dozed for an hour, then showered and changed for dinner. He had seen the grand dining room at Neverglade with its chandeliers and antique oak table long enough to seat twenty – and he was relieved that they would be eating in the conservatory next to the kitchen. This was a pretty room with marble columns, Italian tiles and exotic plants in huge terracotta pots. Nikolei Drevin was already there when he arrived.

"Please come in, Alex. Take a seat." Drevin was drinking wine. He had changed into jeans and a denim jacket, and Alex couldn't help thinking that the clothes didn't suit him. He was somehow too old for them. He was a man born to wear a suit.

"Will you have some wine?" Drevin asked. "Or perhaps a beer?"

"Water will be fine," Alex replied.

"In Russia, children drink alcohol from an early age."

The door opened and a young woman came in, carrying the first course on a tray: melon and serrano ham. Alex had no idea how many people worked at Neverglade; the servants had the knack of staying invisible, except when they were needed. He helped himself to iced water. Paul arrived and sat down without speaking. The servant left and the three of them were alone.

"Has Paul shown you around?" Drevin asked.

"Yes. It's quite a place."

"I bought it when I first came to your country. The original Neverglade was a sixteenth-century manor house. There's a story that Queen Elizabeth I stayed there and saw a production of *Twelfth Night* in the great hall. But I wasn't fond of the architectural style. The house was too dark, and it only had eleven bedrooms. It was too small."

"What happened to it?"

Drevin sighed. "A dreadful accident. It burned down. This present castle rose out of the ashes – or rather, I brought it here. I liked it the moment I saw it. The only problem was that it was in Scotland. But happily I was able to do something about that. Have the two of you decided what you're going to do tomorrow?"

"I thought we might go for a walk," Paul said.

Drevin turned on him and Alex saw something flash in the grey eyes. It was very brief and he couldn't be certain, but it was almost a look of contempt. "Surely you can think of something more adventurous than that!" he said. "Why don't you take the horses out? Or the dirt bikes? Of course, you're both recuperating. Paul from his appendix operation. And you, Alex" – the eyes came to rest on him – "from your cycling accident."

"Yes." Was Drevin questioning his story? "I went over the handlebars and hit a fence."

"You must have been going very fast."

"I was, until I hit the fence."

"Then perhaps dirt bikes aren't the best idea." Drevin thought for a moment. His fingers were tugging at his ring but his face gave nothing away. This was a man who was used to keeping his secrets to himself. "I'll tell you what," he said.

123

"I have a conference call tomorrow morning. With the launch just over a week away, I have to keep in constant contact with my own people as well as NASA and, of course, the British government. But in the afternoon, how would you like to race against me?"

"On horses?"

"Go-karts. You may have seen I have a track here. I built it for Paul, although I'm afraid he seldom uses it."

"I do use it," Paul protested. "But it's no fun when you've no one to race against."

Drevin ignored him. "I have several karts," he went on. "You'll find it quite exhilarating, Alex. You against me. What do you say?"

"Sure." Alex didn't much like the sound of it but there was something about the way he was being asked. He'd felt the same when Drevin had invited him to stay. He wasn't really being given a choice.

"And to make it more fun, why don't we have a bet? If you beat me, I'll give you a thousand pounds."

"I'm not sure I want a thousand pounds," Alex said. It wasn't the money that bothered him; he just wasn't sure he wanted to take it from this man.

"Well, in that case I'll give it to any charity you care to name. But you don't need to worry. There is absolutely no chance that you will win. Paul can be the flagman. Shall we say two o'clock?"

"All right."

Drevin picked up his knife and fork and began to eat. Alex noticed that his son hadn't touched his food. Already he could sense the gulf between them. It was obvious with every word that was spoken, every moment that they spent together. Once again he asked himself what he was doing here. And once again he found himself wondering if it had been such a good idea to come.

Two hours later, Alex was making his way back to his room on his own. Nikolei Drevin had gone out into the garden to smoke a cigar. Paul had announced he was tired and had already gone to bed.

He was walking down the main corridor on the ground floor. There was a fully equipped gymnasium and an Olympic-sized indoor swimming pool at the far end, and Alex was tempted to go for a swim before bed. He wasn't tired any more. He wanted to dive into the warm water and wash away some of the memories of his first day at Neverglade. He was tempted to ring Jack Starbright. She would have arrived in America by now. He was still sorry she had decided not to come with him, and he was worried he had let her down. Maybe he should have gone with her.

His path took him past the double doors of Drevin's study. Paul had pointed it out earlier but they hadn't gone in. On an impulse he stopped and looked left and right. The corridor stretched on, empty, in both directions, its black and white tiles giving it the appearance of the world's longest chessboard. He turned the handle. The door opened. Without quite knowing what he was doing, Alex switched on the light and went in.

The study was enormous, dominated by a massive glass and steel desk shaped like a crescent moon. The wood floor was partly covered by a Persian rug that must have taken years to weave. Behind the desk were glass doors leading out onto the front lawn. Alex counted four phones on the desk, as well as two computers, a printer, several piles of documents and a series of clocks showing time zones all over the world. There was one small picture of Paul in a silver frame.

If Alex had hoped that this room would tell him a little more about his host, he was disappointed. Nikolei Drevin was very rich and very powerful – but he didn't need an oversized desk and a stack of expensive equipment to tell him that. One of the walls was covered with photos and Alex went over to them. This was more like it. He had at least found one tiny chink in the man's impressive armour. Vanity. The wall was a gallery of celebrities.

There were photographs of Drevin with pop stars and actors, photographs taken at glitzy parties and de luxe hotels. He showed little emotion in any of them, but even so Alex could tell that he was quietly pleased to be there. Here was Drevin with Tom Cruise, Drevin with Julia Roberts, Drevin chatting to Steven Spielberg on the set of his latest film.

He was in Whitehall with the prime minister (who was smiling cheesily) and in Washington with the president of the United States. Here he was shaking hands with the Russian president – Alex was surprised to find himself looking at the bloated face of Boris Kiriyenko. The two of them had met when Alex had been a prisoner on the island of Skeleton Key.

The pope had given Drevin an audience. So had Nelson Mandela in Cape Town. Some of the pictures had been taken from newspapers, and the headlines told the story of his life in bold, simple statements:

DREVIN MOVES TO THE UK

DREVIN RICHER THAN THE QUEEN

DREVIN BUILDS £50 MILLION OXFORDSHIRE HOME

DREVIN BUYS STRATFORD EAST

This last headline was accompanied by a photograph of Drevin with Adam Wright, the England striker who had been his first major purchase for his new team. Alex glanced at the other articles.

DREVIN ANNOUNCES ARK ANGEL PLANS

DREVIN BUYS WATERFRONT HOTEL

DREVIN MOVES INTO LONDON PROPERTY MARKET

There was a movement behind him.

Nikolei Drevin had come into the study through the French windows. He was still holding his cigar and was examining Alex curiously. "Alex? What are you doing in here?" There was no anger in his voice. He seemed, if anything, just a little perplexed.

"I'm sorry." It took Alex a few seconds to find the words. He knew he was trespassing. On the other hand, the door hadn't been locked. "I was just on my way to bed. I hadn't been in here and I thought I'd take a look."

"This is my private study; I would prefer it if you didn't come in here."

"Of course. I was about to go but then I saw these pictures." Alex gestured at one of them. "You've met the Queen."

"Several times, as a matter of fact. She spoke a great deal about her horses. I didn't find her very interesting."

"And Nelson Mandela."

"Ah, yes. A great man. He gave me a signed copy of his book."

Silence and suspicion hung in the air between them.

"Well, I'd better go up," Alex said.

"Can you find your way?"

"Yes. Thank you." Alex smiled. "Goodnight."

"Goodnight."

Alex was feeling dizzy. His left arm was throbbing.

He left the study as casually as he could and didn't stop until he'd reached his own room on the second floor. He sat down heavily on the bed. He knew what he had just seen. But he couldn't make sense of it.

The last newspaper cutting had shown Drevin wearing a fluorescent jacket and hard hat, standing outside a derelict building in east London. Alex had recognized it at once and hadn't needed the banner, stretching out high in the background, to tell him its name.

Hornchurch Towers.

The building that had burnt down. The picture had been taken just a few days before he had almost died there.

Either it was an incredible coincidence or Kaspar and his men – the group that called itself Force Three – had deliberately taken him to a block of flats that Drevin had just purchased. They had thought he was Paul Drevin. They had been planning to ransom him for the sum of a million pounds. So why had they taken him to a building that his father owned?

Alex undressed and got into bed. He couldn't sleep. He had thought he was meant to be having two weeks in the lap of luxury. Looked after and safe – that was what Jack had said. He was beginning to feel that both of them might be wrong.

SHORT CIRCUIT

The building was in SoHo, at the southern end of Manhattan. It stood between a delicatessen and a parking garage in a street full of converted warehouses with metal fire escapes, and boutiques that felt no need to advertise. There were no skyscrapers in this part of New York. SoHo prided itself on its village atmosphere, even if you needed a city salary to afford an apartment here. The entire neighbourhood was relaxed. People walked their dogs or ate their sandwiches in the autumn sun. There was little traffic. It was easy to forget the noise and the chaos just twenty blocks north.

Creative Ideas Animation fitted in perfectly. It sold cartoons: cells from the Simpsons and Futurama, original drawings from Disney and DreamWorks. It only had a small front window and there weren't many pictures on display. Unlike the other galleries in the area, its front door was locked. Visitors had to ring a bell. Even so, people would occasionally wander in off the street, but once they were inside they would find that the girl who worked there was unhelpful, the prices were ridiculous and there were better selections elsewhere. In the twenty years the gallery had been there, nobody had ever bought anything.

Which was precisely the idea. The people who worked at Creative Ideas Animation had no interest at all in art of any sort. They needed a base in New York and this was what they had chosen. SoHo suited them nicely. Nobody noticed who went in or out. Not that it mattered anyway. They owned the garage next door and used a secret entrance round the side.

At six o'clock that evening, five men and two women were sitting round a conference table in a surprisingly spacious and well-appointed room on the first floor just above the gallery. The table was a rectangle of polished glass on a chrome frame. The chairs were also made of chrome, with black leather seats. Clocks showing time zones around the world lined two of the walls. A large plasma screen covered a third. The fourth was a single plate-glass window facing a restaurant on the other side of the street. The glass was one way. Nobody at the restaurant could see in.

All the people in the room were formally dressed in dark suits and crisp white shirts. Six of them were young and fit; they could have just come out

131

of college. The seventh, at the head of the table, was more crumpled. He was a sixty-year-old black man with sunken eyes, grizzled white hair and moustache, and a look of perpetual tiredness.

One of the younger men was speaking.

"I have to report a development in England," he was saying. "It may not be relevant, but as you are aware, six days ago Nikolei Drevin was targeted by the environmental group Force Three. They were planning to abduct his son and hold him to ransom but they captured the wrong kid. It seems this other kid got in the way on purpose. He actually got himself kidnapped. Can you believe that?" He coughed. "What happened next is still unclear, but somehow the kid managed to escape and Drevin decided to reward him by making him part of the family. So now he's on his way over here. He'll be travelling with Drevin and Drevin's son down to Flamingo Bay."

"Does this kid have a name?" someone asked.

"Alex Rider." It was the older man who had spoken. "I think you should take a look at him." There was an unmarked file on the table in front of him. He leant forward, flipped it open and took out a photograph. He passed it to the man sitting next to him. "This was sent to me last night," he explained. "This is the kid we're talking about. The woman with him is his guardian. He has no parents."

One after another, the four men and two women

examined the photo. It showed Alex Rider and Jack Starbright as they entered the Waterfront Hotel, and had been taken by a concealed camera at ground level.

"The fact that Alex Rider has gotten himself involved changes everything," the older man went on. "I'm surprised Drevin hasn't checked up on him. It could be his first – and his biggest – mistake."

One of the women shook her head. "I don't understand. Who *is* Alex Rider?"

"He's no ordinary kid. And let me say straight off that this is to go no further than this room. What I'm telling you is classified – but it seems we're in a need-to-know situation." He paused. "Alex is an agent working with MI6 Special Operations."

A mutter of disbelief travelled round the table.

"But, sir..." the woman protested. "That's crazy. He can't be more than fifteen years old."

"He's fourteen. And you're absolutely right. Trust MI6 to come up with an idea like this. But it's worked. Alex Rider is the nearest thing the Brits have to a lethal weapon."

"So how come he's got himself mixed up with Drevin?" the other woman asked.

The older man smiled to himself as if he knew something they didn't. In fact, he was only just beginning to work it out. "Maybe it was a coincidence, or maybe it wasn't," he murmured. "But either way it's a whole new ball game. Alex Rider met Kaspar. He's been at the heart of Force Three. And now he's close to Drevin."

"You think he can help us?"

"He'll help us whether he wants to or not." The man gazed at the photo and suddenly there was a hardness in his eyes. "If Alex Rider comes to New York, I want to see him. Do you understand? It's a number one priority. Use any means necessary to get hold of him. I want you to bring that boy to me."

Over three thousand miles away, at Neverglade, Alex had just finished two sets of tennis with Paul Drevin. To his surprise, he'd been thrashed.

Paul was a brilliant player. If he'd wanted to, he could have served ace after ace and Alex wouldn't even have had a chance. He'd purposely slowed down his serve, but despite Alex's best efforts, the score had been three–six in the first set, four–six in the next. Alex would have happily played on, but Paul shook his head. He had slumped on the grass with a bottle of water. Alex noticed he'd also brought out his inhaler again. At the end of the last set he'd been struggling to breathe.

"You should join a club or something," Alex remarked, sitting down next to him. "Could you play competitively?"

Paul shook his head. "Two sets is all I can manage. After that my lungs pack in."

"How long have you had asthma?"

"All my life. Luckily it's not too bad, but then it kicks in and that's it. My dad gets really fed up."

"You can't help it if you're ill."

"That's not how he sees it." Paul glanced at his watch. "He'll be at the track by now. Come on. I'll walk over with you."

They left the rackets behind and walked across the lawn together. A man drove past on a tractor and nodded at them. Alex had noticed that none of the staff ever spoke to Paul; he wondered if they were allowed to.

"Aren't you going to race?" he asked.

"Maybe later. If it was just you and me, I wouldn't mind. But Dad..." Paul fell silent as if there was something he didn't want to say. "Dad takes it very seriously," he muttered.

"How fast do these karts go?"

"They can do a hundred miles an hour." Paul saw Alex's eyes widen. "They're not toys, if that's what you were expecting. My father had some business friends to stay a few months ago. One of them lost control round a corner and the kart flipped. They can do that. I saw it happen. He must have turned over six or seven times. He was lucky he was wearing a helmet, otherwise he'd have been killed."

"How badly was he hurt?"

"He broke his wrist and collarbone. His face was all cut up too. And you should have seen the kart! It was a write-off." Paul shook his head. "Be very careful, Alex," he warned. "My dad doesn't like to lose."

"Well, I don't think I've got any chance of winning."

"If you want my advice, you won't even try."

There was a question Alex had been dying to ask him all morning and he decided this was probably the right moment. "Why do you live with him and not with your mother?"

"He insisted."

"Do your parents really hate each other?"

"He never talks about her. And she gets angry if I ask her about him." Paul sighed. "What about your parents?"

"I don't have any. They died when I was small."

"I'm sorry." They walked on for a while in silence. "I wish I had a brother," Paul said suddenly. "That's the worst of it. Always being on my own."

"Can't you go to school?"

"I did for a bit. But it caused all sorts of problems. I had to have a bodyguard – Dad insisted – so I never really fitted in. In the end he decided it was easier for me to have lessons at home." Paul shrugged. "I keep thinking that one day I'll be sixteen and maybe I can walk out of here. Dad's not so bad, but I wish I could have my own life."

They had crossed the lawn and there was the track ahead of them: a kilometre of twisting asphalt, with seating for about fifty spectators, and six go-karts waiting in a side bay. Nikolei Drevin was already there, checking one of the engines. There were a couple of mechanics on hand but nobody else. This race was going to happen without an audience.

"Good luck," Paul whispered.

"Ah – Alex!" Drevin had heard them approaching. He looked up. "Have you done this before?"

"A couple of times." Alex had been on the indoor track at King's Cross in London. "I don't think the karts were as powerful as these."

"These are the best. I had them custom-built myself. Chrome Molly frames and Rotax Formula E engines; 125cc, electric starter, water-cooled." He pointed. "You start them by pressing the button next to the steering wheel. I hope you have a head for speed. They'll go from nought to sixty in 3.8 seconds. That's faster than a Ferrari."

"How many circuits do you have in mind?"

"Shall we say three? If you cross the finishing line first, your favourite charity will be richer by a thousand pounds." Drevin picked up two helmets and handed one to Alex. "I hope this is your size."

Alex's helmet was blue; Drevin would be wearing black.

Alex slipped his on and fastened it under his chin. The helmet had a visor that slid down over his face, and protective pads for his neck and the sides of his head.

"This is your last chance, Alex," Drevin said. "If you're nervous, now is the time to back out..."

Alex examined the go-karts. They were little more than skeletons, a tangle of wires and pipes with a plastic seat in the middle and two fuel tanks behind. When he sat down, he would be just inches above the ground. And there was something else missing – apart from the floor. He had already noticed that, unlike the karts he had driven at King's Cross, these had no wrap-around bumpers. Now he understood what Paul had told him. The cars were lethal. The course was hemmed in with bales of straw, but if he lost control, if one of his tyres came into contact with Drevin's, he could all too easily flip over – just like the friend Paul had mentioned. And if the engine scraped along the asphalt and sparks hit the petrol tanks, the whole thing would explode.

Drevin was waiting for his answer. Looking at him casually holding his helmet, one thumb hooked into his designer jeans, Alex felt a spurt of annoyance. He was going to race this man. And he was going to win. "I'm not nervous," he said.

"Good. We'll do two practice circuits before we start. Paul can signal the first and last circuits with a flag."

Alex examined the course. It was a series of twists and sharp turns with two straight sections where he would be able to pick up speed. Part of the track rose steeply on metal legs and then

138

sloped down the other side; it formed a bridge over another section of the track below. Alex realized he would have to slow down as he took it. He would be about six metres up – and although the sides of the bridge were lined by a protective wall of rubber tyres, he didn't like to think what would happen if he lost control and hit them. After the bridge, there was a long tunnel with the finishing line on the other side.

He climbed into his kart and pressed the ignition button. At once the engine burst into noisy life. Already Alex felt horribly exposed. The kart had no sides, no roof. He was sitting with his knees bent, his feet stretched out in front of him. He pulled a seat belt over his shoulder and attached it. It was too late to back out now. Drevin had started his kart and was moving off smoothly. Alex tested the pedals on either side of the steering column. There were just two. The left foot operated the brake, the right foot the throttle. His kart leapt forward, the engine anxious to blast him onto the track. Drevin was already well ahead. Alex gritted his teeth and pressed his foot down.

Nought to sixty in 3.8 seconds. Alex didn't go as fast as that on the first practice circuit but, even so, the power of the engine took him by surprise. There was no speedometer and being so low it was hard to judge how fast he was really going. He guessed he was doing about forty miles an hour, although it felt a lot faster. The track was a blur. The whole circuit seemed to have contracted as his vision telescoped. He saw the grandstand whip past. The mechanics had stopped what they were doing and were watching his progress. His entire concentration was focused on his hands gripping the wheel. His arms were shuddering. He came to a corner and twisted the wheel right. He felt the tyres slide behind him and almost lost control. He was oversteering. Quickly he corrected himself. The kart entered the raised section and he found himself climbing. Halfway over the bridge, the track cornered sharply to the left. Alex swerved round and the wall of black tyres shimmered past. He had almost hit them. Already he regretted accepting this absurd challenge. He had only just come out of hospital. One mistake at this speed and he would be heading right back.

He completed his first circuit and began another. There was no sign of Drevin, and Alex wondered if he had left the track. Then there was a roar behind him and the Russian overtook, his face hidden beneath the black helmet. He had managed two complete circuits in the time that Alex had done one and a half. There was clearly going to be no contest unless Alex put his foot down. How fast had Paul said the karts could go? A hundred miles an hour. Madness!

And there was Paul, positioned on the grandstand, a chequered flag in his hand. Drevin had slowed down, waiting for Alex to catch up. The race was about to begin. Well, at least Alex had had a chance to test the worst corners and bends. He'd begun to work out his race line. And it occurred to him that he might have one big advantage over Drevin. He weighed a lot less than him. That would give him the edge when it came to speed.

But there was no time for further thought. The flag fell. They were off.

Forty miles an hour – fifty – sixty. Just inches above the blur of the tarmac, Alex pressed his right foot down as far as it would go and felt the burst of power behind him. He quickly caught up with Drevin. They came to a bend. Drevin took it tight, hugging the inside. Alex shot round the outside and suddenly he was in the lead as he screamed through the tunnel. So he was right: his weight would make the vital difference. Now all he had to do was stay ahead for the next two laps and he would win.

He had just begun the second circuit when his kart shuddered. For a moment, Alex thought the engine had misfired. Then it happened again, harder this time. He felt himself being jerked back in his seat and the bones in his neck rattled. The tyres slewed and he had to fight for control. A third knock. At this speed it felt as if he had been hit by a sledgehammer. He glanced back and real- ized what was happening. Drevin was bumping him from behind. He was being quite methodical about it; he wasn't trying to overtake. They were doing seventy miles an hour, suspended in the middle of a bare steel frame that offered no protection at all. Did Drevin want to kill them both?

Alex braked and immediately Drevin soared ahead, shooting up the raised section of the track. Alex followed, looking for an opportunity to slip past him. But Drevin was cheating again, zigzagging left and right, refusing to give him any space. They roared down the slope and onto the straight, then plunged into the tunnel. After the bright sunlight, it was very dark inside. Alex accelerated and drew level with Drevin. Drevin twisted his wheel and crashed sideways into Alex.

The whole world leapt. Sparks exploded in the darkness as metal tore into metal. The walls of the tunnel rushed past. Desperately Alex fought for control, and as the two karts burst out into daylight, he dropped back. Once again Drevin had the lead.

Out of the corner of his eye, Alex saw Paul wave the flag, signalling the third and final circuit. The race seemed to have lasted only seconds – and it looked as if Drevin had it in the bag. Alex thought about letting him go. What did it matter who won? After all, this was Drevin's toy. Drevin was paying the bills. It might be polite to lose.

But something inside him rebelled against the idea. He stamped down, urging his kart on. Once more he drew level with his opponent. Now the two karts were side by side, heading up the ramp for the last time. Alex saw Drevin glance across and then wrench at his steering wheel. Alex understood at once what he was doing: Drevin was trying to knock him into the tyres and over the edge! For a horrible moment, Alex saw himself somersaulting sideways in his kart. He saw the world turning upside down and heard the grinding of metal as he hit the tarmac below. Would Drevin really kill him just to win a race? His nerves screamed at him. *Stop now!* This was stupid. He had nothing to prove.

Drevin slammed into him again. That was it. There was no way Alex was going to let the Russian billionaire win. He touched the brake, as if accepting defeat. Drevin shot ahead, swerving round the corner. Then Alex accelerated. But he didn't turn the wheel. Instead he aimed straight for the wall of tyres. He hit them head-on and, yelling out loud, soared into the air. For a brief moment he hung in space. Black tyres cascaded all around him, spinning away like oversized coins. Then he was falling. The tarmac rushed up to greet him. There was a bone-shuddering crash as he hit the track below, and Alex was slammed into his seat. The steering wheel twisted in his hands, trying to pull away as he struggled for control. Somehow the kart kept going. Tyres bounced all around and he was forced to swerve wildly. But he had done it. He had cut the corner and now he was ten metres ahead of Drevin.

The tunnel loomed in front of him. He roared into the darkness and out the other side, across the finishing line. He slammed on his brakes. Too hard. The kart slewed round in an uncontrollable spin and stopped. The engine stalled. But the race was over.

Alex had won.

A few seconds later, Drevin pulled up next to him. He tore off his helmet. He was sweating heavily; his hair was plastered to his scalp. He was furious.

"You cheated!" he exclaimed. "You missed part of the track."

"You pushed me," Alex protested. "It wasn't my fault."

"We will race again!"

"No thanks." Alex had removed his helmet, glad to feel the breeze on his face. "It was a lot of fun but I think I've had enough." He climbed out of the kart. The mechanics were hovering beside the track, wondering if they should approach.

Paul arrived, still carrying the flag. "I can't believe what I just saw! That was amazing, Alex. But you could have been killed!"

"The race is void," Drevin said. "I did not lose!"

"Well, you didn't win either," Alex muttered.

Paul stood there helplessly, looking from one to the other. Drevin considered for a moment, then shook his head slowly. "It was a draw," he muttered. Then he turned and walked away.

Alex watched him go. "I see what you mean," he murmured. "He really doesn't like losing."

Paul turned to Alex, his expression serious. "You should be careful, Alex," he warned. "Don't make him your enemy." He ran after his father.

Alex was left standing alone.

INJURY TIME

By Saturday the race seemed to have been forgotten. Nikolei Drevin was in a good mood as he waited for another of his Rolls-Royces – this one a silver Phantom – to be brought round to the front door. It was an important day for him. Stratford East, the team he had bought for twenty million pounds, were playing Chelsea in the Premiership and, although they had been comprehensively beaten three–nil by Newcastle only the week before, Drevin was in high spirits.

"Have you always supported Chelsea?" he asked Alex as they left the house.

"Yes." It was true. Alex lived only twenty minutes from Stamford Bridge and he had often gone to games with his uncle.

"The club was almost bankrupt when it was bought by Roman Abramovich." Drevin looked thoughtful. "I met him a few times in Moscow.

We did not get on. I hope to disappoint both of you today."

Alex said nothing. There was an intensity in Drevin's voice that suggested that, as far as he was concerned, this was more than a game. The Rolls-Royce pulled up and the two of them got in.

Paul Drevin wasn't coming. He'd had a bad asthma attack the night before and his doctor, who was based twenty-four hours a day at Neverglade, had said he needed a day's rest. And so Alex found himself alone with Drevin in the back of the car as they were driven down the motorway to London.

"You have no parents," Drevin said suddenly.

"No. They both died when I was very young."

"I'm sorry. An accident?"

"A plane crash." It was easy for Alex to repeat the lie that MI6 had been telling him all his life.

"You have no relations?"

"No. Just Jack. She looks after me."

"That is very unusual. But then it seems to me that you are an unusual boy. It would be interesting, I think, to have a son like you." Drevin looked out of the window. "How are you getting on with Paul?" he asked.

"Fine."

"He likes you." Drevin was still looking away, avoiding Alex's eye. "I wish that he was a little more like you. He seems so ... aimless."

"Maybe he'd be happier if you let him go to an ordinary school," Alex said.

"That is not possible."

"Do you really think he's in any danger?"

"He is my son." Drevin spoke the words with no emotion at all. He had summed Paul up. There was nothing else to say. He forced a thin smile to his lips. "But enough of that," he went on. "My team will beat your team. That is all that matters today."

An hour later, they turned onto the Fulham Road and were forced to drive at a snail's pace through the thousands of people who were arriving for the game, the Chelsea fans in blue, the Stratford East supporters in red and black. Alex was glad that Drevin's Rolls-Royce had tinted windows. Nobody could look in. He had come to Stamford Bridge a hundred times on foot and he'd always loved the sense of belonging, that moment when he became part of the crowd battling its way through rain or snow in the hope of seeing a home win. This was too comfortable, too isolated. He would have felt embarrassed if anyone had seen him.

They turned into the complex of hotels, restaurants and health clubs that had come to be known as Chelsea Village, then swept away from the fans, following a narrow passageway to the west stand. The car stopped in front of a revolving door with the words MILLENNIUM RECEPTION in silver above. They got out.

Drevin had become more tense the closer they got to London. His eyes and mouth were three narrow slits and he was twisting his ring in short, jerky movements.

"Here is Miss Knight," he said, and Alex saw Tamara Knight, the over-efficient personal secretary he had met at the Waterfront Hotel. She was still dressed smartly in a jacket and shirt, even though she was at a football match. Alex noticed she was wearing black and red earrings: at least she hadn't completely forgotten her team colours.

"Good afternoon, Mr Drevin. Alex..." She nodded at both of them. "Lunch is being served on the third floor. I have your passes." She gave them two security passes marked ALL ACCESS + T.

"What does the T stand for?" Alex asked.

"I presume it means you can go through the tunnel," Tamara explained. She sounded uninterested. "In fact you can go anywhere you like, except onto the pitch." She turned to Mr Drevin. "Good luck this afternoon," she said.

"Thank you, Miss Knight."

They went into what could have been the foyer of a very smart health club, with a dark wooden desk, a turnstile and a wide corridor with two oversized lifts. A uniformed security guard and a receptionist watched them as Tamara called the lift. They travelled up to the third floor in silence.

Alex realized that he was entering hallowed ground. This was where the directors, chairmen, managers and corporate sponsors came. Normally he wouldn't have been allowed anywhere near.

Yet still he felt ill at ease. Drevin might have forgotten the kart race but he hadn't. It seemed to Alex that the more he learnt about him, the less attractive he became. *An absolutely wonderful man*. That was how Crawley had described him. Well, MI6 had said much the same about Damian Cray. Alex knew that Drevin was a bad loser, and he had dark feelings about this match which he couldn't shake off.

"How are you enjoying your stay with Mr Drevin?" Tamara asked suddenly.

"It's fine."

"I hope you're keeping out of trouble."

Was she trying to tell him something? Alex examined the attractive blue eyes, but they were giving nothing away.

The lift doors opened and they walked out into a corridor lined with dark wooden panels, and into a dining room with a buffet table on one side. Waitresses were circulating with champagne. Unlike the rest of the complex, the room was old-fashioned with a moulded ceiling and a series of ornate, smoked glass windows. But for the two widescreen televisions mounted on the walls, it could have belonged to the nineteenth century.

Drevin accepted a glass of champagne and sat down at one of the tables where about half a dozen people, including the Stratford East chairman and a couple of the footballers' wives, were already seated. There were about fifty people in the room.

Alex recognized a couple of television actors chatting to the Chelsea chairman, who – unlike Drevin – looked completely at ease. A waitress gave Alex a glass of lemonade, and he sipped it in silence.

He found himself standing beside Tamara Knight. "Are you a football supporter?" he asked.

"No." She looked bored. "I've never really understood the British obsession with football. Of course, I want Mr Drevin to win. But otherwise I don't really care."

Alex found himself getting annoyed. Tamara looked like a model or an actress. But she seemed determined to act like a cold-blooded businesswoman. "How did you come to work for Mr Drevin?" he asked.

"Oh, an agency recommended me."

"Do you enjoy it?"

"Of course I do. Mr Drevin is a very interesting man." She was unwilling to say any more and looked relieved when the door suddenly opened and a young woman came striding in. Alex took in the blonde hair, the permanent tan, the diamond collar necklace and the perfect teeth. He recognized her instantly. Her face was rarely absent from the tabloids or the television screen.

Her name was Cayenne James and she had once been a model and an actress. Then she had married Adam Wright, one of the country's most famous strikers and a member of the England squad. Wright had made the headlines himself when Drevin had paid twenty-four million pounds to buy him from Manchester United; he was now the captain of Stratford East. Alex wasn't surprised that his wife had turned up to see him play.

He watched as she went over to Drevin and kissed the air close to his cheeks, then sat down and helped herself to champagne. The conversation in the room had quietened when she came in and Alex was able to hear their first exchange.

"How are you, Niki?" She had a loud, school-girlish voice. "Sorry I'm late. I just popped into Harrods. It's only down the road."

"Was your husband with you?"

"No! Don't worry!" She giggled. "Adam's been concentrating on the big match. He never comes shopping when there's a game coming up..."

More food was served. Alex was feeling increasingly out of place. He was sorry Paul hadn't been able to come. It was half past two. He wished the game would begin.

Half an hour later it did. The smoked glass windows and doors were opened and everyone walked out. Alex went with them, emerging onto a stand with about a hundred seats, one tier up, exactly opposite the tunnel. And at that moment he was able to forget Drevin, Neverglade, go-karting and all the rest of it. The magic of the stadium, moments before kick-off, overwhelmed him.

Stamford Bridge has room for over forty-two thousand spectators and today, in the bright afternoon sunlight, every seat was full. Music was pounding out of the speakers, fighting with the fans, who were already chanting good-humouredly. Alex watched as a Mexican wave travelled in a huge circle in front of him. He had been given seat A10, perfectly placed between the two goals. There were no policemen in sight. Chelsea has its own army of stewards but it didn't look as if anyone was in the mood for trouble.

Then there was a roar as the teams emerged and formed two lines, each one accompanied by a small child. The referee and the two linesmen joined them.

"You're next to me," Tamara Knight announced.

Alex sat down. He was determined to enjoy the next hour and a half.

But it was obvious, almost from kick-off, that it was going to be a hard, unfriendly game. After just ten minutes, one of the Chelsea players was brought down by a vicious tackle that immediately earned Stratford East a yellow card. It was to be the first of many. Chelsea dominated the first half, and but for the hard work of the Stratford East keeper, they would have soon taken the lead. Then, half an hour in, the right winger gathered the ball and sent it in a perfect cross to the penalty area and a second later it had been headed into the goal. The crowd roared; the speakers blared. It was one–nil to the home side, and just five minutes later the Chelsea captain beat two defenders and powered the ball into the back of the net.

Stratford East went into the break two goals down.

There were more drinks served in the dining room during the interval but Alex was careful to avoid Nikolei Drevin. He remembered how he'd behaved at the end of the kart race. This was a thousand times more humiliating. The game was being shown all over the country. Drevin had spent a sizeable fortune building up his team. And the fact that he was being beaten by Chelsea – owned by another Russian – somehow made it all the worse.

Cayenne James didn't help. "Never mind, Niki," she said in her silly, high-pitched voice. "It's not over yet. I'm sure Adam will be talking to the boys in the dressing room."

"It would be nice if your husband were to touch the ball," Drevin replied. He had a glass of champagne but was holding it as though it were poison.

"He does seem a bit tired today. Maybe he's saving his strength for the second half."

In fact, Adam Wright was barely visible when the game began again, and Alex wondered why the manager didn't pull him off. He was playing in the centre but never seemed to be anywhere near the ball, and when he did take possession he didn't create a single opportunity. Alex knew that the Stratford East captain had been given a bad ride by the press. He should never have left Manchester

United. He spent more time modelling clothes and advertising aftershave than playing football. His last outings for England had been dismal. Half the country had turned against him, and perhaps it was now affecting his game.

The next goal, when it came, was more of a fluke than anything else. There was an untidy scrabble in front of the Chelsea goal and for a moment the ball was invisible. Then a Stratford East player got his foot to it. The ball deflected off another player's thigh and sailed past inches away from the Chelsea keeper's outstretched fingers. It wasn't pretty but it made the score two–one with fifteen minutes left to play.

After that, Chelsea rarely lost control of the ball. Alex found himself willing them on, hoping they would keep their lead until the final whistle. He knew it was ungenerous of him; he was here as Drevin's guest. But Chelsea were the better team and he'd been a blue all his life. He kept his emotions to himself, though, resisting the temptation to join the home supporters as they urged their team on.

Full time. It seemed that Chelsea had it in the bag. But then, out of nowhere, three minutes into injury time, came the chance to equalize: a foul inside the Chelsea penalty area. One of the Stratford East players went down, gripping his leg in agony, and although Alex suspected he was faking, the referee believed him. There was a blast of the whistle. Another yellow card. A roar of disbelief from the crowd. But Stratford East had been awarded the penalty. It had to be the last shot of the game.

Adam Wright stepped forward to take it.

He couldn't miss. He had taken penalties for England countless times. Alex had watched him perform brilliantly against Portugal in the last European Championships, firing the ball into the net with breathtaking ease. Surely he would do the same now.

A peculiar hush had descended on the stadium. After making so much noise, it was astonishing that over forty-two thousand people could be so quiet. Alex glanced at Drevin sitting four seats away. The man's entire body was tense but there was something close to a smile on his face. He knew there was no way Stratford East could win this game. But a draw would be enough. There was no humiliation in a draw.

Adam Wright settled the ball on the penalty spot.

The other Stratford East players were ranged behind him. The Chelsea keeper was crouching, rubbing his hands together. The moment seemed to stretch out to an eternity. The crowd held its collective breath.

Adam Wright ran his hands through his hair. It was long this season, with blond highlights. The referee blew his whistle. A single, short blast. Wright ran forward almost lazily and kicked.

Alex watched in disbelief.

Something had gone terribly wrong. The keeper had been misdirected and had dived to the left, but the ball hadn't gone anywhere near the goal. A clump of grass and mud sailed in one direction while the ball soared in the other, passing at least a yard over the crossbar. Adam Wright realized what had happened and, even at this distance, Alex thought he could see the shock in his eyes. Then, slowly, everything seemed to unfreeze. The keeper got to his feet, punching the air with both fists. The other Stratford East players stood where they were, stunned. The Chelsea fans roared their pleasure; the visiting supporters sat in paralysed silence.

And Drevin? He had gone very pale. His hands were clasped together, his eyes empty.

A few seats away from him, Cayenne James giggled nervously. "Oh dear!" she squealed.

Drevin turned to look at her and Alex could see that he made no attempt to disguise the contempt in his face.

And then it was all over. The referee didn't even bother with another kick-off. He blew the final whistle and the two teams came together, shaking hands and swapping shirts. More music pounded out as the screens flashed up the final score. Two–one to Chelsea. The stewards reappeared and the crowd started to trickle out of the stadium.

Drevin was suddenly very much alone. As Alex watched, he dug a hand into his trouser pocket and took out a mobile phone. He pressed a speed dial button and spoke briefly. Alex got the feeling that he was talking in Russian, but even if it had been English, he wouldn't have been able to hear above the general din. Drevin's face was colourless. Whatever he was saying, Alex doubted he was sending his team a congratulatory message.

Drevin put his phone away and stood up. He seemed to notice Alex for the first time.

"I'm sorry," Alex muttered. He didn't know what to say.

"There will be other games." Drevin's voice was heavy. "If you don't mind, Alex, I will ask Miss Knight to accompany you home. The driver is waiting outside. I have some business to attend to."

Tamara nodded. "Whatever you say, Mr Drevin."

Drevin went back into the dining room. Alex took one last look at the stadium, at the great rectangle of bright green grass, at the departing spectators. He knew it was unlikely he would ever have this view of Stamford Bridge again.

Something caught his eye.

The sun glinting off something. Somebody in the crowd.

No. It wasn't possible.

Alex looked again, then hurried down the steps to the edge of the terrace and looked more carefully, his eyes searching the milling crowd. He knew what he had seen. He just hoped he was mistaken.

He wasn't.

Silver Tooth was standing on the edge of the pitch. Alex looked down, shocked. The man he'd knocked out with the defibrillator and who had been there with Force Three when he was interrogated was there, in the crowd! He had been watching the game as if that was what he did on a Saturday afternoon when he wasn't kidnapping people. Alex watched as he slipped something into his jacket pocket and then began moving slowly towards the south stand.

Tamara Knight called out to him. "Alex?"

What should he do? Alex didn't want any more involvement with Force Three. He was meant to be on holiday, recuperating. But he couldn't just let the man walk away.

He made his decision. He turned and ran past her. "I'll meet you at the car!" he called out.

And then he was gone, through the glass doors into the dining room, searching for the way back down.

BLUE MURDER

Force Three were here at Stamford Bridge.

As Alex burst out into the open air, he knew they hadn't come to watch a football match. They had already attacked Drevin once – through his son. Was it possible they were going to try again, this time by targeting his football team?

Alex reached the edge of the pitch and looked around. The crowd was slowly disappearing through the various exits, like sand trickling out of a leaking bucket, but there must still have been at least ten thousand people in the stadium. Now that he was at ground level, he wondered if he would have any chance of spotting the man he knew only as Silver Tooth again.

Up on the giant television screens, Adam Wright was being interviewed about the missed penalty. The Stratford East captain had a boyish face; he could have been about nineteen. He looked and sounded as if he was sulking.

"...so I don't really know what happened," he was saying. "I thought the ball moved just before I kicked it. The soil was a bit soft around the penalty spot. I don't know. It's just one of those things, I suppose. There's always next time..."

Alex glanced away from the image and that was when he saw him. Silver Tooth was wearing an orange Gore-Tex jacket. Perhaps he thought it was going to rain. There was a large gap between the terraces and the pitch, and Alex saw Silver Tooth as he separated from the crowd. He was walking purposefully round the front of the south stand, not making for any of the exits. Alex was able to examine him properly for the first time. He was in his twenties. Not English. His looks were Middle Eastern. His hair was long and dirty. It wasn't just his teeth that needed attention. Alex followed him behind the goal and towards the players' tunnel. What was the man doing here? He turned the question over and over in his mind.

Silver Tooth reached the tunnel and disappeared from sight. Alex quickened his pace, grateful for the security pass around his neck. A couple of stewards glanced his way but neither of them tried to stop him. It occurred to him that Silver Tooth must have a pass too. If so, how had he got it? Or was his simply forged?

He reached the tunnel, which was surrounded by a sea of empty blue seats with the press box just above. Nine steps led down to an old-fashioned metal and wire gate. In normal circumstances Alex would have given anything to be here. He had watched his team emerge countless times from right where he was standing. He could picture the spectators in their thousands, hear the chanting and clapping swelling into a roar of excitement as the players appeared. This really was the lion's mouth. But he couldn't feel any excitement. Despite all his resolutions, Alex knew that he was getting into trouble once again. Trouble, it seemed, just wouldn't let him go.

Alex entered a modern, surprisingly empty area with a ceiling so low it was oppressive, and grey tiles on the floor. There was no sign of Silver Tooth. There were a couple of gleaming silver bins and a bench where injured players could receive immediate physio. The air was cold and sterile, endlessly recycled by a powerful air-conditioning system. Everything smelled brand new, and Alex recalled that the owner of Chelsea had spent millions of pounds smartening the place up. He pushed open a door and found himself looking into the press room, a rectangular space with about twenty seats facing a narrow platform. The journalists had already left. There was an outer room with two walls covered in carefully placed advertisements and he recognized the spot where Adam Wright had been interviewed only a few minutes before.

He tried another door. As he pushed it ajar, he heard voices coming from inside. One was all too familiar. He held the door open a crack and looked through. Yes. Combat Jacket was there. The last time Alex had seen him, he had been shooting at him with an FP9 single-action pistol, blocking his escape from a blazing building. Now he was standing with his back to the door, hands on hips. Silver Tooth and Spectacles were with him. They were surrounding a fourth man who was sitting on a bench, a towel wrapped around his waist.

It was Adam Wright. This was the visiting team's changing room. Peering through the narrow crack – Alex didn't dare open the door any wider – he took in the blue padded benches, the lockers, the vending machine filled with water and Lucozade, the ultra-modern showers and toilets on the far side. The ceiling was low here too. Alex could almost feel the weight of the seating in the stand directly overhead.

The Stratford East captain was the only player in the room. The others must have left while he was being interviewed, getting out as fast as they could after losing the game. Adam Wright was looking up at the three men towering over him. He was clearly surprised to see them.

"If you guys don't mind," he said, "I was just going to take a shower. We don't usually have visitors in the players' changing room."

"We represent the Stratford East Supporters'

Club," Combat Jacket said. "And we have some-thing for you."

"A thank-you present," Spectacles added.

"That's right. To thank you for everything you've done for the team." Combat Jacket took a sealed plastic box from his pocket and held it out.

Adam Wright took it. "Well, that's very kind of you guys. But if you don't mind, I'll open it later."

"We'd prefer you to open it now."

Alex was only a few metres away from the Stratford East captain, who was sitting facing him. He watched as the player opened the box and took out a gold medallion on a chain. It was an appropriate present. Adam Wright wore more jewellery than most women: earrings, bracelets and a different necklace every day of the week. But none of this made any sense. The three men in the dressing room were killers. What were they doing offering gifts to a footballer who'd just blown a game?

"It's really nice," the Stratford East captain said, holding up the medallion. It was round and chunky, about four centimetres across, like an oversized coin. There was a figure engraved on the front. Himself, heading a ball into a net. "It's great!" he exclaimed. "Can you tell the fans that, you know, I really appreciate this."

"Aren't you going to put it on?" Combat Jacket asked.

"Sure!" Wright slipped it over his head. The

medallion rested on his muscular chest. "It's quite light. What's it made of?"

"Caesium," Combat Jacket said.

Adam Wright looked blank. "Is that rare?" he asked.

"Oh yes. Getting hold of it can be murder..."

Something nudged the back of Alex's neck. Alex stepped backwards, allowing the door of the changing room to close, and he heard no more of the conversation.

There is something about the touch of a gun that is unmistakable. It's not just the coldness of the metal; it's the whisper of death that comes with it. Very slowly, Alex turned round. He saw the gun clasped in two hands, one of them swathed in bandages. He knew that the man who held it had broken at least a couple of his fingers. Alex remembered him from the magnetic resonance imaging chamber at St Dominic's. He was short and very well built. Alex had nicknamed him Steel Watch, but the watch was no longer there. It must have been broken when the man crashed into the MRI machine. Alex was a little surprised that the same thing hadn't happened to his neck.

"You!" Steel Watch was shocked to see Alex.

Alex raised his hands. "I don't suppose you've got the time?" he asked.

Steel Watch grimaced. He seemed unsure what to do. He had been about to enter the changing room; the other members of Force Three were waiting for him. But he had a personal score to settle with Alex.

He made up his mind. "You and I are going to leave quietly together," he ordered. "I am going to walk behind you. The gun will never be more than a few inches away. You will not speak; you will not stop. If you try anything – *anything* – I will put a bullet in your spine. Do you understand?"

"Where are we going?"

"There's a van. I'll show you. Now move."

Alex had no choice. He could see that Steel Watch meant exactly what he said. He was going to force him out of the stadium and make him a prisoner for a second time. Alex knew if he got in the van, he'd be dead anyway. Both Combat Jacket and Steel Watch had a score to settle with him. They were adults. Professional killers. He was a child. But he had beaten them twice. They were going to enjoy making him pay.

Steel Watch gestured with his gun and Alex walked down a corridor leading away from the tunnel. He had noticed that the man was wearing a security pass just like his. It had to be fake. There was nobody around, but even if one of the stewards did appear, there would be nothing Alex could do. If he called for help, Steel Watch would kill him and then run. There were still hundreds of people milling around Stamford Bridge; it would be simple to disappear into the crowd.

Briefly Alex thought about Adam Wright and

wondered what was going on inside the changing room. But there was nothing he could do for the footballer. He was more worried about himself.

They left the building. The east stand was now behind them, the terraces slanting up at an angle from the ground. There was a high wall straight ahead. Alex knew that the railway ran behind it – the wall had been built to keep out the noise. On the other side of the tracks was a cemetery. Alex had been there when his uncle, Ian Rider, was buried. He had to think. If he didn't do something soon, he might well end up joining him.

Steel Watch jabbed the gun into the small of his back, deliberately hurting him. He had seen a couple of policemen standing on the other side of the gates that led into the Fulham Road. There was an endless queue of people filtering slowly out of the gates. The bars, restaurants and hotels were open. Alex paused. He couldn't believe they were about to walk through the middle of it all.

Steel Watch sensed his hesitation. "We are going to start walking now," he hissed. "Remember. The gun is out of sight. There'll be one shot and nobody will know where it came from. You'll be lying in the gutter and I'll be gone. Head out of the gates and across the road. I will tell you where to go after that."

Alex began to walk with the wall on his left. He turned the corner and saw the ticket booths and souvenir shop just ahead. The Stratford East fans seemed to have gone, taking their disappointment with them. But the Chelsea supporters were in no hurry. It was a mild evening and this was the place to be, meeting friends, savouring the victory. Alex knew that his situation would get worse with every step he took. Right here, now, there might be something he could do. There were the two policemen, chatting together, unaware that anything was wrong. There would be dozens more on the Fulham Road. But once Alex moved away from the crowds, he would be totally exposed. Steel Watch had mentioned a van. Alex imagined the steel door slamming shut behind him. At that moment he would be as good as dead.

He had to do something now, before it was too late. He glanced over his shoulder. Steel Watch was being careful, keeping a safe distance between them. The man had his hands tucked under his jacket. It didn't even look as if the two of them were together, but Alex knew that the gun was trained on him. If he tried anything, Steel Watch would fire through the fabric. He couldn't speak; he couldn't turn. He had to keep moving.

The gates were getting closer. The Fulham Road was beyond. One of the policemen was giving somebody directions. But they weren't going to help him. What about the crowd? Ahead of him, next to the exit, he caught a glimpse of red and black. Two Stratford East supporters in team shirts. One of them was a skinhead with small, red eyes and a ruddy, pock-marked face. He was scowling at the departing Chelsea fans and Alex could see that he would love to cause trouble. He was swaying on his feet. He'd probably been drinking. But there were too many policemen around. All he had was attitude – and he was showing as much of it as he could.

Alex was heading straight towards him with Steel Watch close behind. And suddenly he had a thought. Steel Watch was keeping an eye on his every movement. But he couldn't see his face. He couldn't see what he did with his hands.

But the Stratford East supporter could.

Alex slowed down.

"Keep moving," Steel Watch ordered in a low, ugly voice.

Alex stared at the skinhead. He had once read somewhere that if you stared at another person hard enough, they'd become aware of you. He had tried it often enough when he was bored in class. Now he focused all his attention on the man even as he continued walking forward, weaving through the crowd.

The man looked up. It wasn't telepathy; there was no real way he could avoid him. Alex was about fifteen metres away, getting closer all the time. People were crossing in front of him – fathers with their sons, couples, fans dressed in the blue Chelsea strip – but Alex ignored them. His eyes drilled into the Stratford East supporter.

The skinhead noticed him. His own eyes narrowed.

Alex's hand was against his chest. With his gaze still fixed on the man, he raised two fingers slowly and deliberately, then dropped one of them. Unseen by Steel Watch, he had signalled the score: two–one. And he had left his middle finger standing offensively upright. Alex sneered at the supporter, trying to look as aggressive as he could. The supporter stared. Alex repeated the sign. This was the worst insult he could throw at the man without opening his mouth.

Alex had been right. The Stratford East supporter was drunk. He had watched his team lose with almost as much disgust as Drevin himself, and the botched penalty in the final seconds had enraged him. And here was some cocky little sod, a Chelsea supporter, making fun of him! Well, to hell with the police. To hell with the crowd. He wasn't going to stand here and take it. He was going to sort him out.

He lumbered forward. Alex felt a spurt of excitement as he saw that his tactic had worked. Behind him, Steel Watch hadn't realized what was going on. Things had to happen very quickly; Alex needed the element of surprise.

The Stratford East supporter stopped in front of him, blocking his path. "What's your problem?" he demanded.

Alex came to a halt – he had no choice – and

he felt Steel Watch bump into him. There was no longer any distance between them.

"I said – what's your problem?"

Alex said nothing. He had been instructed not to talk. Instead he twisted his face into a sneer of amusement, mocking the man who stood in front of him.

It worked. The supporter swore at him and lashed out with his right fist. Alex ducked. The fist flew past his head and slammed into the throat of Steel Watch, who had been standing right behind him. The gun went off. The bullet hit the Stratford East supporter in the arm, spinning him round. Panic erupted. Suddenly everyone was screaming and running, aware that somebody had been shot but not knowing who had fired. The two police-men charged in through the gates. Behind them a third policeman appeared on horseback. The horse whinnied and began to push through the scatter-ing crowd.

The Stratford East supporter was sitting on the ground, clasping his injured arm. Alex felt sorry for him, but he wasn't going to hang around. The instant the gun had been fired, he had darted away, diving into the crowd, weaving left and right, hoping Steel Watch wouldn't have a chance to shoot again.

He had timed it perfectly. Steel Watch didn't dare try another shot. There were already too many people between him and Alex. And he couldn't bring out the gun without drawing attention to himself. There were police everywhere. There was nothing more he could do.

Alex ran on, past the Chelsea shop and on towards the entrance where the car had dropped him before the match. Tamara Knight was standing there. She was looking alarmed, and Alex wondered if she had heard the shot. Then he realized she was staring at him. She could tell from his face that something was wrong.

"Alex? What is it?" she demanded.

"Get help!" he exclaimed. "Call the police. Whatever." He took a deep breath. "You've got to send someone to the changing rooms. Adam Wright. I think he's in trouble."

"What? What are you talking about?"

"Force Three." It was too complicated to explain. Drevin's personal assistant was looking at him as if he were deranged. Where was he meant to begin? "Just trust me," he begged. "You need to get security over to the changing rooms. Please! Believe me..."

Tamara gazed at him for a few more seconds, summing him up. She didn't look as if she believed him. But then she nodded. "All right, then. There's a steward inside." She turned and hurried back into the west stand.

But it was already too late.

The three men had left the changing room.

Adam Wright was on his own. He fingered the new medallion they had given him. He had more than a dozen of them – in gold and platinum. He'd always liked medallions, even when he was a boy growing up in Essex. He thought they suited him.

It was strange, though. Receiving a gift after a game like that. Adam Wright thought about the missed penalty as he went over to the showers. However you looked at it, he wasn't having a good season. Maybe it was time to think about another transfer. He had to be careful. If his game began to slip, he might lose some of his advertising and sponsorship deals. And if that happened, how would he pay for his next Ferrari?

He dropped his towel. Glimpsing himself in a mirror, he smiled. He had a perfect body and he liked the way the new medallion lay against his chest. He was looking forward to showing it to Cayenne.

He turned the shower on full. Hot water blasted down. He stepped into the spray and water battered his neck and shoulders. He turned round.

The men who had given Adam Wright the medallion had told him that it was made of caesium. What they hadn't told him was that caesium is an alkali metal found in group one of the periodic table. It does not occur naturally. It has only one electron in its outer shell. And, like all alkali metals, it reacts extremely violently when exposed to water. The medallion had been given a coating of

173

wax to protect it from the atmosphere, but the wax was now melting in the shower.

Adam Wright knew there was something wrong when he felt an intense burning. For a moment, he thought the water was too hot. Then he looked down and, to his astonishment, he saw a brilliant flame bursting out in front of him. He opened his mouth to scream, and at that moment the caesium medallion exploded. The scream died in his throat. With the water rushing down, he fell to his knees, his hands outstretched, and for a brief instant he looked just like a keeper seconds after he has let the ball into the back of the net. Then he pitched forward and lay still.

Two minutes later, the door of the changing room crashed open and a group of security men rushed in. There was nothing they could do. Adam Wright was lying on the floor with water all around him. Smoke was rising up beneath his chest, creeping through his armpits.

The Stratford East captain and England striker had taken his last penalty.

And the people who had come for him hadn't missed.

EXPIRY DATE

The following day, Alex was playing table tennis with Paul Drevin. Once again Paul was beating him. The score was fifteen–eighteen and it was his serve. He fired the ball down the table, trying to put some spin on it. Paul lobbed it back. Alex went for the slam and got it. The ball hit the corner of the table and bounced over Paul's bat. Sixteen–eighteen. He was in with a chance.

The two boys were playing in the most extraordinary room Alex had ever been in. It was more than sixty metres long but only six metres wide, an oversized cigar tube with porthole windows running along the whole length. Part of the room was carpeted, with luxurious leather chairs arranged around a coffee table, a drinks cabinet and a widescreen TV. Then there was the games area: complete with table-tennis table, snooker table, PlayStation and gym. Next to it was a small but well-equipped kitchen and, on the other side, closed off, a study area with a library and conference table where Nikolei Drevin was now working.

And the whole thing was thirty-six thousand feet above the ground.

Alex and Paul were on their way to America, flying in Drevin's private 747 which he had adapted to his own needs. Forget cramped seating and microwaved food on plastic trays. The interior of this plane was beyond belief. But for the noise of the engines and the occasional turbulence, it would have been hard for Alex to believe that he was in the air.

He was glad to be out of England.

The death of Adam Wright had naturally made the front page of every newspaper. It had also been the lead story in all the news programmes on TV. This time, Alex had not been involved – and for that he had to thank Tamara Knight. She alone knew that he had seen and followed one of the killers at Stamford Bridge, and when the body in the shower had been discovered, she had decided to keep this information to herself. As she said to Alex, he'd been through enough. Force Three had already claimed responsibility for the murder, explaining that the footballer had been another victim in their war against Drevin. What difference would it make if Alex was dragged into it once again?

Tamara was on the plane too, sitting in one of the leather chairs, reading a book. Alex had glanced at the cover and seen the title. She was reading a history of space travel, obviously preparing herself for the launch that was to take place in just three days' time. She glanced up briefly as he prepared to take his next serve, then turned a page.

Alex lost the serve and, two points later, the game. He wondered if they'd reached the coast of Canada yet. It had been almost five hours since they had left Heathrow, and even with all the comforts of the 747, he was aware that he was in that strange, empty space, hovering on the edge of the world between two time zones.

"Are you hungry?" Paul asked him.

"No thanks," Alex replied. The plane had a cook and two stewardesses, who had served a brunch of fresh fruit, coffee and croissants just after they had taken off.

"We can watch a film if you like."

"All right."

Paul put down his bat and slumped into one of the nearby chairs. "It's a shame we won't have more time in New York," he said. "I really wanted to show it to you. It's a cool city just to wander around in. And it's got great shops. I was going to buy a whole load of gear."

"How long are we there for?" Alex asked.

"Dad says just one day. He's got some people to see – or we'd be going straight to Flamingo Bay." Paul pressed a button in the arm of his chair and a moment later one of the stewardesses appeared.

"Can we watch a film?" he asked.

"Of course." The stewardess smiled. "I'll bring you the menu. And would you like something to drink?"

"I'll have a Coke. Alex?"

"No. I'm fine."

Alex sat down opposite Paul, avoiding the other boy's eye. It seemed to him that Paul was more like his father than perhaps he realized. Despite his protests, he fitted comfortably into this billion-aire lifestyle, taking the private plane, the houses all over the world and the complete freedom for granted. Right now the two of them should have been at school. Alex thought of Brookland and a big part of him yearned to be with his friends, lark-ing around and getting into trouble – back in the real world.

He was feeling guilty because, although he'd said nothing to Paul, he had already made his deci-sion. As soon as he arrived in New York, he was going to leave the Drevin household. He felt sorry for Paul. More and more the other boy seemed to be relying on his friendship, taking him for granted like everything else. Paul hadn't chosen any of this but he was stuck with it, and one day it would be him jetting around the world, making all the important decisions.

But Alex had had enough. Nikolei Drevin had nothing he wanted. More than that, Alex was becoming increasingly uneasy, aware of an invisible net closing in. He had now encountered Force Three twice. He might not be so lucky a third time. Whatever their argument with Drevin, he didn't want to be any part of it.

And then there was the question of Drevin himself. There was so much about the man that didn't add up. If he was so concerned about Paul's safety, why hadn't he put any guards in place at St Dominic's? And was it just coincidence that the kidnappers had taken Alex to a building that Drevin – or one of Drevin's many companies – actually owned? Alex thought about his meeting with Kaspar. The Force Three leader had been about to cut off one of his fingers – and would have if Alex hadn't convinced him who he really was. If Paul Drevin had been kidnapped, he would have been maimed. Why? Was there some sort of private vendetta between Nikolei Drevin and Kaspar that both men were keeping concealed?

Alex didn't trust Drevin. That was the simple truth. When they had raced against each other, Drevin had tried to kill him. If Alex had flipped over inside the tunnel, he might have been crushed – and all because the Russian didn't like losing. He had lost again at Chelsea, and as a result a man had died. Was Drevin responsible for that too? Alex remembered seeing him talking on his mobile seconds after the game had ended. And when Alex had spotted Silver Tooth, he had been slipping something into his pocket. Could it have been a phone?

Was it possible that he had been taking his orders directly from Drevin?

Well, he had decided. As soon as he arrived in New York, he was going to call Jack Starbright, who was only a couple of hours away in Washington. He knew she'd be happy for him to join her, especially if she thought he was in any danger. He would tell Nikolei Drevin that he was homesick. It didn't matter what excuse he made up. When Drevin and his son flew to Flamingo Bay, they would be travelling without him.

"Is everything all right, Alex?"

Alex looked up and realized that Tamara Knight had been examining him. He still hadn't worked her out. She had never been particularly friendly to him and seemed completely devoted to Nikolei Drevin. On the other hand, as far as he knew, she had never told Drevin about his involvement in Adam Wright's death. Right now, she was studying him suspiciously. Maybe she was trying to work him out too.

"I'm fine, thanks," Alex said.

"Are you looking forward to the launch?"

Alex shrugged. "I suppose so."

Paul had chosen a film. The lights in the centre of the cabin dimmed and a few minutes later it began.

It was just after one o'clock, New York time, when they touched down at JFK Airport. Nikolei Drevin had come out of his study for the last hour of the flight, dictating a letter to Tamara and chatting to Paul. Part of the conversation was in Russian and Alex got the feeling that father and son were talking about him.

The 747 taxied to a holding area. Looking out of a window, Alex saw a chauffeur-driven limousine waiting to meet them. He guessed that a man as rich and influential as Drevin wouldn't have to queue up at immigration with everyone else, and he was right. The door of the plane opened electronically and two men in suits – customs and immigration – were shown in. One of them had a metal attaché case which contained a computer and an old-fashioned passport stamp.

"Good afternoon, Mr Drevin, sir," the man said. He was young, clean-shaven, with short blond hair and dark glasses. "Welcome to New York."

"Thank you." Drevin held out his passport.

The man ran it through the scanner on his computer without so much as glancing at it, then stamped one of the pages. He did the same for Paul and Tamara. He took Alex's last, gazed at the photograph and lowered it behind the lid of his case. For a moment it was out of sight as he scanned it, but then he was holding it up again with a look of polite puzzlement.

"I'm sorry, sir," he said to Drevin. "We have a problem here."

"What problem?" Drevin was annoyed.

"This passport is out of date. It expired two days ago."

"That's not possible." Drevin reached for the passport. He looked at the expiry date, then at Alex. "The man is correct," he said.

"No." Alex was shocked. It was true he hadn't looked closely at his passport for a long time, but he was certain he'd only had it four years. There was an absurd photograph of him aged ten; he remembered going with Jack to have it taken. "It can't be!" he protested.

Drevin handed him the passport. Alex studied it. It was the same photo. The terrible haircut embarrassed him as it always did. There was his signature, and Ian Rider's name and address as next of kin. But the immigration man was correct. His passport had expired the day before he left London.

"But how can it have happened?" Alex asked. He couldn't believe he'd been so stupid. "Why didn't they notice at Heathrow?"

"I guess they didn't look closely enough," the American said.

"What does this mean?" Drevin asked. His voice was cold.

"Well, sir, I'm very sorry but we can't allow your guest to enter the United States. In normal circumstances he'd be sent back home, but I guess we can work something out. How long do you plan to be here?"

"Less than twenty-four hours," Drevin replied. "We leave tomorrow."

"In that case, we can hold Mr Rider here at the airport. It'll be like he's in transit. You can pick him up again when you leave."

"But the child only wishes to stay here one night. Surely he can't be such a threat to American security that you won't allow him to stay with me!"

"I'm very sorry, Mr Drevin. It's like I say. Really he should be on his way back to the UK. I'm stretching things as it is. But I can't allow him in."

"I don't understand it," Alex insisted. "I only got it four years ago – I'm sure of it." He was feeling wretched. Both Drevin and his son were staring at him as if this were all his fault, which, he supposed, in a way it was.

"It seems we have no choice in the matter, Alex," Drevin said. He turned to the immigration officer. "Where will you hold him?"

"We have rooms here at the airport, sir. He'll have a TV and a shower. I can assure you he'll be fine."

"Then it seems we'll have to pick you up tomorrow, Alex."

Drevin got up and left the aircraft. Paul and Tamara followed. The assistant had said nothing throughout the discussion. Alex looked out of the window as they got into the limousine. A moment later they drove away and he found himself alone with the two Americans.

"Do you have any hand luggage?" the immigration man asked.

"No."

"OK. My name's Shulsky, by the way. Ed Shulsky. You'd better come with me."

Alex followed the American down onto the tarmac, the customs official close behind. There was another car waiting for them and Alex climbed into the back. Shulsky took the front seat. The other man stayed behind.

"Just relax. This won't take long," Shulsky said.

The doors had locked themselves automatically. Feeling far from relaxed, Alex sat back and watched where they were going.

They drove out of the airport, passing through a double barrier and a gate. That already struck him as odd. Hadn't Shulsky just said he was going to have to spend the night at JFK? But it seemed they were heading for Manhattan. The driver joined the traffic on the freeway that led to Brooklyn Bridge, and suddenly Alex found himself looking across the water to the most famous skyline in the world. Even now, even in these circumstances, the view couldn't fail to thrill him, the magnificent arrogance of the skyscrapers packed together on the cramped, chaotic island a monument to power and success and the American way of life.

Alex leant forward. "Where are we going?" he demanded.

"We'll be there soon," Shulsky answered.

"I thought you said we were staying at the airport."

"Relax, Alex. We'll look after you just fine."

Alex knew something was going on. There had been nothing wrong with his passport. He was sure of it. But there wasn't anything he could do. He was locked in a car on the other side of the world and he might just as well sit back and – as the Americans would say – be taken for the ride.

He looked out of the window as they crossed the bridge and turned north, heading past the terrible empty space where the World Trade Center had once stood. He had visited New York a couple of times and had happy memories of the city. Now he was being driven through SoHo, in south Manhattan.

The car slowed down and he noticed an art gallery with a window full of cartoons, its name printed in gold letters on the glass. They turned into a parking garage. Alex sighed and shook his head. Now he knew exactly where he was.

In Miami they had called themselves Centurion International Advertising. The gallery here in New York was called Creative Ideas Animation. Two different names but the same three letters.

CIA.

The car drove up to the first floor of the garage

and stopped. Shulsky got out and opened the door for Alex. "This way," he announced.

Alex followed him to a bare metal door that could have led into a storage cupboard or perhaps an electric generator room. A keypad was built into the wall and Shulsky entered a seven-digit code. There was a buzz and the door opened. Alex walked through into an empty corridor with a CCTV camera pointing down at him from above and another locked door at the end. It swung open as he approached.

There was a comfortable reception area on the other side, and, beyond that, open-plan offices filled with phones and computers. Two telephonists sat behind the main desk, and men and women in suits walked along the carpeted corridors. A black man with white hair and a moustache was waiting to greet him. Alex recognized him at once. His name was Joe Byrne. He was the deputy director for operations in the Covert Action section of the Central Intelligence Agency of America.

"Nice to see you again, Alex," he said.

"I'm not so sure," Alex replied. He remembered how his passport had briefly disappeared into Shulsky's attaché case. "You swapped my passport," he said. "The one you showed Drevin was a fake."

Joe Byrne nodded. "Come this way. Let me show you to my office. I think it's time you and I had a little chat."

THE BIGGEST CRIMINAL IN THE WORLD

Byrne's office was identical to the one that Alex had visited in Miami. It had the same ordinary furniture, the same blank walls, the same air-conditioning turned up one notch too high. Only the view was different. Alex guessed he probably had something similar in just about every major city in America.

"You fancy a drink?" Byrne asked as he sat down behind his desk.

"Some water, thanks." There were a couple of bottles on a sideboard. Alex helped himself.

"It's good to see you again, Alex." Byrne sounded tired. He looked as if he hadn't been to bed for a week. "I was never able to thank you for the work you did for us on Skeleton Key."

"I was sorry about your agents."

"Tom Turner and Belinda Troy. Yeah, it was too bad. I was sorry to lose them. But that wasn't your fault. You did a great job." Byrne ran his eyes over Alex. "You look in good shape," he went on. "I was sorry to hear you got hurt in London. I told that boss of yours, Alan Blunt, that it wasn't a good idea getting a kid involved in this sort of work. Of course, he didn't listen to me. He never does. In a way, that's why you're here now."

"Why *am* I here now?"

"We had to get you away from Drevin without alerting him to the fact that the CIA was involved," Byrne explained. "Like you said, we swapped your passport, so now he thinks you're tied up with customs and immigration. That gives us a chance to have a talk. As a matter of fact, I was rather hoping you might be able to help us."

"Forget it, Mr Byrne." Alex shook his head. "I'd already made up my mind before we landed. I don't want anything more to do with Drevin. So if you don't mind putting me on a plane to Washington, I'll say goodbye."

"Washington?" Byrne raised an eyebrow. "It's funny you should mention that. But I'm afraid you can't just walk out of here, Alex. Apart from anything else, you're an illegal immigrant, remember?" He quickly raised a hand in a conciliatory gesture. "Just hear me out. What I've got to say may be of genuine interest to you. And when I've finished, then you can tell me what you think. The truth is, right now you're in a unique situation. You could be very useful to us. And you have no idea how much is at stake."

Alex sighed. "Where have I heard that before?" He opened the bottle of water and sat down opposite the CIA man. "OK. Go ahead."

"Well, as you've probably guessed, this is all about Drevin," Byrne began. "Nikolei Vladimir Drevin. By our count, he's the fourth or fifth richest man alive and, of course, the British just love him. He's bought a soccer team; he's a big businessman; he gives money to charity. And then there's Ark Angel. Thanks to him, you British are going to corner the market in space tourism, and that's a prize worth having. But I'm afraid it's not as easy as that. You see, for the last eighteen months the CIA and the State Department have been investigating Drevin, and we've discovered that he isn't quite what he seems. I'm talking about organized crime, Alex. And all roads lead straight to him. To put it in a nutshell, we think he's just about the biggest criminal in the world."

Byrne paused. Alex showed no reaction. After all he'd been through, he no longer had it in him to be surprised.

"It's complicated," Byrne went on. "And even though you flew over here on Drevin's sky palace, I guess you're probably jet-lagged. So I'll give it to you in broad strokes.

"To understand Drevin, you have to go back

to the break-up of the Soviet Union in the early nineties. Communism was finished and the whole country was looking forward to a fresh start. But there was a problem. The new Russian government was broke. It needed money badly and it decided to sell off all its assets, which is to say, its car manufacturing centres, its hydroelectrical plants, its airline and – most crucial of all – its oilfields. They sold them cheap, often for a fraction of their real value. They had no choice, because they needed the money fast and they needed it up front. In the next few years a new group of businessmen appeared. They were in the right place at the right time and they saw that this was a fantastic opportunity. These people weren't going to become millionaires overnight. As share prices rose, they were going to become *billion*aires – and that's exactly what happened.

"Nikolei Drevin was one of these people, but he was very different to the rest. We don't know a lot about his past. It's hard to find out anything that's happened in Russia in the last twenty years. We believe that Drevin started off in the army. He was certainly a senior figure in the KGB – which used to be their main security service. Then we lose track of him until he re-emerges with a successful business selling – of all things – gardening equipment. He also dabbled in shares, particularly oil. He was doing well, but not that well, and when the sale of the century started he didn't have enough money to cut himself a slice.

"And this was when he had his big idea. His work with the army and the KGB had brought him into contact with the Russian underworld – I'm talking about the mafiya. He knew all the big names and so he went to them for a loan. You see, he was a respectable businessman. He'd seen the future, and with their support he could buy into it big time. He needed about eighty million dollars, enough to buy a controlling interest in Novgerol, one of the big Russian oil companies. The mafiya met with him and decided they liked him, but they didn't have enough money, so they turned to their friends in Japan. You've heard of the yakuza? Well, they were interested too, and just to round things off, the Chinese triads also decided to join the party. Between the three of them they raised the finance and Drevin was in. Suddenly he was a major player.

"So he bought into Novgerol. He got it for a song and the people who suffered in the end were the Russian people. It was their oil and it was more or less stolen from them. I doubt that Drevin lost any sleep over that. His shares doubled and trebled and multiplied by about a hundred, and he was able to pay back all his criminal friends with interest, and that was the end of that. Of course, there were people who got in his way. There were protesters. The police launched an inquiry. And do you know what? They were all murdered. You only had to sneeze at Drevin and someone would call round at your house with a machine gun. Kill you. Kill your family. Kill everyone who knew you. It was easier to keep quiet and, believe me, after a while, people did just that.

"So Drevin is in with the mafiya. He's in with the yakuza. And he's in with the triads. And of course, once these people know him, they're not going to leave him alone. Not that Drevin cares. He's got as much money as anyone could possibly want; but the funny thing is, people like that – they always want more. So he keeps working with them. He becomes, if you like, the banker for half the criminal organizations in the world. The yakuza are selling Russian energetics weapons to terrorist groups; the triads are running drugs out of Burma and Afghanistan; the mafiya are moving into drugs and prostitution throughout the West: Drevin provides the cash flow. I would say that around the world there are hundreds of dirty deals done every day and Drevin's money is behind just about all of them."

"If you know so much about him, why don't you arrest him?" Alex asked. His head was spinning. He had just spent almost a week living with this man and he was trying to marry what Byrne was saying with what he had himself observed. He had guessed that Drevin was no saint; but he had never suspected anything like this.

"We're going to arrest him," Byrne replied. "I

told you. We've been investigating him for over a year. But when you're dealing with the really big criminals, Alex, it's not as easy as you might think. I mean, look at Al Capone. He was one of America's worst gangsters. Nobody knows how many people he had killed. But despite all the work of the FBI, in the end all they could get him for was fiddling his income tax. It's the same with Drevin.

"He's clever; he's covered his back. A deal here, a deal there – he leaves no trace. We get whispers and hints that he's involved, but it's like trying to build a castle out of individual grains of sand. Witnesses are too scared to talk. Anyone who comes forward gets killed. Even so, slowly but surely, we've been building a case against him. The State Department has collected over two thousand documents. There are transcripts, tape and video recordings, photographs. There's been a team of thirty people working round the clock for months; there still is. And they've all had to be protected. From the start, we've been afraid that Drevin might try to get to them. He might even send people in to destroy the evidence. Mercenaries. Suicide bombers. I wouldn't put anything past him. So we've stored it all somewhere really safe."

"Where?"

"That's why I was interested just now when you mentioned Washington. The case against Drevin is lodged in probably the safest place in the United States. Inside the Pentagon."

Byrne got up and helped himself to a bottle of water. All the talking had made him look more exhausted than ever.

"We plan to arrest Drevin one week from today. I hardly need tell you that this information is highly classified. The real problem is Ark Angel. The British government's invested billions in the space station, and when we arrest Drevin, the whole project could collapse. That's why we've had to wait. We've had to be absolutely sure that we've tied up all the loose ends before we make our move.

"Of course, MI6 know what we're doing. There's no way we could stop them finding out. We've shown them the evidence but they don't want to believe it. They can't afford to believe it. When Drevin goes down, there's going to be a scandal that'll rip the whole financial market apart. But that's too bad. The man is a crook; he belongs in jail."

"So why do you need me?" Alex asked.

Byrne sat down again. "Because something's happened," he admitted. "Something we don't understand – and you seem to be in the middle of it."

"Force Three."

"Exactly. Here's a group of people who call themselves eco-warriors and who seem to have picked a fight with Drevin, supposedly because he wiped out a few bird species on Flamingo Bay. But we don't know where they came from. We don't know who they are. We even wonder if Drevin himself isn't using them as some sort of diversion to distract us from our investigation. Your Mrs Jones is trying to get to the bottom of it right now – but we're running out of time. I'm worried Drevin is going to pull some kind of stunt in the next seven days and slip through our fingers. Maybe he's going to disappear. He could head off to South America, or there are parts of Australia where we'd never find him. A man with his connections wouldn't find it difficult to build himself a new identity. We need to know if he's planning to leave and, if so, where he might be going. That's where you come in.

"I've already got one agent inside his organization, but that's not enough. Drevin's too careful. He's not giving anything away. But you're different. You're right in the middle of the family. You're buddies with Paul Drevin. And the best thing is, they don't know anything about you. You're above suspicion. They certainly don't know about your connection with us.

"Tomorrow they're going to take you with them to Flamingo Bay. It's like Skeleton Key all over again. We can't get anyone in there. He's got the rocket base on the south of the island and the whole place is protected by his own private security force. It's not even American soil. The island is ten miles off the coast of Barbados and it just happens to belong to the British. Drevin leased

195

it from your government when he built his space centre there. So we can't go storming in.

"All I'm asking is for you to hang in there for one more week and report back if you see anything going on. It'll just be a vacation as far as you're concerned. You're Drevin's guest—"

"I *was* Drevin's guest," Alex cut in. "I told you. I'm leaving."

"Why?"

Alex shrugged. "What you've told me about him – I didn't much like him anyway. And now I don't want to go anywhere near him."

"You won't be in any danger."

"That's what you said last time, Mr Byrne. And I nearly got killed. Two of your agents *did* get killed."

"And if you hadn't helped us, thousands more people would have died too." Byrne looked genuinely puzzled. "What's the matter, Alex? Are you scared? Is it because of what happened with the sniper?"

Alex felt a twinge of pain in his chest. It happened every time anyone reminded him of his bullet wound. Perhaps it always would. "I'm not scared," he said. "I just don't like being used."

"We only use you because you're so damn good," Byrne replied. "And this time I'm not lying to you. You're not working for MI6 and you're not working for us. I just want you to continue with your vacation and if you see Drevin packing his suitcases or

196

if a submarine turns up in the middle of the night, give us a call. I've already told you, I've got an agent on the island and there'll be a back-up team just ten miles away on Barbados. You'll be watched all the time. Nothing's going to happen to you. I'm only afraid that somehow Drevin is going to get off the hook. Seven more days, Alex. Then we can make the arrest and you can go home."

"What about Paul?" It was only now that Alex thought about Paul Drevin. He wondered if he knew the truth about his father.

"Nothing will happen to him. He'll be well looked after. I guess he'll go back to his mother."

Alex didn't speak. He wanted to refuse but something was stopping him. He didn't want Byrne to think he was afraid. Maybe it was as simple as that.

"One week," Byrne promised. "Drevin won't suspect a thing. And just in case you do run into trouble, we've got someone here who might be able to help you."

"Who?"

"He's waiting for you outside."

He stood up and Alex followed him out of the office and down a corridor to an open-plan area. There was a man sitting at a table and Alex recognized him instantly. It would have been hard not to. The man was enormously fat. He was bald with a black moustache and a round, smiling face. He was wearing a brightly coloured Hawaiian shirt that couldn't have looked more inappropriate among the dark suits of the CIA operatives. Alex had never seen so many flowers on one piece of material.

"Hello, Alex!" the man boomed.

"Hello, Mr Smithers," Alex replied.

"What a great pleasure to see you again. You're looking tremendously well, if I may say so. Mrs Jones sends her best wishes."

"She knows I'm here?"

"Oh yes. We've been keeping an eye on you. As a matter of fact, it was she who sent me here." Smithers lowered his voice, although it could still be heard across the room. "We thought you might like one or two new gadgets, and although the Americans do produce a few of their own, I rather think we lead the field. Not that they'd agree, of course!"

"Gadgets..." Alex watched as Smithers reached down and lifted a briefcase onto the table.

"Absolutely. It wouldn't be any fun without gadgets, would it? And I've come up with some quite interesting ideas. This, for example." He produced an object that Alex recognized immediately. It was an inhaler, identical to the one Paul Drevin used. "Now, we happen to know that Drevin's son has one of these," Smithers explained. "So if anyone notices this in your luggage, they'll simply assume it's his. But it's fingerprint sensitive and I've programmed it for your personal use. When you press the cylinder, it'll send out a puff of knockout gas. Effective up to about five metres. Alternatively you can twist the cylinder round twice clockwise; that turns it into a hand grenade. Five-second fuse. I tested it on one of my assistants. Poor old Bennett ... he should be out of hospital in a couple of months."

He passed it across and dived back into the case.

"Eavesdropping," he went on. "Part of your brief is to listen to anything interesting that Mr Drevin may be saying, and for that you'll need this." He brought out a slim white box with a set of headphones. Alex picked it up. It was an iPod. At least, it looked like one. "This uses microwave technology," Smithers explained. "Point the screen at anyone up to fifty metres away and listen through the headphones. You'll hear every word they say. You can also use it to contact the CIA. Rotate the click wheel three times anticlockwise and speak into it. I've got another version, by the way, packed with enough plastic explosive to blow up a building, but Mr Blunt said you weren't to have it. Shame, really. I call it the i-x-Plod.

"And one last thing. Flamingo Bay is a tropical island with lots of creepy-crawlies. So this might help..." Once again he reached into the case and this time came out with a glass bottle marked:

STINGO
Jungle-strength mosquito lotion

"Mosquito repellent," Alex said.

"Absolutely not," Smithers replied. "This is a very powerful formulation and it actually does the exact opposite. It attracts mosquitoes. In fact, once you open the bottle, it'll attract just about every insect on the island. You might find it useful if you need a diversion." He closed the case and stood up. "I'm off to St Lucia," he announced. "A little holiday – and it'll give me a chance to test my shark-repellent swimming trunks. So I won't be too far away if you need me, although I'm sure you won't. Chin-chin!"

Smithers wandered off down another corridor. Alex was left with Joe Byrne.

"So will you do it?" Byrne asked.

Alex stared at the three gadgets on the table. "It looks like everyone's already made up my mind for me."

"That's great, Alex. Thank you." Byrne gestured and the blond-haired man who had brought Alex from the airport came over. "You've already met Special Agent Shulsky," he said.

"Call me Ed," the agent said. Without the dark glasses and the intimidating manner, he seemed a lot more pleasant. Alex guessed he was still in his twenties; he looked as if he hadn't long graduated from college.

"Agent Shulsky will be heading the back-up operation," Byrne explained. "He and a dozen people will be based on Barbados. That's where you'll be landing, by the way. Flamingo Bay doesn't have its own airstrip. The moment you call, they'll come running."

Shulsky smiled. "It's a real pleasure to be working with you, Alex," he said. "They showed us your file. I have to say, it's more than impressive."

"Is there anything else you want to know?" Byrne asked.

"Yes. There is one thing," Alex said. "This all came about because I just happened to be in the room next to Paul Drevin at St Dominic's Hospital. But it was no coincidence, was it? Mr Blunt put me there because he hoped I'd meet Paul and become friends with him."

Byrne hesitated. "I can't answer that for sure, Alex," he said. "But I will say this much: Alan Blunt does have a knack of making events work his way."

So it was true. Alex could have been taken to any hospital in London. But even as he lay there bleeding with a bullet in his chest, the MI6 chief had been planning ahead, engineering his next assignment. It was almost beyond belief. No. Where Blunt was concerned, it was to be expected.

"Shulsky will take you back to the airport," Byrne added. "We'll sort you out a temporary passport and Drevin will pick you up tomorrow. Good luck on Flamingo Bay."

"Just don't expect any postcards," Alex said.

He and Ed Shulsky left together. Byrne shook his head and walked slowly back the other way.

FLAMINGO BAY

The six-seater Cessna 195 seaplane circled the island almost lazily before it came in to land. Alex, along with Paul and his father, had been flown from New York to Grantley Adams International Airport on the south-east corner of Barbados. From there they had been taken by car a few miles up the coast to Ragged Point, where the seaplane had been waiting for the final ten-mile flight to Drevin's private island.

Alex could see it now, his face pressed against the window with the single propeller buzzing noisily and the starboard wing stretching out above his head. From the air, Flamingo Bay looked as ridiculously beautiful as every Caribbean island, the colours almost too intense to be true. There was the dazzling blue of the ocean, the immaculate white beaches, the rich, elemental green of the pine trees and rainforest. The weather couldn't have been more perfect for the coming launch. As the plane arced for a second time, tilting towards the stretch of water that would be its landing strip, brilliant sunshine blazed in through the window.

"There it is!" Paul Drevin leant past Alex and pointed. "You can see the launch site!" he exclaimed.

The island was about two miles long and shaped like a leaping fish. The rocket gantries stood where the eye should have been. There were two of them, right next to the sea, with about a dozen brick buildings, many of them surmounted with satellite dishes, about a quarter of a mile away. The ground in this area was quite bare, all the vegetation burned away, presumably by rocket exhaust. Alex remembered what Kaspar had told him when he had been a prisoner of Force Three. Four bird species had been made extinct on the island. He was surprised it hadn't been more.

If the head of the fish was naked, the rest of it was covered with dense rainforest separated by a narrow track which ran the full length of the island. The track led to a tall fence running north to south, with a checkpoint and a series of wooden cabins near by. This was the only way into the launch site. There were watchtowers all over the island, making sure that nobody could approach unseen by sea.

Drevin's house had been built on what Alex thought of as the fish's tail. It was a simple white structure, and even from this distance he could see that it was ultra-modern with giant glass windows giving uninterrupted views of the sea. The arched belly of the fish was one long beach with palm trees leaning towards the water. As the plane dipped down, Alex saw a brightly painted wooden jetty, three motor launches and a couple of sailing boats anchored in the shallows. He couldn't hear music from steel drums or smell the rum – but it was easy to imagine them.

"Fasten your seat belts," Drevin said. "We are about to land."

Drevin was sitting on the other side of the aisle, wearing a pale yellow open-necked shirt. He hadn't spoken much on the journey from New York, not even when he had fetched Alex from the departure lounge at JFK. Alex got the impression that Drevin blamed him personally for the mix-up over the passport. Or perhaps he was annoyed with the American authorities for inconveniencing one of his guests. Now he was deep in thought, tugging at his ring. In the bright sunlight his face looked more pale than ever.

Alex was grateful for the silence. He wasn't sure how to behave with Drevin any more. Everything Joe Byrne had told him was tumbling around in his head. In the space of just a few days, Drevin had gone from being a reclusive billionaire who didn't like losing, to the biggest criminal in the world. He was involved with the mafiya and the triads, who

– only a few months ago – had tried to kill Alex. People who got in his way died. He was another monster and here he was, sitting just a few seats away.

The Cessna swept down and landed smoothly, water spraying up towards the windows. It taxied towards the jetty and came to a halt. Paul Drevin was the first to stand up, followed by Tamara Knight, who had been sitting directly behind Alex. They made their way out into the soft heat of the Caribbean afternoon.

There was an electric buggy waiting for them, the sort that was normally used on golf courses. Drevin had already explained that there was very little petrol on the island; electric vehicles were easier. Now that he was back on land, he seemed more cheerful.

"We'll go to the house first and change," he announced. "Alex, I'm sure you'd like to see around the island. We can do that before dinner. Tomorrow I'll be busy with preparations for the launch, so the two of you will have to amuse yourselves. But there's plenty to do. Swimming, scuba-diving, sailing... Welcome, you might say, to paradise."

Drevin drove them the short distance to Little Point, the corner of the island where the house stood. The building was as impressive in its own way as every property that Drevin owned. It was almost futuristic, white with huge windows that retracted into the walls, so that at the press of a button it could be either open to the elements or enclosed. It had been raised about half a metre above the ground, presumably to allow the air to circulate. Thick, wooden legs supported it on a rocky shelf facing west. Alex guessed that the sunsets would be spectacular. There were only three bedrooms. Tamara would be staying on the other side of the island. Alex was next door to Paul. His room had two single beds, an en suite bathroom and plenty of space.

Ten minutes later, dressed in a T-shirt, knee-length shorts and sandals, Alex was back in the buggy next to Paul. It was early in the afternoon and the sun was still strong. Drevin drove them along the single track. Although the island couldn't have been more than half a mile wide, the sea had disappeared from view, lost behind a seemingly impenetrable screen of vegetation. Here the atmosphere was damp and heavy, and Alex could hear thousands of insects already active among the leaves.

They passed the cabins that Alex had seen from the air, and immediately afterwards came to an electric gate with a checkpoint and three guards on patrol. They were the first guards Alex had seen. They were dressed in pale grey overalls with a logo – a pair of wings and a streak of light – printed on the left side of their chest. They wore combat boots and carried black Mini Uzi 19mm sub-machine guns. Seeing the vicious weapons, Alex felt a twinge of unease. Joe Byrne had made this visit to Flamingo Bay sound very safe and straightforward. He was there to make sure Drevin didn't run away. Nothing more than that. But if something *did* go wrong, if Drevin found out that Alex had been in contact with the CIA, he would be trapped. He had no doubt that the motor boats would be neutralized at night. The plane had already left. Barbados and the CIA back-up team were ten miles away. Once again Alex found himself surrounded by an enemy army and, as usual, he was on his own.

The buggy stopped and a man appeared, dressed in the same grey uniform as the guards. He was an ugly man, aged in his thirties, with round cheeks, thick lips and curling, ginger-coloured hair. There was something about his face that didn't look quite real. His skin was deathly pale, as if he never stepped out into the sun. Alex could see the man's paunch pressing against his overalls. He wasn't just unfit. He looked ill.

"Good afternoon, Mr Drevin," he said. His voice suited his appearance. The words came out in a strained, unpleasant whisper as if he had something caught in his throat.

"Good afternoon." Drevin turned to the two boys. "This is one of the most important people on the island," he explained. "His name is Magnus Payne and he's the head of security." He looked at Payne. "You haven't met my son, Paul; and his friend, Alex Rider."

The security man nodded at Alex. "Nice to meet you, Alex," he said, and at that moment Alex was conscious of two things. Although he knew it was impossible, he wondered if he'd met Payne before. And there was something else. Something that felt wrong. But what?

"I should warn you that Payne has complete control over this side of the island," Drevin was explaining. "You must do what he tells you. And please don't try to get past here without his authorization."

"What's the point of a security barrier?" Alex asked. "This is an island. If someone wanted to break in, they could just swim round."

"Razor wire," Magnus Payne rasped. "Under the water. They could try, but it would be rather painful."

He raised a hand and the gate slid open, activated from inside the checkpoint. Payne climbed into the buggy next to Drevin and the four of them continued to the launch area.

Alex had seen many amazing things in his life, but the sight before him was something he knew he would never forget.

The rocket was right in front of him, on the edge of a flat, empty area, pointing towards the sky and supported by two steel arms reaching out from a huge gantry. It was at least fifty metres tall, slender and more beautiful than anything Alex could have imagined. He had seen rockets in museums; he had watched launches on TV. But this was different. It was surrounded by a vast, blue sky which seemed suddenly endless. And yet, sitting there, it seemed to radiate the power that was contained in the four solid rocket boosters that would, very soon, blast it into space. About twenty people were working around it. The rocket dwarfed them, making them look tiny.

"We call it *Gabriel 7*," Drevin said, and he couldn't keep the excitement out of his voice. "It's an Atlas 2AS rocket. You can just make out the payload." He pointed to a bulging shape close to the rocket's tip. "It's covered with an aerodynamic fairing," he went on. "It has to survive the ascent through the atmosphere. But underneath, there's a glass and steel observation module weighing 1.8 tonnes. It will take the Atlas just fifteen minutes to carry it into space, and the day after tomorrow it'll be up there, three hundred miles above our heads. The heart of Ark Angel!"

Paul shook his head. "It's really cool!"

"Cool?" Drevin snapped. "I despise this modern teenage slang! You use the language of the street to describe what you can't even begin to imagine. *Cool?* Is that all you can say?"

"What about the other rocket?" Alex asked.

He had seen the second gantry from the plane. It was further along the shore, a clear distance from the Atlas. The second rocket, slightly smaller, also seemed to be waiting for blast-off. More people surrounded it, working on the final preparations.

"Mr Payne?" Drevin turned to his head of security.

"We've brought forward the launch," Payne explained in his rasping voice. "We plan to send it up immediately after *Gabriel 7*."

"Why?" Alex wondered.

"We are involved in a series of long-term experiments," Drevin said. "We need to know more about the effects of weightlessness on the human body. The second rocket is a Soyuz-Fregat. It will carry a model of the human system into space."

"What does that mean?" Alex asked.

"An ape."

"I didn't realize you were still allowed to use animals."

Drevin shrugged. "It's not ideal. But there's no other way."

They drove to the first of the brick buildings. It was the largest in the compound, with three satellite dishes pointing up at the sky. "This is the control centre," Payne told them. "The other buildings are for storage and construction. We also have sleeping quarters and recreation facilities. There are more than sixty people working on the island."

They went in, along a corridor and into a large room with slanting windows looking out onto the launch site. Above the windows was a giant screen, blank at the moment but ready to transmit pictures of the launch itself. There were about twenty computers, arranged in two groups, facing each other. One group was marked COMMAND, the other TELEMETRY. To one side Alex noticed a conference table, a dozen chairs and another screen. A huge board with hundreds of light bulbs spelt out various information including LTST – local true solar time – the space equivalent of GMT. There was less to the control centre than Alex had imagined. In many ways it was like an oversized classroom.

A man had stood up as they came in. He was short but thickset, and looked either Chinese or Korean with neat black hair, wire-framed spectacles and a pencil moustache. He was dressed like a businessman in a smart jacket and tie. The clothes couldn't have been less appropriate on a Caribbean island, but of course the climate in the control room was conditioned. Alex could feel the sterile air blowing cold on his bare arms and legs.

Drevin introduced him. "This is Professor Sing Joo-Chan, the flight director here on Flamingo Bay. We were very lucky to be able to recruit him from the Khrunichev Space Centre."

"How do you do." Sing spoke with a cultured English accent. He shook hands with Alex and Paul, but the dark brown eyes behind the glasses showed no interest in them at all. They were children. They had no place here. That was what the eyes seemed to say.

"This is where it all happens," Drevin went on. "We'll be controlling both the launch and the docking procedure from here. Of course, most of the procedure is computerized. But we have a camera fitted into *Gabriel 7*'s nose. Travelling three hundred miles at the speed of light, it takes about 0.001 seconds for the images to be relayed back here. It's a bit like a giant computer game, except when you press a button here you're manoeuvring about four tonnes of equipment in outer space. You can't afford mistakes."

Sing shook his head. "There will be no mistakes," he assured them.

"Have we had the latest weather reports?" Drevin asked.

"Yes, Mr Drevin. I've gone over the meteorological charts myself and the conditions are exactly as predicted."

"Good." Drevin was pleased. "Nine o'clock on Wednesday morning. It's a sight you boys won't forget."

"Can't we get any closer?" Paul asked.

Professor Sing looked away, as if the question was too stupid to answer. Alex wondered what it was about the man that he didn't like. Perhaps it was his complete lack of enthusiasm. There was no emotion in his face – and none in his voice. How could he be in charge of such a huge project and not feel the excitement of it?

"If you were any closer you'd be deafened,"

Drevin said. "When *Gabriel 7* is launched, the vibration levels will be huge. They'd destroy your eardrums if you were too close. Even in here we'll need to be completely insulated."

"I'm afraid I must ask for some time with you, Mr Drevin," Sing interrupted. "I need to discuss the launch trajectory dispersions."

Drevin turned to Alex and Paul. "Magnus will show you around the rest of the base if there's anything else you wish to see. We'll meet again at dinner."

"Sure." Alex tried to smile, but he didn't look up. He could no longer trust himself to meet Drevin's gaze. And there was something else that was worrying him. The more he saw of the island – the rockets, the launch pad, the space centre – the more he felt a nameless sense of dread. It was hard to explain, but Alex was beginning to think that Joe Byrne and the CIA had got it all wrong. Drevin wasn't behaving like a man about to run away. He had something else in mind. Alex was sure of it.

There were less than forty-five hours until the launch. That might be all the time he had left to find out what it was.

But later that afternoon, Alex was able to forget some of his worries. Paul took him down to the beach and, as promised, gave Alex his first lesson in kite-surfing.

The sport, very simply, combined surfing and kite-flying. As Paul said, you stood on a board and flew a kite, and the wind did the rest. Of course, there was more to it than that. The kite was actually a giant polyester wing – nine metres across – which had to be inflated with a pump. It was connected to Alex by four lines which clipped onto a rubber harness around his waist. Then there was the board, similar to a surfboard but with four fins and twin tips, making it bidirectional. And finally there was the control bar, which he held in front of him. The mechanics were simple enough. The control bar was his steering wheel, which he could raise and lower, turn left and right. The rest was balance and nerve.

Alex was lucky. There wasn't much wind and the sea was fairly calm. But even so, he soon felt the power of the new sport. He started on the edge of the water with Paul about twenty metres behind him, holding the kite. Paul released it and Alex quickly brought it up until it reached the zenith, directly over his head. While it was there, the kite was essentially in neutral. Carrying the board, Alex waded into the sea until the water was up to his ankles. He put one foot on the board. Then he lowered the kite into the wind.

And he was away. It was an incredible sensation. He could feel his arms straining at their sockets, his whole body tensing against the pull of the kite. Before he knew it, he was moving very fast, skimming over the surface with the spray flying into his eyes. The board was incredibly flexible. All Alex had to do was pull on the control bar and he could change direction instantly. With the late afternoon sun beating down on him and the palm trees rushing past, all his worries about Drevin, the CIA, Ark Angel and Force Three were forgotten. For the next two hours he was happy, finally enjoying the holiday he had been promised.

After the two boys had exhausted themselves with the kite, they flopped down onto the sand and watched as the sun began its descent. It was still very warm. The breeze, blowing gently across the beach, carried the scent of pine and eucalyptus. From this part of the island it was impossible to see the launch pad and the two waiting rockets. A single grey heron perched sedately on the end of the jetty, its eyes fixed on the water, searching for fish. The sailing boats and motor launches bobbed up and down, jostled by the waves.

Alex was lying on his back, enjoying the warmth of the setting sun. He glanced sideways and noticed Paul staring at his bare chest. The scar left by his surgery had healed quickly but it was still very red.

"You must have really hurt yourself," Paul said.

"Yes." Alex was reluctant to talk about his fake bicycle accident.

"You've got lots of other cuts and bruises too."

Alex didn't even look. Every time MI6 had sent him out on a mission, his body had come back with more souvenirs. He sat up and reached for his T-shirt. "I'm starving," he said, changing the subject. "When's dinner?"

"Not for another hour. But we can grab a snack, if you like."

"No. I'll wait."

Alex pulled on his shirt. The sun was a perfect disc, cut in half by the edge of the world. The sea had turned blood red.

"Do you like it here?" Paul asked.

"It's fantastic. Really great." Alex did his best to inject some enthusiasm into his voice.

"It makes a real change to have someone like you here." Paul stared at the horizon as if searching for the right words. "It must be awful not to have parents," he went on. "But you don't know what it's like having a dad like mine. He's got so much money, and everyone knows who he is. But sometimes I think I don't even know him myself."

"Do you enjoy being with your mother?" Alex asked. He wanted to steer the conversation away from Drevin.

Paul nodded. "Yes. I wish he'd let me see more of her. And it doesn't help being on my own all the time. I sometimes wonder what I'm doing in the middle of all this. It would be a lot easier if there was someone else around."

Alex was feeling increasingly uneasy. Paul had no idea that his entire life was about to self-destruct and that he – Alex – had been sent here to help make it happen. In less than a week's time, the CIA would arrest his father. All Drevin's assets would presumably be seized by the American government. Drevin would go to prison.

And what would happen to Paul? The story would be on the front page of every newspaper all over the world. He'd have to change his name. He'd have to begin all over again, adapting to a completely different life. Somehow he'd have to get used to the fact that he was the son of a ruthless criminal. A killer. But none of this was Alex's fault. He forced himself to remember that. And Paul had a mother who'd be there to look after him when this whole thing exploded. He'd get through it.

The sun had almost disappeared. A great shadow seemed to stretch out across the sea, and Alex watched as the heron flew off, soaring effortlessly over the palm trees. Paradise? Perhaps the bird knew otherwise.

Alex stood up. "Let's go in," he said.

They walked along the beach together, the waves lapping softly near by.

On the other side of the island, another conversation was taking place.

The head of security, Magnus Payne, was standing in a large office overlooking the launch site.

Drevin was sitting on a leather sofa, reading the email that Payne had just handed him.

"Alex Rider is an MI6 agent," Payne was saying. "He may not be working for them now, but he has certainly worked for them in the past – and not once but several times. If they know he is here, it is quite possible that they have already approached him and asked him to spy on you. I have searched his luggage and found nothing. But that does not mean he isn't equipped in some way."

Drevin lowered the email. "It's not possible!" His fingers began to play with his ring. "A spy? He's fourteen!"

"I agree, of course, that it is unusual." Payne's lips twisted in a sneer. "But I can assure you, Mr Drevin, that my contact is completely reliable. After what happened at the hospital, then at Hornchurch Towers and a third time at Stamford Bridge, I felt that the boy was simply too good to be true. There was something about him ... so I made enquiries." He gestured at the email. "That's the result."

"The bicycle accident?"

"In fact a bullet wound from his last assignment. That's what my contact tells me."

Drevin fell silent. Payne could see his mind at work, turning over the possibilities, making evaluations. It was all there in the watery grey eyes.

"That business with the passport in New York," he said. He snapped his fingers angrily and swore briefly in Russian. "They must have wanted to make contact with him. He was out of my sight for nearly twenty-four hours. They could have been briefing him, telling him what to do."

"They?"

"The Central Intelligence Agency." Drevin spoke the words with loathing. "They're hand in hand with MI6. The boy could be working with either of them. Or both."

"The question is, what do you want to do with him?"

"What do you suggest?"

"He's dangerous. He shouldn't be here. Not now."

"We could send him away."

"Or we could kill him."

Drevin thought for a little longer. He barely seemed to breathe. Magnus Payne waited patiently.

"You're right," Drevin said suddenly. "Paul won't be too happy about it, but that can't be helped. See to it tomorrow, Mr Payne."

He got to his feet.

"Kill him."

DEEP TROUBLE

It was another perfect day. Alex Rider was eating breakfast with Drevin and his son on a terrace perched on the edge of the sea, the waves lapping below them. A servant – all the staff had been brought in from Barbados – had served them cold meat, fruit, cheese and freshly baked rolls. There was a jug of Blue Mountain coffee from Jamaica, one of the most delicious and expensive blends in the world. This was the millionaire lifestyle, all right. A stunning house, a private island, Caribbean sunshine ... a snapshot of another world.

Drevin was in an unusually good mood. It was the day before the launch and Alex could sense his excitement.

"What have you boys got planned for today?"

"Do you want to take the kite out again?" Paul asked Alex. "There might be a bit more wind."

Alex nodded. "Sure."

"Why don't you do some waterskiing?" Drevin suggested.

"We could do that too." Paul was obviously pleased that his father was taking an interest. It seemed to Alex that if Drevin had suggested a sandcastle competition, the other boy would have agreed.

Drevin turned to Alex. "Have you ever dived?"

"Yes." Alex had been a qualified diver since he was twelve.

"Then why don't you go out this afternoon? We have all the equipment you need – and you can visit the *Mary Belle*." Alex looked puzzled. Drevin went on. "It's an old transport ship; it was sunk in the Second World War while carrying supplies to the American bases in the Caribbean. Now it's an excellent dive site. You can swim into some of the holds."

Alex had been on wreck dives before. He knew that there was nothing more strangely beautiful, more eerie, than the ghost of an old ship. He turned to Paul. "Do you want to come?"

"I can't," Paul said. "My asthma..."

"Scuba is one of the many things Paul is unable to do," Drevin said. "But I can ask one of the guards to be your buddy. It would be a shame not to see it."

"Don't let me stop you, Alex," Paul added. "Everyone says the *Mary Belle* is amazing, and I've got some homework I'm supposed to do. So you go ahead."

At that moment, Tamara Knight appeared on the terrace, dressed in a linen jacket and trousers with a pair of sunglasses dangling around her neck. She was carrying a bulging file.

"You've got some important correspondence to deal with, Mr Drevin," she said.

"Thank you, Miss Knight. I'll be with you in a few minutes." Drevin nodded at Alex. "Enjoy the dive," he said, and went into the house.

"You're diving?" Tamara asked. She sounded surprised.

"Yes." Alex wasn't sure what to say.

"Where?"

"The *Mary Belle*."

"Oh yes." Tamara still wasn't smiling. "You'd better be careful. I understand it's very deep. And I hope you don't see any sharks."

After breakfast, Alex went back up to his room to fetch his trunks. The shutters had been drawn back and the windows were wide open. He had a spectacular view of the whole of Little Point. Looking out, Alex saw Drevin standing by his buggy, talking into a phone. Alex thought for a moment, then went over to his case and drew out the iPod Smithers had given him. He put on the headphones, turned it on, then pointed the screen in Drevin's direction. Almost at once, he heard

Drevin's voice. It was so clear, he could have been standing right next to him.

"...for the final preparations. I am going over everything again today. I want all the programming to be double-checked." A pause. "The boat is coming in tonight at eleven. Not at Little Point. The western tip of the island, behind the launch site. I'll be waiting for it there..."

There was a movement at the door. It was Paul. "What are you doing, Alex?" he asked.

Alex took off the headphones. "Nothing."

Paul saw the iPod. "Are you taking that down to the beach?"

"No. I'm just checking it's working."

The two of them left together. For the rest of the morning they swam and snorkelled and went out with the kite. This time there was a little more wind and Paul taught Alex a few tricks – jumps and the handle pass. But Alex found it hard to concentrate. All he could think about was the conversation he'd overheard. A boat was arriving that night at eleven. Why? Drevin obviously didn't want it to be seen. That was why he wasn't using the jetty near the house. Could it be that he was planning to leave, and, if so, should Alex alert the CIA now? No. It was too soon. Better to get over to the other side of the island once darkness had fallen and see for himself. That was the reason he was here. It would mean slipping past the checkpoint, but of course, he couldn't swim round.

Alex remembered what the head of security had told him. There was razor wire concealed in the water. There had to be another way.

Lunch was at one o'clock: delicious shrimp roti served with salad and rice. Then they rested for an hour, avoiding the worst heat of the sun. At half past three there was a knock on Alex's door and a young black man appeared, wearing the grey overalls of the security staff.

"Mr Rider?" he asked.

Alex got to his feet. "I'm Alex."

"My name is Kolo. Mr Drevin said you needed a diving buddy."

"That's right."

"You a certified diver?"

"Yes."

"Then let's go!"

Paul wasn't around. Alex followed Kolo outside and down to an equipment store underneath the house. It was a large room, a cross between a garage and a boathouse. Here there was spare equipment for the various boats, a few nets and, in a separate area, scuba tanks, BCDs, wetsuits, fins and everything else needed to go diving.

"The water's warm out there," Kolo said as he hauled out a couple of tanks. "But the *Mary Belle* is deep, about twenty-two metres. So I'm going to give you a half-body wetsuit and I'll check out some weights."

Half an hour later, Alex was dressed in a bright blue neoprene wetsuit that came down to his thighs and halfway down his arms. Kolo was dressed in black. Carrying his equipment, Alex staggered out onto the beach, where a boat with a Bajan skipper was waiting to take the two of them out to sea.

"Good luck, Alex!"

Alex turned to see Paul Drevin standing on the terrace above him, waving. He waved back, then climbed into the boat.

The journey only took a few minutes. In that time, Alex went over his equipment, running through the usual checks. His mask fitted. The BCD was brand new. He turned on his air supply and checked his gauge. He had been given just under 3,000 psi. Alex made a quick calculation. The deeper he went, the more air he'd use. But he was a light breather. At twenty-two metres, the depth of the *Mary Belle*, he guessed he would have a bottom time of at least half an hour.

He noticed Kolo watching him as he finished his preparations. Alex had been looking forward to visiting the wreck, but suddenly he felt uncomfortable. He had been diving many times with his uncle and once with friends, and each time it had been a happy, sociable affair. Now he was in a boat with a captain who hadn't said a word and a buddy who had barely spoken either. Two hired hands taking the rich kid for a ride. For a moment, he understood the loneliness that Paul must have felt all his life.

The boat slowed down and the anchor was lowered. The captain raised a flag – red with a white stripe – signalling that there were divers in the area. Kolo helped Alex put on his equipment. Then it was time for the briefing.

"The *Mary Belle* is right underneath us," Kolo told him. "We'll enter the water over this side and then if everything's all right, we'll go straight down. The sea's a little choppy today and visibility's not so good, but you'll soon see the wreck. We'll start at the stern. You can see the rudder and propeller. Then we'll swim up the deck and into the second hold. There's plenty of fish down there. Glassfish, hatchetfish, groupers – maybe you'll be lucky and see a shark. I'll signal when it's time to come back up. Any questions?"

Alex shook his head.

"Then let's do it."

Alex drew his mask over his face, checked his respirator one last time, then sat on the edge of the boat with his hands crossed over his chest. Kolo gave him a thumbs up and he tipped over backwards, splashing down into the sea. It was a moment which he always enjoyed, feeling his shoulders pushing through the warm water, rolling in a cocoon of silver bubbles with the fractured light high above. Then his BCD, partly inflated, dragged him back to the surface. He was bobbing in the water, face to face with Kolo. The captain was watching them over the pulpit rail.

"All right?" Kolo shouted.

Alex gave him the universal diver's sign: finger and thumb forming an O, the other three fingers pointing up. *Everything OK*.

Kolo responded with a clenched fist, thumb pointing down. *Descend*.

Alex released the air in his BCD and let his weight belt drag him down. The water rose over his chin, past his nose and eyes. Gently he began a controlled descent, listening to the sound of his own breathing amplified in his ears. It was only now that he remembered he had been operated on just three weeks ago. What would Dr Hayward think about him scuba-diving? Well, at least it wasn't something that had been forbidden.

A triggerfish – green with brilliant yellow stripes and a yellow tail – swam past, taking no notice of him. The water was a deep tropical blue that became darker and murkier the further he descended. He looked at his depth gauge. Eleven metres, twelve metres, thirteen... He was comfort-able, in full control. Kolo was a few metres above him, legs crossed. Great bubbles, each one containing a pearl of used air, rose in clusters to the surface.

And suddenly the *Mary Belle* was there, appearing in front of him as if projected onto a screen. It was always the same underwater. Objects, even ones as big as a sunken cargo ship, seemed to loom out of nowhere. Alex squeezed a little air into his BCD to slow his descent. He checked that he had neutral buoyancy, then he kicked forward and swam to examine this silent witness from the Second World War.

The *Mary Belle* lay in the sand, slanting to one side. It was in two halves, separated by a jagged, broken area that could have been made by a German torpedo. It was about a hundred and thirty metres long, twenty metres wide, the whole ship covered in algae and brightly coloured coral that would one day turn it into an extraordinary artificial reef. As he swam over the deck, heading for the stern, Alex looked down on the dark green surfaces, the twisting ladders and rails, the anchor winches and blast roof. He passed two railway freight cars lying side by side. Part of a locomotive lay shattered, a few metres away on the sand. At the far end he saw what had to be an anti-aircraft gun, now pointing helplessly at the seabed. Once, the deck would have been full of life, with young marines running back and forth, the tannoy system barking orders, the wind and the sea spray blowing in their faces. But the *Mary Belle* had been hit. It had lain here for over half a century. There was nothing in the world more silent. It was the very definition of death.

Alex noticed Kolo signalling to him and he swam under the stern. He had disturbed a shoal of snappers which darted away, zigzagging rapidly out of sight. The propeller was directly above him. When the ship had broken in two, the stern had turned on its side, otherwise it would have been buried in the sand. Kolo signalled again. *Are you all right?* Alex glanced at his air supply. He had used 500 psi. He signalled back. *Fine*.

Slowly they swam round the side of the wreck. Alex had his arms crossed over his chest, his hands clasping opposite arms. This was how he always dived. It helped retain body warmth and stopped him being tempted to touch anything. They rose up over the bridge and followed a ladder – each rung encrusted with new life – back to the upper deck. Kolo pointed at an opening beside one of the freight cars Alex had noticed. A hatchway, with a ladder leading down. It was the entrance to the second hold.

It seemed that Kolo wanted him to go in ahead of him. Alex took out his torch, then kicked down and cautiously swam through the opening, head and shoulders first. Wreck diving is entirely safe provided you know what you're doing, and Alex knew that the only real danger was getting his air pipes caught or slashing them on a sharp edge. The solution was to do everything very slowly, checking for any obstructions. But the hatch was easily wide enough for him. He followed the ladder down, turned on the torch and looked around him.

He was in a large, cavernous space which ran the full width of the ship and about twenty-five metres of its length. A ghostly green light streamed in through a series of small portholes and Alex flicked off the torch, realizing he wouldn't need it. The light illuminated an array of objects instantly recognizable even after sixty years beneath the sea. There was a Jeep, parked against a wall, a stockpile of Winchester rifles, a row of boots, a pair of motorcycles. It occurred to Alex that if he had come upon these on land, they would have been rusting and ugly, nothing more than junk. But their long stay underwater had given them a strange beauty. It was as if nature was trying to claim them and magically transform them into something they had never been.

Sound is also different underwater.

Alex heard the clang of metal hitting metal but for a moment he was unsure where it had come from, or indeed what it was. He glanced left and right but nothing was moving. Then he looked back the way he'd come. There was no sign of Kolo. Why hadn't the other man swum into the hold? Then Alex realized. The hatch that he had come through had been closed. It had swung shut – that was the sound he had heard.

He twisted round and swam back up the ladder. He wasn't wearing gloves and he was afraid of cutting himself, but when he reached the hatch he put his hand against it and pushed. It didn't budge.

It was so securely fastened it could have been cemented into place.

What the hell was going on? Alex felt the first stirrings of unease which could all too easily become panic. But he knew the most important rule of scuba-diving was to remain calm, and he forced himself to breathe slowly, to take everything one step at a time. The support holding back the hatch must have broken. But it didn't matter. Kolo knew he was here. There was a dive ship directly overhead. He'd just have to find another way out.

Alex backed away from the hatch and swam the length of the hold. He came to a steel wall on the other side of the truck, and although it was pitted with holes, some big enough to get an arm through, there was no way the rest of his body would be able to follow. But there was a door – and it was ajar. Once it would have allowed the crew access from one hold to another. Now it was the exit that Alex needed. He swam over to it and pushed. The door opened about five centimetres but no more. It had been chained shut on the other side. Alex saw something glint. The chain was brand new. That was when he really began to worry.

A new chain on an old door. It could only be there for one reason. Somehow Drevin had found out who he was. Alex had thought he was so clever, eavesdropping with his iPod and snooping round the island. But he had let them put him on a boat and take him out to sea. He had done exactly what they wanted, swimming down into this death trap. And now they had locked the door. They were going to leave him here to drown.

Fury, black and irresistible, surged through him. His heart was thundering; he couldn't breathe. For a brief moment he was tempted to take the regulator out of his mouth and scream. He was helpless. At the mercy of a single pipe and a diminishing supply of air.

The next ninety seconds were possibly the most difficult of Alex's life. He had to fight for control, twenty-two metres below sea level, aware that he was quite probably in his tomb. Somehow he had to channel his anger away from himself, back towards Drevin, who had dealt with him as ruthlessly as anyone else who had ever crossed his path.

Another sound. An engine overhead. Alex felt a flicker of hope but quickly clamped down on it. It wasn't the sound of someone coming to rescue him. Kolo had returned to the surface. He had done his job and now he was leaving.

Sure enough, the noise faded and died away.

Alex was alone.

There was one thing he had to know, although he dreaded looking. He reached down for his instrument console. How much air had he used? The needle told him the worst. He had 1,750 psi left. At 500 psi, the gauge turned red. At that point, a spring-operated shut-off valve inside the tank's J-valve would close. He would have a few minutes left. And then he would die.

When he was sure he was back in control, he swam forward again. Alex knew that at this depth, he would soon get through what air he had left. But moving too fast, using too much energy, would only quicken the process. How long did he have? Fifteen minutes at most. Already he knew that his situation was hopeless, and he forced himself to ignore the dark whispers in his mind. Nobody knew he was here. There was no way out. But he still had to try. Better people than Drevin had tried to kill him and failed. He was going to find a way out.

The hatch was sealed shut. The windows were too small. The floor, the ceiling and the walls were solid. There was just the single door that might lead him to safety, and that was chained. Alex looked around, then picked up one of the Winchesters. There was no chance it would fire after all these years underwater, but it might still do. Carrying the old rifle, he swam over to the door and, holding onto the stock, slid the barrel through. He would use it as a crowbar. Maybe he could prise the door open; the chain was new but it was attached to a handle that was old and might be rotten. Using all his strength, Alex pulled. Briefly he thought he could feel the metal giving. He pulled harder and jerked back as something snapped. The rifle. He had broken the barrel in half.

He swam over to the pile and picked up another. He could feel his gauges dragging behind him, but he didn't look at them again. He was too afraid of what he would see. He could hear his every breath; it echoed in his ears. And every time he opened his mouth he could see his precious air supply disappearing in a cloud of bubbles. He was hearing and seeing his own death. It was being carefully measured out all around him.

The second rifle broke just as the first had done. For a moment, Alex went mad. He grasped the door with his hands and wrenched at it as if he could tear it off its hinges. Bubbles exploded around his head. Blackness swirled around his eyes. When he calmed down, little had changed. His fingers were white, and he had cut the palm of one hand.

And his air supply had dropped to 900 psi. Only minutes left.

He had to move fast. No, moving fast would only bring the end closer. But there had to be another way out. He examined the windows again. The largest of them was irregular in shape – some of the metal had worn away. Alex could just about fit his head and half his shoulder through the gap. But that was it. Even if he took off his tank, his waist and hips would never make it through. He jerked back, fearful that he was going to get stuck and cut through his own air pipe. He hadn't achieved anything.

And his supply was now down to 650 psi. The

needle was only a millimetre above the red.

Alex was cold. He had never been so cold in his life. The wetsuit should have been trapping some warmth for him but his hands and arms were turning blue. There was no sunlight in the hold. He was at the bottom of the sea. But it was more than that. Alex knew he was going to die. He would be found floating in this hellish place, surrounded by rusting machinery and memories of a war long over. This time there was no way out.

500 psi.

How had that happened? Had he somehow missed the last two minutes – two precious minutes when he had so few left? Alex forced himself to think. Was there anything else in the hold that he could use? Maybe the ship had been carrying artillery shells. He had seen an anti-aircraft gun on the deck. Could he perhaps blow his way out of here?

He began to search desperately for ammunition. As he did so he felt something in his throat and knew that it was becoming more difficult to breathe. His air supply was finally running out. He wondered if he would faint before he drowned. It seemed completely unfair. By a miracle, he had survived an assassin's bullet in London. And was it just for this? For another even worse death just a few weeks later?

Something grey flashed past one of the windows. A large fish. A shark? Alex felt a sense of total despair. Even if by some miracle he did find a way out, the creature would be waiting for him. Perhaps it already knew he was there. In just a few brief seconds, his situation had become doubly hopeless.

But then he saw the grey shape again and with a shock of disbelief realized that it wasn't a shark at all. It was a diver in a wetsuit.

Someone was looking for him.

He had to force himself not to cry out. He kicked hard with his fins and reached the last window just as the diver was about to swim by. Alex's arm pushed through the jagged gap and he caught hold of the diver's leg. The diver twisted round.

Brown hair floating loose. Blue eyes full of worry behind the mask that covered them. The diver hovered on the other side of the window, and Alex recognized Tamara Knight.

Desperately he made the distress signal that he had been taught years before, chopping with his hand in front of his throat. *Out of air. Help!* He was finding it more and more difficult to breathe, straining to draw what was left in his tank, aware that his lungs were never more than half filled. Tamara reached into the pocket of her BCD and pulled something out. She passed it through the window. Alex was confused. He was holding one of Paul Drevin's inhalers. What good was that? Then he realized she must have taken it from his room. It was the gadget Smithers had given him in New York. How had she known about it?

And would it work underwater?

Dizzy, barely in control, Alex swam over to the chained door. He had to struggle to remember how the inhaler worked. Twist the cylinder twice clockwise. Why hadn't Tamara set it off herself? Of course, she couldn't. It was fingerprint sensitive. Alex had to do it. Breathe! Now the inhaler was armed. He rested it on the chain, then swam back further into the hold.

10 psi. The needle on his air gauge didn't have much further to travel.

The door blew open. There was a ball of flame, instantly extinguished, and Alex felt the shock wave hit him, throwing him against the truck. He wasn't breathing any more; there was nothing left to breathe. Where was Tamara? Alex had assumed that there was a way out through the next hold, but what if he was wrong?

Everything was going black. Either the blast had knocked him out or he was suffocating.

But then he felt Tamara's arms around him. She was pulling his regulator out of his mouth. It was useless, and he let it go. He felt something touch his lips and realized she had given him a second regulator, the octopus attached to her own tank. He breathed deeply and felt the rush of air into his lungs. It was a wonderful sensation.

They stayed where they were for a few minutes, their arms wrapped around each other. Then Tamara gently nudged Alex on the shoulder and pointed up. He nodded. They were still a long way down and with the two of them sharing a single tank, it wouldn't be long before Tamara's air supply also ran out.

Tamara swam through the broken door and Alex followed. There was an open hatch and they slipped through it, travelling slowly up. They paused when their gauges showed five metres. This was the safety stop that would allow nitrogen to seep out of their bloodstream and prevent them from getting the bends. Five minutes later they completed their ascent, breaking through the surface into the brilliant afternoon sun.

Alex had no air to inflate his BCD, so he unfastened his weight belt and let it fall. Then he tore off his mask.

"How...?" he began.

"Later," Tamara said.

It was a long swim back to the island and Tamara wanted to make sure they weren't seen. They allowed the current to carry them round Little Point, then kicked in for the shore behind the house. Tamara checked there were no guards in sight before they ran across the beach and into the shelter of the palm trees.

Alex heaved off his tank and threw himself down onto the ground. He lay there panting. Tamara was lying next to him. In her wetsuit, with her hair loose and water trickling down her face, she didn't look anything like a personal secretary ... and suddenly

Alex realized that she had never really been one.

"That was too close for comfort," she said.

Alex stared at her. "Who are you?" he asked. But already he knew the answer. "CIA."

Of course. Joe Byrne had told him he had someone on the island.

"I'm sorry I've had to be so unfriendly to you," Tamara said. She gave him a dazzling smile, as if it was something she had been wanting to do all along. "I'm sure you understand. It was my cover."

"Sure." It all made sense. "How did you find me just now?" he asked.

"You'd already told me where you were going," Tamara explained. "I don't know why, but I was nervous and I decided to follow you. I went into your room and grabbed the inhaler. I thought it might be useful and I was right. Then I swam out. I was just nearing the site of the wreck, when I saw the boat heading back without you and I guessed what must have happened. So I came down to find you."

"Thank you." Alex was feeling drowsy. The late afternoon sun was beating down on him and he was already dry. "So what happens now?" he asked.

"You tell me."

"I think Drevin may be planning to leave tonight." Quickly Alex told her about the phone call he had overheard.

But Tamara looked doubtful. "I can't believe that," she said. "The launch tomorrow ... Ark Angel.

It means everything to him. He's been working on it for months. Why disappear now?"

"I agree. But he definitely mentioned a boat. It's arriving at eleven o'clock."

"Then we have to be there. There's a back-up unit waiting in Barbados. If Drevin tries to leave, we can contact them and they'll be here in minutes."

"What do we do until then?"

"You'd better wait here. I'll go back to the house and get you some clothes. And something to eat and drink." She studied Alex closely. "Are you OK?"

"I'm fine. Thanks, Tamara. You saved my life."

"It's great to be working with you, Alex. Joe told me all about you."

Tamara slipped away, leaving Alex on his own. He watched the waves breaking gently on the white sand. The sun was beginning to set and the first shadows were already stretching out, reaching towards Alex and silently warning him of the dangers of the coming night.

TROPICAL STORM

At ten o'clock that night, Alex and Tamara were waiting on the edge of the rainforest, looking down the track towards the wooden cabins where the guards got washed and changed. Both of them were dressed in dark clothes. Tamara had picked out stone-coloured chinos and a long-sleeved black T-shirt for Alex. He was too hot. The night had brought with it a clammy heat that clung to his skin, and he could feel the sweat snaking down his back. But this way there was less chance of being seen, and he was protected from the worst of the mosquitoes.

Tamara was also in black. From somewhere she had produced a gun, a slim Beretta, which she was wearing in a holster under her arm. She also had a radio transmitter with which she was planning to contact the CIA back-up team – although she was worried about the reception. The clouds were thick, obscuring the moon, and it looked as if it was going to rain. Getting a decent signal in the middle of a tropical storm wouldn't be easy.

Alex was glad she was with him. He had been alone too long and it seemed to him that the two of them were well suited. Tamara had told him that she was one of the youngest agents working for Joe Byrne; she had been recruited when she was just nineteen. She didn't look much older than that now, crouched beside a giant *flamboyant*, the umbrella-shaped tree common to much of the eastern Caribbean. He sensed that this was one big adventure for her. Maybe that was the difference between them. She enjoyed her work.

There were three cabins, connected by covered walkways, beside the track. They were fairly primitive: dark wooden planks for walls, roofs made from palm fronds. About twenty metres further down, Alex could make out the electric gate and the checkpoint guarding the launch area on the other side. There were three guards on constant patrol, one of them inside the control box, the other two shuffling back and forth in front of the ten metre high metal fence. The whole area was illuminated by a series of arc lights shining down from metal watchtowers. Alex could see hundreds of moths and mosquitoes dancing in the beams.

The guards were relieved at ten fifteen. As Drevin's personal assistant, Tamara had been able to see the roster and she knew that the second night watch would be arriving at any moment. Alex glanced back down the track in the direction of Drevin's house. He thought briefly of Paul. Presumably he would have been told that Alex had drowned ... a terrible accident. He wondered what Paul would be thinking, and he was sorry that Tamara hadn't seen him when she'd gone back to the house to fetch him some clothes.

But he couldn't worry about that now. It was time. The track was still empty; there was no sign of any electric buggies coming either way. Tamara nudged him and he crept forward, keeping close to the undergrowth, making his way to the first of the three cabins. Very carefully he opened the door. There had been no sound or movement for twenty minutes, but even so there could still be someone asleep in there.

The cabin was empty. Alex slipped inside and found himself in a small, rectangular space. There were a couple of old sofas, a fridge and a table with empty beer bottles, some pornographic magazines and a deck of playing cards strewn across the surface. A fan stood in one corner but it was switched off. The room reeked of stale cigarette smoke, and the air was sluggish and still.

He passed through this cabin and into the next, an even smaller one with four shower cubicles and a row of wooden benches. The floor was tiled. Damp towels hung on hooks. Again, there was nobody in sight.

It was in the third cabin that he found what he was looking for. This was where the guards got changed for work. Uniforms, freshly ironed, hung in metal lockers; polished boots were neatly lined up against the wall. Exactly as Tamara had described.

Alex couldn't help smiling to himself as he reached into his pocket and took out the bottle that Smithers had given him. He glanced at the name on the label – STINGO – then opened it and sprinkled the contents over the guards' uniforms. The liquid was colourless and didn't smell of anything. The guards wouldn't have any idea what was about to hit them.

He heard a low whistle from outside: a warning from Tamara. There was a second door leading out of the cabin and Alex slipped through it into the darkness. Outside, he heard an approaching buggy. Perfect timing.

It was the changing of the guard. As Alex rejoined Tamara, a buggy drew up and three men dressed in baggy shorts and T-shirts got out. Alex recognized one of them. It was Kolo, the diver who had left him to die. He was pleased. If anyone deserved to suffer, it was Kolo.

"Is this going to work?" Tamara whispered as the three men disappeared into the changing room.

"Don't worry," Alex replied. "Smithers has never let me down."

About five minutes later, the three men reappeared, now dressed in their grey overalls.

Alex and Tamara watched as they approached the checkpoint to swap places with the three guards there. They exchanged a few words in low voices, then took up their positions. The three who had been relieved went back into the cabin to change and drove off in the buggy a few minutes later.

"Let's get closer," Alex whispered. He was keen to see whatever was going to happen.

Kolo was sitting in the control box, in front of a bank of telephones and monitors. The window was open so that he could communicate with the other two, who were now armed and standing together in front of the fence. It was a thankless task, Alex thought, hanging around all night, waiting for something to happen. And although none of them knew it, it was about to get worse.

Alex noticed it first. The cloud of insects visible in the beams of the arc lamps had thickened. Before there had been hundreds of them. Now there were thousands. It was impossible to tell what kind of bugs they were: beetles, flies, cockroaches or mosquitoes. They were just black specks made up of frantically beating wings, antennae and dangling legs. There were so many that the light was almost obliterated.

Kolo slapped his face. The sound was surprisingly loud in the thick heat of the night. One of the other guards muttered something and scratched under his arm. Kolo slapped his face a second time, then the back of his neck. The other men were beginning to shuffle around edgily, as if performing a weird dance. One ran the stock of his machine gun down his chest, then reached over his shoulder, using it to scratch his back. Inside the control box, Kolo was swatting at the air in front of his face. He seemed to be having trouble breathing, and Alex could see why. The air all around him had been invaded by thousands and thousands of insects. Kolo couldn't open his mouth without swallowing them.

The mosquito lotion that Smithers had created was awesome. Every insect on the island had been attracted to the three unfortunate men. The two outside were out of control, slapping themselves, whimpering, jerking around like electric shock victims. Kolo screamed. Alex could see a huge centipede clinging to his neck. Very little of the man's skin was visible now. He was covered in a mass of biting, stinging insects. They were crawling into his eyes and up his nose. Still screaming, he punched himself frenziedly. The other two men were doing the same.

There was a small explosion and a shower of sparks as one of the television monitors, invaded by insects, short-circuited. It was the final straw. Blind and swearing, Kolo staggered to his feet and tumbled out of the control box. The other two guards fell onto him, clinging to him for support, and the three of them began to grope their way towards the showers and the changing room.

A huge cloud of insects followed them.

Suddenly everything was silent.

"You were right," Tamara observed. "Your Mr Smithers *is* pretty good."

The two of them hurried past the now deserted checkpoint, through the gate and along the track on the other side. The rainforest soon ended and they could make out the gantries with the rockets ahead. There was still no moon.

Tamara looked up. "We're going to get wet," she announced.

She was right. A few minutes later, the clouds opened and they were instantly drenched. The rain was warm and fell from the sky as if poured from an enormous bucket. A sheet of lightning pulsed over the sea, reflected in the ground that was being churned up all around them. Everything had become black and white.

"What will happen to the launch?" Alex shouted. There was no longer any need to whisper. Tamara could hardly hear him against the crashing rain.

She shook water out of her eyes and shouted back, "It won't make any difference. The rain won't last long. Everything will be dry by tomorrow morning."

In fact, the storm couldn't have broken at a better time. The launch area was a quarter of a mile of completely open land and Alex had wondered how they would cross it without being seen. He had no doubt that there would be other guards on patrol and probably CCTV. The rain provided perfect cover. In their dark clothes, he and Tamara were invisible.

The second jetty was on the western point of the island, connected to the rocket gantries and the various control buildings by a white cement track. Alex and Tamara were jogging towards it when a light suddenly burst out, cutting through the rain. It was mounted on a boat that was heading towards the shore, fighting its way through the tumultuous waves.

"This way!" Tamara yelled and pulled Alex towards a brick outbuilding with a tangle of metal pipes and gauges outside. As they ran, she tripped. Alex managed to catch her before she fell, and a few moments later they were safely concealed behind a water tank. The jetty was right in front of them. Alex wondered if Drevin was about to appear.

The boat reached the jetty. The rain was coming down even more heavily and it was difficult to see what was happening. Someone jumped down with a rope. More figures appeared on the deck. Alex had thought that Drevin was planning his exit from the island, but it looked as if the boat had brought new arrivals – people who didn't want to be seen.

Alex heard a sound behind him and turned to see Magnus Payne and two guards drive down the track towards the boat. The ginger hair and lifeless skin of the island's head of security were unmistakable even in a tropical storm. They reached the jetty and Payne got out. Four men climbed down from the boat. Alex grabbed hold of Tamara, shocked. He knew who the men were, even though he had never learnt their real names.

Combat Jacket. Spectacles. Steel Watch and Silver Tooth.

Force Three had come to Flamingo Bay. But why? What did it mean? Magnus Payne was shaking their hands, welcoming them. This was the terrorist group that had sworn to destroy Drevin. But they were being greeted like old friends.

And then a voice crackled out of the storm, amplified by hidden speakers, echoing all around.

"Do not fire! We know you are there. Drop your weapons and come out with your hands up."

The five men froze. Two of them pulled out guns. But the words weren't being addressed to them.

If Alex had any doubts that it was he and Tamara who were being targeted, they were dispelled a few seconds later. Four more buggies had come racing out of the rain. They slid to a halt, facing him, their headlights dazzling him. A dozen black shadows came tumbling out and took up positions around them. Next to him Tamara tensed, then sprang into action, drawing her gun. There was a single shot, fired from one of the buggies. Tamara cried out. Her gun spun away. Blood began to seep from a wound in her shoulder, spreading rapidly down her sleeve.

"That was your last warning!" the voice boomed. "Stand up and move slowly forward. If you resist, you will be shot."

How had they been found? Alex thought back and remembered Tamara stumbling. A tripwire. That had to be it. As they had run, she had triggered an alarm.

Magnus Payne pushed his way through the line of guards. The four members of Force Three followed. The whole area had been empty only minutes before; now it was swarming. Tamara was clutching her wounded shoulder. Alex stood next to her, sick at heart.

And then Nikolei Drevin appeared, dressed in a light raincoat and – bizarrely – holding a brightly coloured golfing umbrella that shielded him from the downpour. He seemed relaxed, as if he'd simply decided to go for a late-night stroll. He stood in front of Alex and Tamara. There was very little emotion in his face.

"Miss Knight," he said, and although he spoke softly, the words carried even above the sound of the rain. "I always did have my doubts about you. Or rather, I suspected that the CIA would try to infiltrate my operation, and you seemed the most likely choice. How very sad I am to have my fears confirmed."

"The boy..." Magnus Payne had reached Drevin's side.

"Yes. It seems your man didn't quite finish the

job." Drevin stepped forward until he was centimetres away from Alex. Alex didn't flinch; rain streamed down his face. "Tell me, Alex," Drevin asked. "I'd be interested to know who you're working for. Is it MI6 or the CIA? Or perhaps both?"

"Go to hell," Alex replied quietly.

"I'm truly sorry that you chose to make yourself my enemy," Drevin continued. "I liked you from the start. So did Paul. But you have abused my hospitality, Alex. A great mistake."

Alex was silent. Next to him Tamara had gone very pale. She had one hand clamped over her wound and was obviously in pain. But she was still defiant. "The CIA know we're here, Drevin," she said. "You do anything to us, they're going to be crawling all over you. You're not getting away; you've got nowhere to go."

"Whatever made you think I was planning to go anywhere?" Drevin retorted. "Lock the girl up," he ordered. "I don't want to see her again. Magnus – bring Alex Rider to the main hangar. I want to talk to him."

Drevin turned and walked away. It only took three paces and he had disappeared into the rain.

PRIMARY TARGET

The main hangar was huge. Perhaps this was where the Cessna was kept when it wasn't in use. The roof was a great curve of corrugated iron. One wall slid back to allow access to the launch site. There were various pieces of machinery and a few oil drums scattered around, but otherwise the hangar was bare. Alex was tied to a wooden chair. Drevin was sitting opposite; Magnus Payne was standing beside him. Combat Jacket, Silver Tooth, Spectacles and Steel Watch were grouped together a short distance away. They had been invited to the party but it was clear that Drevin didn't expect them to join in.

The rain had stopped as suddenly as it had started. Alex could hear the water still gurgling in the gutters and there were a few last drops pattering on the roof. The air in the hangar was warm and damp. He was soaked. Payne had used a length of electrical wire to bind him to the chair and it was cutting into his flesh. His hands and feet were numb.

Drevin was wearing a light blue cashmere jersey and cords. He was relaxed, holding a giant brandy glass in one hand, two centimetres of pale golden liquid forming a perfect circle in the bottom. He raised it to his nose and sniffed appreciatively.

"This is a Louis XIII cognac," he said. "It's thirty years old. A single bottle costs thousands of pounds. It's the only cognac I drink."

"I knew you were rich," Alex said. "I also knew you were greedy. But I didn't know you were boring as well."

"There are five men here who would be only too glad to deal with you if I were to allow it," Drevin replied mildly. "Perhaps you would do better to keep your mouth shut and listen to what I have to say."

He swirled the brandy and took a sip.

"I have to confess, I'm fascinated by you." The grey eyes studied Alex closely. "When Magnus told me you were an MI6 agent, I laughed. I simply couldn't believe it. But when I look back over everything that's happened, it makes perfect sense. I met Alan Blunt once and thought him a most devious and unpleasant individual. This confirms my impression. Even so, I find it hard to accept that he sent you after me. Is that what happened, Alex? Were you planted from the very start?"

"He'd been shot," Payne growled. "I've seen copies of his hospital records. That was real enough."

"Then perhaps it was no more than an unhappy coincidence. Unhappy, that is, for you. But I'm glad we have this time together. Although I'm afraid that both you and Miss Knight must be dispensed with soon, at least I've been given the opportunity to explain myself to you. You see, Alex, I'd like Paul to know about me. I'd like to tell him everything I'm about to tell you. But he's weak. He's not ready yet. He might even end up hating me for what I am. But you, I know, will understand."

Drevin lowered his nose into the glass and breathed in deeply.

"I am, as you mentioned just now, a rich man. One of the richest men on the planet. I employ a team of accountants who work for me full-time all the year round, and even they are unsure quite how much I am worth. You have no idea what it's like, Alex, to be able to have anything you want. I can walk into a shop to buy a suit and decide instead to buy the shop. If I see a new car or ship or plane in a magazine, it can be mine before the end of the day. At the last count I had eleven houses around the world. I can sleep in a different country every day of the week and wake up in yet another little bit of paradise.

"Of course, as you've probably been told, this wealth did not come to me in a way that you might describe as honest. Such terms are of no interest to me. I am a criminal; I freely admit it. I have killed many people personally and countless more have died as a result of my orders. Many of my associates are criminals. Why should this trouble me? There's not a successful businessman alive who has not at some time cheated or lied. We all do it! It's just a question of degree.

"I have been hugely successful for the past twenty years, and I fully intend to become richer and more successful in the years to come. However" – Drevin's face grew dark – "about eighteen months ago I became aware of two small problems, and these have forced me into a particular course of action. They are the reason why you are here now, Alex. They are problems that could all too easily destroy me and which I have spent a great deal of time and money seeking to overcome."

"Why are you telling me all this if you're planning to kill me?" Alex asked.

"It is *because* I'm planning to kill you that I can tell you," Drevin replied. "There will be no danger of you repeating what you hear. But please don't interrupt again, Alex, or I shall have to ask Magnus to hurt you."

He closed his eyes briefly. When he opened them again, he was fully composed.

"The first problem," he said, "concerns the State Department of the United States, which decided to investigate some of my financial dealings, particularly those involving the Russian mafiya. Of course, I have been aware right from the start that they were building a case against me. I have always been a careful man. I avoid written evidence and make sure there are no witnesses who might incriminate me. But even so, it would not be possible to act on the scale that I do without leaving some trace of myself, and I knew that the Americans were squirrelling away the bits and pieces, talking to anyone who'd ever met me – and that sooner or later they were planning to bring me to court.

"The obvious solution to this seemed to be to destroy the US State Department and in particular the men and women whose job it had been to meddle in my affairs. It occurred to me that in one respect they were actually being quite helpful. They had gathered all the evidence together: a case of putting all their eggs in one basket! With a single, well-aimed missile, I could kill all the investigators and destroy all the tapes, files, scraps of paper, telephone records, computer printouts – everything! I could begin again with a completely clean sheet. The more I thought about it, the more grateful I became to the Americans for what they were doing.

"Of course, it wasn't going to be easy. Because, you see, the investigation was based in one of the most secure buildings in the world – the Pentagon in Washington. The place is nothing more than a huge slab of concrete – and much of it underground. It employs an anti-terrorist force that operates twenty-four hours a day. Every form of monitoring device you could imagine can be found there, and since 9/11, no commercial plane can get anywhere near. The Pentagon is thoroughly protected against chemical, biological and radiological attack. I know, because I considered them all. But even a brief examination showed me that any such approach was doomed to failure.

"And now, if you'll permit me, I'll move on to the second problem that I mentioned. It may seem completely unrelated to the first. For a long time, I thought it was. But you will see in a minute how it all connects."

Alex said nothing. He was aware of Magnus Payne and the men who made up Force Three watching him. He was still wondering how they fitted into all this. And where was Kaspar, the man with the tattooed skull? Even now, nothing quite added up. Alex shifted in the chair, trying to get some feeling back into his hands and feet.

"My other problem was Ark Angel," Drevin went on. "Space tourism has always interested me, Alex, and when the British government approached me to go into partnership with them, I must confess I was flattered. I would benefit from the money they would put into the project. I would be at the forefront of one of the most challenging and potentially profitable enterprises of the twenty-first century. And it would provide me with the one thing I most needed: respectability! The Americans might view me as a criminal, but it would give them pause for thought when they saw that I was having supper with the Queen. It occurred to me that they might find it rather more difficult to drag me off to prison when I was Sir Nikolei Drevin. Or even Lord Drevin. Sometimes it helps to have the right contacts.

"And so I agreed to become partners with your government in the Ark Angel project, the world's first space hotel. It's above us right now. It's always above us. And I can never forget it. Because, you see, it has become a nightmare, a catastrophe. Even without the Americans and their investigation, Ark Angel could easily destroy me."

Drevin frowned and took a large sip of brandy.

"Ark Angel is billions of pounds over budget. It's sucking me dry. Even with all my wealth I can no longer support it. And it's all the fault of your stupid government. They can't make a decision without talking about it for months. They have committees and subcommittees. And when they do make a decision, it's always the wrong one. I should have known from the start. Politicians have no experience of business. They know nothing. It's why everything the British government builds costs ten times as much as it should and doesn't even work.

"Ark Angel is the same. It's late, it's leaking and it's lost any hope of ever being completed. The whole thing is falling apart. And for months now I've been thinking, if only the wretched thing would simply fall out of the sky. I could scrape back at least some of my money because, like every major project, it is insured. More than that, I'd be able to wipe my hands of it. I'd be able to wake up without having it, quite literally, hanging over my head. There were days when I seriously considered paying someone to blow it up.

"And that, Alex, is when I had my big idea. It's as I told you. Two problems that came together with one single solution."

Drevin leant forward and at last Alex saw quite clearly the madness in his eyes.

"I wonder how much you know about physics, Alex. Even as we sit here now, there are hundreds of objects orbiting above us in outer space, from small communications satellites to giant space stations such as the ISS and Mir before that. Have you ever wondered what keeps them there? What stops them from falling down?

"Well, the answer is a fairly simple equation consisting of their speed balanced against their distance from the earth. You might be amused to know that, theoretically, it would be possible for a satellite to orbit the earth just a few metres above your head. But it would have to go impossibly fast. Ark Angel is three hundred miles away. It's therefore able to maintain its orbital velocity at just seventeen and a half thousand miles per hour. But even so, every few months it has to be reboosted. The same was true for Mir when it was in orbit, and for the International Space Station now. Every few months, rockets which are known as progress vehicles have to push all these large satellites back into space. Otherwise they'd come crashing down.

"In fact, some of them do exactly that. The Russian space probe Mars 96 fell out of the sky on 17 November 1996 and the pieces rained down across South America. In April 2000 the second stage of a Delta rocket narrowly missed Cape Town. The world has been very lucky that so far there has been no major catastrophe. Well, almost three quarters of the planet is water. There are huge deserts and mountain ranges. The chances of a piece of space junk hitting a populated area are relatively small. Even so, most astronomers would agree, it is an accident waiting to happen.

"Are you finding this hard to follow? I'll make it easy for you. Imagine swinging a conker on a piece of string around your hand. If you slow down, the conker will fall and hit your hand. And there you have it. The conker is the space station; your hand is the earth. It doesn't take a great deal to cause one to crash into the other.

"And that is exactly what I intend to do.

"Tomorrow, when *Gabriel 7* blasts off, it will be

carrying a bomb which has been exactly timed and which must be exactly positioned within Ark Angel. Everything has been worked out on computers and the program is locked in. If you look at a map, you will find that Washington is positioned at around thirty-eight degrees north. The angle of inclination followed by Ark Angel – its flight path – is also thirty-eight degrees. This means that every time it orbits the earth, it passes directly over Washington.

"The bomb will go off two hours after *Gabriel 7* has docked with Ark Angel – at exactly half past four. This will have the effect of knocking Ark Angel out of its orbit. The space station will begin to topple towards the earth. It will enter the earth's atmospheric drag and after that things will begin to happen very quickly. The more atmosphere that surrounds it, the faster it will fall. Soon it will be tumbling out of control. Or that is how it will seem. In fact, I have secretly programmed what are known as de-orbit manoeuvres into Ark Angel. Although it will seem to be moving haphazardly, it will be as accurate as an independently targeted nuclear missile.

"Can you imagine it, Alex? Ark Angel weighs about seven hundred tonnes. Of course, much of it will burn up as it re-enters the earth's atmosphere. But I estimate that about sixty per cent of it will survive. That's about four hundred tonnes of molten steel, glass, beryllium and aluminium travelling at around fifteen thousand miles an hour. The

Pentagon is the primary target. The building will be destroyed. All the people working there will die, and every last scrap of information will be incinerated. I rather suspect that the shock wave will destroy most of Washington too. The Capitol. The White House. The various monuments. The parks. A shame, because I've always thought it a rather attractive city. But very little of it will be left."

Alex closed his eyes. Jack Starbright was in Washington, visiting her parents. Maybe she would survive the hideous explosion that Drevin had planned. But thousands of people – hundreds of thousands – would not. Once again Alex found himself wondering how he had got himself into this. Had it really all begun with a doctor ordering him two weeks' R & R?

"And now I must tell you about Force Three," Drevin said.

"You don't need to," Alex replied. He had worked this part out for himself. "You need someone to take the blame. Force Three don't exist. You invented them."

"Exactly." Drevin waved his glass at the four men standing near by. "I consider Force Three to be the most brilliant aspect of the entire operation. Obviously, if Ark Angel is sabotaged, if it falls on the Pentagon, I will be the main suspect. So I had to create a scapegoat. I had to make sure that I was above suspicion.

"I created Force Three. I hired the men you see

here now. Under my instructions, they committed several acts of terrorism that seemed to be directed against capitalist concerns. They blew up a car manufacturing plant in Dakota, a factory in Japan, a GM research centre in New Zealand. I also paid a journalist working in Berlin and a lecturer in London to speak out against Force Three, to warn the world about them. I then promptly had them murdered. Do you see? I was creating the illusion of a ruthless group of eco-warriors who hated anyone involved in big business – and who particularly hated me."

"You kidnapped your own son!" Alex exclaimed. At last the events at the hospital and Hornchurch Towers were beginning to make sense.

"I told you. I had to be seen to be above suspicion. The world had to believe that Force Three were my enemy. What sort of father would allow his own son to be kidnapped just days after an operation—"

"But they got it wrong," Alex interrupted. "They took me instead of him." He thought back to the time when he had been held prisoner and his head swam. "They were going to cut off Paul's finger! Did you really order them to do that?"

"Of course." For the first time, Drevin looked troubled. Alex could see him struggling with his emotions, forcing them down. "The threat had to be credible. If Paul had been maimed, nobody would have suspected that I had anything to do with it. And when Force Three attacked me here on Flamingo Bay, I would be the victim."

"But that's monstrous!" Alex protested. "He's your son!"

"Maybe a little pain would have toughened him up," Drevin retorted. "The boy is too soft. And one day he is going to inherit billions. The whole world will be his. Is one little finger too much to ask in return?"

"It must be great having you as a dad!" Alex sneered.

"You will die very painfully if you continue to speak to me in that way!" Drevin finished his brandy. He was suddenly flushed and out of breath. "The only mistake I made was not providing Kaspar with a photograph of Paul. We knew his room number; we knew there would be no security at the hospital. How could we know that another boy – *you* – would decide to get involved?"

"Is that why you tried to kill me in the fire?" Alex asked.

"No." Drevin shook his head. "We needed you alive. That was the whole point. Paul had been saved from his ordeal but we still needed someone to tell the world that it was Force Three behind the kidnap attempt. Killing you would have been no use to us at all. You were meant to escape. There was a chair in the room so that you could climb up through the ceiling and over the wall into the corridor. The fire was deliberately started away from the stairwell so

264

that you could get out of the building."

"But one of your people was waiting for me with a gun." Alex looked at the man he knew only as Combat Jacket. This was the man who had shot the night receptionist at the hospital. He was gazing at Alex with watery eyes that were too small and too close to his broken nose.

Drevin was obviously hearing this for the first time. "Is this true?" he asked.

"He's lying," Combat Jacket said. It was the first time he had spoken. "I let him go like you said. I never went near him."

Alex understood. He'd humiliated Combat Jacket. And the man had disobeyed orders to get his revenge. He was the one who was lying. It was obvious to everyone there; they could hear it in his voice.

Drevin shrugged. "It makes no difference," he said, and Combat Jacket relaxed. "You may be wondering why Force Three have come to the island, Alex. It's because I have one last use for them. The launch is timed for nine o'clock tomorrow morning. The bomb will go off at half past four in the afternoon. And as Ark Angel comes crashing down on Washington, a fight will break out here on Flamingo Bay. Intruders will have been discovered. My men will shoot to kill. And when the authorities come calling and the investigation begins, I will be able to give them the final proof that Force Three were responsible. You have described the men who kidnapped you, Alex. Tomorrow their bullet-ridden bodies will be on display."

Now it was Silver Tooth who spoke. Spectacles and Steel Watch were also looking uneasy. "How are you going to fake that?" he asked.

Drevin smiled. "Who said I was going to fake it?"

The chatter of gunfire was so loud and so close that Alex nearly toppled over in the chair. The four fake terrorists didn't stand a chance. They were dead before they could react, blown off their feet onto the cold concrete floor. Alex twisted round. Magnus Payne was holding one of the Mini Uzis. There was a dreadful smile on his face. A cloud of smoke hovered around his hands.

"You're insane!" Alex spat out the words without knowing what he was saying. "You're never going to get away with it! They'll know it was you..."

"They may well suspect it was me, but it's going to be almost impossible to prove," Drevin retorted. "I'm afraid I'm the victim in all this."

"But what about me? What about Tamara? If you kill us, the CIA will come after you!"

"The CIA are already after me. What difference will another couple of bodies make? I'm afraid you and Miss Knight will be found on the beach. Accidentally caught in the crossfire. A terrible shame. But not my fault."

"And what about Kaspar?" Why had Alex thought of him? He was the one piece missing from this

266

crazy jigsaw. If Force Three had been working for Drevin all along, then so had Kaspar. But where was he?

"Show him," Drevin ordered.

Magnus Payne put down the sub-machine gun. He reached up and took hold of his ginger hair. A wig. He pulled it off, then ripped at his skin. Alex should have recognized the latex. He had recently worn a similar disguise himself. He watched in dismay as the head of security seemed to tear his own face apart and the dreadful tattoos appeared underneath. In just a few seconds the magic trick was complete. Magnus Payne was gone; Kaspar stood in his place.

"The tattoos were rather painful and unpleasant," Drevin commented. "But we had to create a terrorist leader people would remember. I'd say we succeeded, wouldn't you?"

Alex felt utterly defeated. He remembered now his first meeting with Payne on Flamingo Bay. The head of security had disguised his voice, of course. But even so, Alex had been sure he'd seen him somewhere before. And Payne had known immediately who he was. Both he and Paul had been in the buggy when Drevin introduced them, and Payne was supposed to be meeting them both for the first time. But he had known immediately which was which. Of course. He had recognized Alex.

"We'll arrange the bodies on the beach after the

launch," Drevin said to Kaspar. "And we'll add the boy and the woman then." He put down his glass and stood up. "Goodbye, Alex. I enjoyed meeting you very much. I would have liked to get to know you better. But I'm afraid we've reached the end."

He tugged at his ring one last time as if there was something he had forgotten to say. The men who had pretended to be Force Three, and whose names Alex would never know, lay sprawled on the floor.

Kaspar stepped forward and grabbed hold of the chair. Alex was helpless as his chair was tilted backwards and he was dragged away.

WIND AND WATER

Kaspar drove Alex across the compound to a flat, rectangular building with barred windows and a door with steps leading down, just below the level of the ground. Alex could no longer think of the other man as Magnus Payne. Drevin's head of security hadn't bothered to replace his wig or mask, and even in the darkness the hideous map of the world still glowed livid on his skin. Alex wondered how much he had been paid to disfigure himself. Whatever the sum, it would probably cost him just as much one day to pay for the laser surgery to remove the tattoos.

Alex had been untied from the wooden chair but his hands were still bound. As they got out of the buggy, he tested the wire, attempting to find some slack. It seemed to him that, given time, he might be able to free himself. Not that it would do him much good. The building in front of him looked like a prison. And Kaspar knew what he was capable of. He wasn't going to make any more mistakes.

They went down the steps into a large area filled with electronic equipment, computers and workstations. A model of a space probe – gleaming steel with circuitry spilling everywhere – took up most of the room. Alex noticed two sets of what looked like tracksuits hanging on a rail. They both had the Ark Angel logo stitched onto the sleeve. He supposed they must be the outfits worn by astronauts.

"This way," Kaspar grunted. He gestured with his gun towards another flight of stairs leading down.

Alex obeyed and found himself in a wide corridor with two solid-looking cages on either side. As he stepped forward, he heard a screeching and jabbering from the first cage, and to his surprise an orang-utan bounded towards him, crashing its fists against the bars. Then he remembered. Drevin had said he was planning to send an ape into space – some sort of endurance experiment.

"Meet Arthur," Kaspar said. There was an ugly smile on his face.

"Is he any relation?" Alex asked.

The remark earned him a sharp jab with the gun. But the pain was quickly forgotten. He had looked into the next cage and seen Tamara Knight, still very pale but alive. She smiled at Alex but said nothing while Kaspar opened the door of the cage opposite.

"In here," he ordered.

Alex had no choice. He stepped inside and waited while Kaspar locked the door behind him. He looked around. The cage was about two metres square. The bars were solid steel. The lock was brand new. Alex had no gadgets on him and his hands were still tied. He was going nowhere.

Kaspar removed the key and slipped it into his pocket. "I'll leave the three of you together." He glanced at his watch. It was almost one o'clock in the morning. "You'll hear the rocket launch," he said. "And as soon as it's gone, someone'll come for you. They'll take you to the beach and that'll be the end." The corner of West Africa twisted in a grimace of pure hatred.

Alex had seen it all before. The bigger the criminals, the more they resented being beaten by a teenager. And Alex had beaten Kaspar twice. "I'm just sorry I won't be the one holding the gun," Kaspar went on. "But I'll be thinking of you. I hope it won't be too quick."

He walked away. Alex heard his footsteps on the stairs. The main door opened and closed. Arthur the orang-utan stalked to the back of his cage and sat down.

"Charming guy," Tamara muttered.

"Tamara, are you OK?" Alex had been worried about her, and he was relieved to see her now.

"I've been better," she admitted. "Was that Magnus Payne just now?"

271

Alex nodded.

"I thought I recognized his voice. What happened to his head?"

Alex told her. He also told her about his meeting in the hangar and Drevin's plan to destroy Washington. Tamara was kneeling against the door of her cage, listening closely. When he finished talking she let out a deep sigh. It seemed to Alex that even more colour had drained from her face.

"We thought he was going to cut and run," she said. "We thought he was finished. We never figured he was going to come up with something like this."

"Can he really do it?" Alex asked.

Tamara thought for a moment, then nodded. "Maybe. I don't know. He'd have to work everything out right down to the last second. The explosion. All the rest of it. But, yes ... I'm afraid he probably can."

"We have to contact Joe Byrne."

"The guards took my radio transmitter. I imagine they'll have taken your iPod too."

"What about the phones?"

"There are radio phones on the island but Drevin will have disabled them, just in case. And ordinary mobiles are no good; you can't get a signal. I don't know, Alex. Either we're going to have to stop him ourselves or one of us is going to have to go for help."

"Barbados..."

"It's only about ten miles from here. Ed Shulsky is waiting at Harrison Point; he's got plenty of back-up. Maybe you could steal a boat."

"Why me? Why not both of us?"

Tamara shook her head. "I'm sorry, Alex. But I've got a bullet in my shoulder. I'd only slow you down."

Alex lashed out at the cage door with his foot. The bars rattled. It was obvious to him that he wasn't going anywhere, and he said so.

"Maybe I can help you," Tamara said. She was wearing trainers and as Alex watched, she reached down and pulled out the laces. "Catch!" She slipped her uninjured arm between the bars of her cage and threw the laces over to Alex.

"What—"

"You're not the only one with gadgets. There's tungsten wire inside the laces. Diamond-edged. You can cut through the bars."

"That's neat," he said, though secretly he wished that the CIA had come up with something less clumsy and perhaps a little more efficient.

"They removed my exploding earrings," Tamara added, as if reading his mind.

Alex took one of the laces and examined the door. The steel bars were strong but they were thin and he would only have to cut through three of them to squeeze through. His job wouldn't be made easier by the fact that his hands were tied, but perhaps he could deal with that too.

"How much time do we have?" he asked.

"Not much. It gets light around six, and if you're not out by then, I don't think you'll have much chance."

"Right."

Alex looped the lace over the wire between his wrists, then grabbed the dangling ends with his teeth. He pulled the lace tight and began to jerk his hands in a vague sawing motion. In less than a minute his wrists were free. He saw Tamara smile. Now he could begin work in earnest.

The bars weren't so easy. It took well over half an hour to make the first cut, and Alex was disappointed to discover that even after it had been severed near its base, the bar wouldn't bend. He had to make a second cut – another half-hour's work – before it finally fell to the floor with a clang. Alex cursed himself. If there were any guards upstairs, the noise would have alerted them. But he was lucky. Nobody came. It seemed that the two of them were on their own.

Tamara hadn't spoken while he was working but now she nodded at him. "Keep going!" she encouraged.

"What time is it?"

"I don't know. They took my watch."

That was the worst of it. As Alex started on the second bar, he had no idea how much time had passed. All he knew was that he was worn out. He needed to sleep. And he had blisters on his thumbs, his fingers and the heels of his hands where they had rubbed together.

The night dragged on. He sat hunched up in the cage, sawing back and forth. Tamara was watching him. The orang-utan had turned his back on both of them and seemed to be asleep.

At last it was done. The third bar came loose, leaving enough space for Alex to slip through into the corridor. He went over to Tamara.

"I'm going to get you out," he said.

"No, Alex."

"I can't just leave you here."

Tamara shook her head. "You don't have a lot of time. Get to Barbados. Find Ed." She leant back. Although she was trying not to show it, Alex could see that she was in a lot of pain. "I'll be all right," she went on. "I've got Arthur to keep me company. Now go, before someone comes."

Alex knew she was right. He picked up one of the loose bars and climbed back up the stairs. Looking through the window, he was alarmed to see streaks of pink light stealing across the inky sky. It must be well after six o'clock, less than three hours to the launch.

He went over to the door and opened it a crack. There was a guard sitting in a chair, wearing grey overalls and a cap. Alex smiled to himself. For once luck was on his side. The man was fast asleep. He gripped the metal bar more tightly. He had thought it might come in useful.

*   *   *

Ten minutes later, dressed in the guard's uniform
and with the cap pulled down low over his forehead, Alex drove an electric buggy back towards
the checkpoint. Without slowing down, he held out
the guard's ID, angling his arm so that it covered
most of his face. He was prepared to crash through
the gate if he had to, and he was relieved when it
opened to let him pass. It seemed that security on
Flamingo Bay needed a serious overhaul. But then
again, he and Tamara were supposed to be locked
up. The place was an island, ten miles away from
the nearest land. What was there for Drevin or anyone else to worry about?

The buggy was easy to drive, with only two
pedals – accelerator and brake – and no gears. He
put his foot down and sped through the rainforest,
aware that the sky was getting lighter all the time.
Drevin's house and the far end of the island, Little
Point, appeared in the distance. Alex turned the
wheel and spun off the track, steering the buggy
down between the palm trees towards the beach.
It made it about halfway before it got stuck in the
sand. That was good enough for Alex. He jumped
out and ran down to the jetty.

There were two canoes and a boat moored there
– a Princess V55 motor cruiser. A canoe would be
too slow. But the boat? It was a beautiful craft,
very low in the water, its bow shaped like a knife,
built for speed. Alex looked for the key in the

276

ignition. Why not? One guard had been asleep. Another hadn't even looked at him as he drove past. A third might have made the clumsiest mistake of all.

But this time he was disappointed. There was no key. He searched all the cupboards and lockers in the main cabin, but there was nothing. Frustrated, Alex rested his hands on the wheel and forced himself to think calmly. Drevin's house was in sight. He was tempted to steal in and try to get hold of a telephone. But Tamara had warned him that all the phones on the island would be disabled, and Alex believed her. Might he find a key to the Princess in the house? It was possible but the risk was too great. Alex looked up. The sky was brightening rapidly, the darkness trickling away like spilt ink. Dawn had broken. Drevin might wake up at any moment.

No phones. No boats. Barbados was ten miles away – too far to swim or to paddle in a canoe. Alex knew what he had to do. He had worked it out when he was sawing through the bars of the cage, but he'd hoped he would be able to find another way. Well, there was no other way. He might as well get on with it.

He jumped down from the boat and ran along the beach, making for the house. But he wasn't going in. Instead, he went round the back to the equipment store where Kolo had taken him before the dive. It occurred to Alex that he might find a key to the motor launch somewhere inside, but he wasn't going to waste any more time looking. The store was where Paul Drevin kept his power kite and board. That was what Alex had come for.

But even as he found the kite and began to bundle it out, he wondered if it would be possible. Ten miles was a long way, and after the storm the sea might be rough. At least there was a strong breeze. Alex had felt it when he was on the jetty – and it was also blowing offshore. Most kite boarders avoid an offshore wind; it's lumpy and difficult, and there's always a danger it will blow you out to sea. But that was exactly what Alex wanted. He needed to get away. Fast.

He reached for the board and at that moment the door swung open behind him. Alex was already spinning round, his fists raised, preparing for a karate strike, when Paul stepped inside.

"Alex?" The other boy had obviously only just got up. He was wearing shorts and nothing else. He stared at Alex, shocked. "What are you..." He couldn't find the words. "I thought you'd gone," he said.

"I'm afraid not." Alex wasn't sure how much Paul knew, and he didn't know what to say. He was aware that the whole situation had changed. Where did he go from here?

"What's happened to you?" Paul asked. "What are you doing here? And why are you dressed like that?"

"I'm sorry," Alex said. "I can't tell you." He desperately wished Paul hadn't found him. "How did you know I was here?"

"I couldn't sleep. I went to the window to get some air – and there you were, on the beach."

"Do you have a key to the boat? Do you know where it is?"

"No." All of a sudden Paul was angry. "Dad told me that you'd been sent here to spy on him. I said that couldn't be true, but he was sure of it. He said he had enemies in New York and they'd paid you to come here, to make trouble."

"Did he tell you what he did to me?" Alex cut in. He was getting angry himself. Here was Paul, accusing him. But he knew nothing.

"He said he put you on the plane out of here." Paul looked at Alex uncertainly. "Is it true, Alex?" he demanded. "Are you spying on us?"

"I haven't got time to talk about this now." He took a step and Paul's arm shot out, his hand reaching for a button built into a panel on the wall. Alex hadn't noticed it before.

"This is an alarm," Paul told him. "If I press it, there'll be a dozen guards here in less than a minute. I want you to tell me the truth. What are you doing here? What's been happening?"

"If you press that button, I'll be killed."

"You're lying..."

"Your father will kill me, Paul. He's already tried once."

"No!" Paul was staring at Alex and now there was something else in his face. It wasn't just disbelief. It was anger. And Alex understood. There was nothing he could say. He could tell Paul everything he knew about Nikolei Vladimir Drevin, and it would make no difference.

Drevin had lied to him. He had taunted him and shown him little affection. But he was still Paul's father. It was as simple as that. And no matter what the feelings were between them, Paul would defend him. Because he was Drevin's son.

Alex knew that he had only seconds before Paul sounded the alarm. He raised his hands, palms upward, as if to prove that he meant no harm. "OK, Paul," he said. "I'll tell you everything."

"Don't come any closer..." Paul's hand hovered centimetres from the alarm.

Alex risked another step forward. "It's not what you think. Your dad was wrong about me. So are you. Your mother asked me to come here."

"What?"

Alex had mentioned Paul's mother because he knew the effect it would have. Paul froze, uncertain, and in that split second, Alex lashed out, driving his elbow into the other boy's temple. Paul crumpled instantly; Alex caught him and lowered him to the ground. He had been learning karate since he was six years old but this was the first time he had struck anyone the same age as himself. He felt ashamed. All Paul had ever wanted was a friend, someone he could look up to – and it had come to this. But what else could he do? He had to leave the island. He had to prevent a whole city from being destroyed.

He forced himself to ignore the unconscious boy, picked up the kite and the rest of the equipment and dragged it down to the beach. The sun was already well above the horizon. Alex pumped up the kite and laid it out along the shore, all the while looking out for any approaching guards. How long would he have before Paul came round? Fifteen minutes, perhaps twenty. No matter which way he looked at it, he was running out of time.

And there was still the problem of launching the kite. With two people it had been easy. On his own it would take more time. Quickly Alex stripped off the grey uniform; underneath he was wearing swimming trunks. He picked up the harness and clipped it on. It was a Mystic Darkrider, made out of black rubber with a foam shell. Paul had chosen all the equipment himself and he'd made sure he'd got the best. If only he could have been here to help Alex with it.

How to do it?

Alex checked the wind direction, then laid the kite out on the ground with the lines stretching towards the water's edge. He scooped up several handfuls of sand and dumped them on the upwind tip of the kite. The other tip he left free.

He picked up the board and control bar and began to walk backwards into the sea. The water, surprisingly cold, lapped around his ankles. The kite, shaped like a crescent moon, was lying flat behind him. It was already flapping like a wounded animal, trying to rise up into the air. Only the sand was holding it down.

Alex laid the board down beside him and pulled one of the lines attached to the downwind tip, gently nudging it into the breeze. Almost at once it began to rise, and the kite inflated, the wind rushing through the vents. Alex stepped deeper into the water. The kite was pulling more strongly, the fabric jerking and throwing off the sand. And then, suddenly, it rose. Alex steered it carefully into the air and neutralized it above his head. It had taken him several minutes to get to this point and he was painfully aware of the time ticking away. But he had done it. He was ready to go.

He hooked the control bar to his harness and then stepped onto the board. Carefully he lowered the kite into the wind. Almost at once he felt the pull, fierce and irresistible. He leant back, letting it take him. He was powered up. A moment later, he was away.

The kite was flying in front of him, about fifteen metres above the sea. Despite everything, Alex experienced the same exhilaration that he had felt with Paul when the two of them were fooling around. He seemed to be going incredibly fast.

The wind was rushing over him, the spray almost blinding him as it swept into his face. The sun was already hot; he could feel it beating down, warming his arms, chest and shoulders. If he was out here too long, he would burn. But Alex knew that was the least of his problems. Somehow he had to cover the ten miles. And Drevin would be coming after him very soon.

He was heading past Little Point; once round it he would find himself in less friendly waters. He eased the control bar, raising it slightly to slow himself down, then pulled on the two front lines, tilting it to the left. The moment he rounded the headland, he felt the difference. The waves were suddenly much larger. The view ahead was obstructed by solid blue walls that rose up with alarming speed and threatened to come crashing down on him. Somehow he managed to climb them, one after another. But his arms, taking most of the strain, were already aching. And when he did catch a brief glimpse of the horizon, there was nothing on it, not even so much as a speck. Barbados was still a long way away.

Ten minutes passed. Alex was a good surfer but the experience was very different with a kite. All his concentration was fixed on the soaring black and white Flexifoil wing. If he allowed it to stray outside the wind envelope, he knew it would fall into the sea. He would come to an immediate halt and it would be almost impossible to launch the kite again. He had to stay upright. He was exhausted from lack of sleep. *Ignore it. Stay focused.* Gritting his teeth, he willed himself on.

The wind was coming at him sideways now, gusting at around thirty miles an hour. The spray was lashing into him. He wondered if he was going in the right direction and risked a glance behind him. Flamingo Bay was already small and distant. He figured that so long as he kept it over his left shoulder, he must be heading more or less straight.

He looked back again, and felt a sickening lurch in his stomach. He had to fight to keep his balance. He must have travelled at least five miles, he was sure of it. But there was still no sign of Barbados and the worst had happened.

He was being pursued.

Paul must have come round and raised the alarm. Either that or someone had spotted the kite and guessed what had happened. The Princess V55 was knifing through the water, its sleek form powering towards him. It was incredibly fast, moving at almost thirty-nine knots. Forty-five miles an hour. It wouldn't take very long to catch up with him. And there was more to come. There were two smaller boats with it. As Alex risked another glance behind him he saw them peel away from it, leaping ahead and rapidly closing the distance between the Princess and him.

They were brand-new Bella 620 DC speedboats, Finnish-made and shipped out to the Caribbean.

They were twenty feet long, squat and mean-looking with silver pulpit rails shaped like the nostrils of an angry bull. Each one was equipped with a single 150 horsepower Mercury Optimax Saltwater outboard and Alex knew that they had to be going almost twice as fast as him. They were less than a minute away.

There was nothing he could do. His hands were clamped tight round the control bar and he lowered the kite as much as he dared, desperately trying to pick up speed. Now he could hear the motors above the wind. More walls of water rose up in front of him. His legs trembled with the strain as he fought his way over the waves. The boats flew along, carving through them.

There were two men in each of them, one steering, the other holding a machine gun. They hadn't come to capture him and take him back. They were here to kill him. Alex heard the first rattle of machine-gun fire, almost lost in the roar of the waves. He slammed the bar into his chest, steering the kite up. At the same time, he transferred his weight to the flat of the board, tensed himself and jumped. Now he was in the air, ten metres above the water. The bullets passed underneath him. The hang time seemed to stretch on for ever. He was flying, his whole body tilted backwards, the soles of his feet towards the sky. The men in the speedboats had been taken by surprise. Thrown around by the sea, they were off balance, half blinded by the spray, unable to aim at a target high above their heads. For a few seconds, Alex was safe.

But he couldn't defy gravity for ever. Alex braced himself for the splash down, trying to ignore the two boats, which were horribly close. He landed between them, bending his knees to absorb some of the impact, lowering the kite to maintain speed. If he toppled over, he would die. But while he remained standing, the men couldn't fire. There was too much risk that they would hit each other in the crossfire.

And then Alex saw Barbados. It was there, ahead of him, no bigger than a one-penny piece. If he could survive just a few more minutes, he would be all right.

He was being pulled along between the two boats, all three of them doing the same speed. He was so close to the men that but for the scream of the engines and the booming of the waves he would have been able to call out to them. He could sense his strength beginning to fail him. His arms were aching. All his muscles were straining. He could barely feel the board beneath his feet.

And then the boat on his left edged ahead, allowing the one on his right a clear line of fire. Alex saw the guard raise his machine gun, preparing to shoot. He was a sitting duck skimming across the water, totally unprotected, just a couple of metres away from the man who was about to mow him down.

Alex did the only thing he could. Once again he took to the air, but this time he didn't jump as high. The man with the gun might think he'd miscalculated. But Alex knew exactly what he was doing. Everything depended on surprise.

As he took off, he let go of the bar with one hand and reached down. There was a handle in the middle of the board and he grabbed hold of it. He was hanging in the air and the board fell away, coming free of his feet. Holding it tightly, Alex swung it beneath him like a club. The board slammed into the man's head. Alex knew that it was made of Kevlar, the same material that the SAS used for their body armour. For the man with the machine gun, it was like being hit with a slab of metal. He crumpled. But his finger was still on the trigger. Alex saw the muzzle flash. Bullets tore into the deck of the boat, shattered the windscreen and hit the driver. He jerked and fell forward. The boat went out of control.

Alex slid the board back under him, and managed to get his feet into the straps a second before he hit the water.

The Bella 620 DC had an unconscious passenger and a dead driver slumped over the wheel. It performed a fantastic S-bend, veering first to the right, then back to the left, crossed the open expanse of water and smashed at full speed into the other boat. Alex watched as the two craft collided. There was an explosion of splintering metal and fibreglass, and the second boat was flipped into the air. For a brief moment, it seemed to hang there, and Alex glimpsed the face of the terrified driver, upside down, as he gazed at his own death. Then it pancaked down and there was a huge splash.

It was over. Alex allowed the kite to drag him out of danger. He was suddenly alone.

But not for long. The Princess had been hanging back, waiting for the two speedboats to finish their work. Now it surged forward. As well as the driver, it was carrying three guards armed with machine guns. The men had seen what had happened; they would be more careful. All they had to do was move into range and they would be able to cut him down.

Alex didn't have the strength for another jump. Barbados was looming up in front of him but, as if taunting him, the wind had died down. He could feel himself losing speed. He brought the kite as low as he dared but it made no difference. There was nothing more he could do.

He braced himself, waiting for the chatter of the guns and the searing agony that would follow.

There was another explosion. A blast of smoke and burning petrol. Alex toppled sideways, deafened. He wondered for the briefest of moments if he had been hit. Then he plunged into the water as fragments of broken, blackened fibreglass ricocheted all around him like a swarm of bees. His hands no longer had the strength to hang onto the control bar. He was sucked beneath the surface, twisting round and round, broken, finished.

He surfaced.

The Princess was on fire. There was no sign of the driver, no sign of the three armed men. The boat swerved, trailing black smoke, and began to slow down.

Alex was choking. He coughed up water and twisted round. Another boat had appeared, some sort of naval vessel. There was a man standing in the bow, holding a bazooka. Alex recognized the blond hair and chiselled features of Ed Shulsky, the CIA agent he had met in New York.

"Alex!" Shulsky called out. "You want a ride?"

Alex was too weak to respond. His shoulders and face had been burnt by the sun but he was shivering. The boat drew up alongside him and he was pulled on board. There were a dozen men on the deck, all young and tough-looking. Someone produced a large towel and wrapped it around him.

"We were watching the island," Shulsky told him. "We saw you coming, although we didn't know it was you at first. To be honest, we couldn't believe what we were seeing. I still don't believe it! So we came over to help..."

It was all the explanation Alex needed. "Drevin has Tamara Knight," he said. "She's a prisoner. And there's something you need to know—"

Just then, it happened.

A blinding light so bright that it seemed to blot out the sun, sucking the blue out of the sea and the sky, turning the whole world white. A noise like an explosion, only ten times louder and more sustained. A shock wave that shivered across the water, sending new waves punching into the side of the boat. The very air seemed to vibrate and Alex felt a bolt of pain in both ears.

He turned in time to see a silver pencil blasting into the sky, flame scorching out of its base, rising as if on a cushion of smoke. It was ten miles away, tiny, but even so Alex could sense its awesome power and majesty. He watched as it disappeared, effortlessly penetrating the upper atmosphere.

He was too late. *Gabriel 7* had been launched.

The bomb that was going to bring Ark Angel crashing down onto Washington was on its way.

THE RED BUTTON

It sometimes seemed to Alex that the whole universe was against him. Getting away from Flamingo Bay had almost killed him. It had been an exhausting struggle against time, the elements and Drevin's firepower.

And now he was going back.

It was the CIA agent, Ed Shulsky, who had made it happen.

"Alex, you know the place. I need you to tell me where they're holding Tamara. You can give me the layout of the island. Anyway, we don't have much time. You saw for yourself. The rocket is on its way, and if what you've told me is true..."

"It is." Alex felt a spurt of annoyance. Why should the American doubt, even for a moment, what he had said? Was it perhaps because he was only fourteen?

Shulsky noticed his reaction. "I'm sorry. That was out of line. But this plan of his, Ark Angel ... Washington..." He shook his head. "It's beyond anything we could have imagined. And that's why we have to take him out. Right now. We don't have time to drop you off."

"But you're too late," Alex argued. "*Gabriel 7* has gone. What are you going to do? Shoot it down?"

Shulsky smiled. "There's no need for that. All we have to do is find the red button." Alex looked puzzled. "The self-destruct! If something went wrong with the launch, Drevin would have had to have a fallback. We'll be able to blow it up before it gets anywhere near Ark Angel."

Alex was standing at the bow of the armour-plated Mark V Special Operations Craft, the sleek, streamlined vessel used primarily to carry SEAL combat swimmers into operations. It was equipped with 7.62mm Gatling guns and Stinger missiles and the dozen men had been drafted in from the Special Operations Force, fully armed and ready to invade the island.

He was wearing combat clothes that were a little too big for him; someone had found a spare set on board. Now he watched as the island drew closer, the familiar landmarks coming into focus. The strange thing was, deep inside, he knew that he would have wanted to come back, even if Shulsky hadn't made any argument pointless. Tamara Knight was waiting for him. And then there was Paul Drevin. Alex wanted a chance to explain himself. He still felt bad about what he'd done.

"Two minutes!" Shulsky called out.

The men began to check their weapons and body armour. They were heading for the old wooden jetty near the house. Shulsky intended to approach the control centre through the rainforest. It would mean a forced march along the length of the island and would take longer, but after Alex had described the launch area, Shulsky had decided a frontal attack would be too risky. There was no shelter; they would be cut down the moment they left the boat.

Shulsky rejoined Alex at the bow. "I want you to stay on board until the fighting's over," he announced.

"What do you mean?" Alex protested. "I thought you wanted me to help."

"You *have* helped. Thanks to you, we know where we're going and what we're going to do. But this is going to be a war, Alex. And I can't afford to have my men worrying about you. Stay on the boat and stay out of sight."

It was too late to argue. They had reached the jetty, and Alex had to admit that Shulsky was right about one thing. This side of the island was deserted. If Drevin had seen them coming, he had concentrated his forces around the launch site; nobody so much as blinked as the boat drew up at the jetty. Alex watched the thirteen Americans disembark. They stomped across the beach and disappeared through the palm trees. He still wished he had gone with them. He had told them where to find Tamara but he would have liked to be the one to release her himself.

He was left behind. Forgotten. He could see Drevin's house in the distance, the sunlight sparkling off the windows. Someone had dumped some waterskis and two tow ropes on the sand, but otherwise the beach was empty. The Cessna 195 was bobbing in the shallows but there was no sign of the pilot.

The Cessna.

It hadn't been there when Alex had set off with the kite. He felt a sense of misgiving. If Drevin knew that the Americans were on their way, his first thought would be to save his own skin. Shulsky and his men had rushed off without stopping to think. They should have disabled the seaplane first.

Alex looked around, searching for a weapon or anything he could use to do the job himself. But the Americans had taken everything and he had no doubt that the Gatling guns would be locked in their mounting positions. What else? Nothing. Just the two canoes sitting peacefully beside the jetty, the waterskiing equipment, and a pelican watching him from a distant wooden post.

The silence was broken by a rattle of machine-gun fire and the pelican took off in fright. It had begun. Alex listened as the shooting intensified. There was an explosion and a column of flame rose up briefly above the trees. A movement caught his eye. A buggy was racing along the track. Alex glimpsed it between the palm trees. Then it broke out into the open and he froze. The buggy was being driven by Nikolei Drevin. He was alone.

Alex assumed Drevin would make for the seaplane, but he continued to the house. Maybe there was a safe there. Maybe he needed to pick up a few last things. Or perhaps he'd come back for Paul. Alex tried to work out what to do. He wished more than ever that Shulsky had taken him with him – or at least left one of his men behind.

Five minutes later, he approached the house.

Alex knew he was making a mistake, but he had to see for himself what Drevin was doing. Anyway, it was against his nature to sit there, skulking away in an American boat while the fighting continued all around him. He could smell burning. Black smoke was drifting across the forest. There was more gunfire. Alex hurried across the hot sand, knowing that he had arrived at the endgame. The last moves were about to be played.

He reached the side of the building and pressed himself against the wall, keeping out of sight. The terrace where he had eaten breakfast with Drevin and Paul was directly above him. A wooden staircase curved up from the beach and Alex was just considering whether he could risk climbing it to look in through the window, when Drevin appeared round the side of the house, an attaché case in one hand, an automatic pistol in the other.

He saw Alex and stopped. "Alex Rider!" he exclaimed. His eyes were curiously empty. In the last few hours he seemed to have shrunk. "Why did you come back?"

Alex shrugged. "I forgot to say thanks for having me."

"I am glad to see you one last time. I wonder what it was that brought you and me together. Was it fate? Was it destiny?"

"I think it was Alan Blunt."

"MI6? Well, they've failed. *Gabriel 7* will reach Ark Angel; it can't be stopped. The bomb will explode and Washington will be destroyed, along with all the evidence against me."

"They don't need any evidence against you now," Alex said. "They all know you're mad."

"Yes. It will be necessary for me to disappear. But it will be easy. A man with my wealth, with my contacts..."

"The world's too small for someone like you to hide."

"We'll see." Drevin raised the gun. "But one thing is certain. We won't meet again."

He fired.

Alex had been ready for it. He dived down onto the sand. He felt the first hail of bullets pass centimetres over his head – and knew there was no way he could avoid the second.

Drevin groaned.

It was the most terrible sound Alex had ever heard, an animal cry that seemed to come from the very depths of the man's soul. He looked up, brushing sand out of his eyes. He saw Drevin standing there, quite limp, his eyes staring. Then he looked behind him.

Paul Drevin had come out of the house. He must have heard them talking, and walked round the side of the building just as Drevin had fired. Alex had dived out of the way but Paul hadn't been so lucky. He had taken the full impact of the bullets, and he was lying on his back, arms and legs spread wide, blood soaking into the sand.

"You...!" Drevin screamed the single word. Then he began to babble. Not in English but Russian. His face was white, twisted in pain and hatred. Tears were seeping out of the corners of his eyes. He pointed the gun at Alex once more. But this time Alex was ready for him.

Before Drevin could pull the trigger, Alex began to roll, spinning over and over, propelling himself towards the house. Bullets kicked up the sand, then slammed into the nearest wall. But Drevin had been caught by surprise. Still rolling, Alex disappeared into the crawl space underneath the house. It was cold and damp here. There might be spiders or scorpions nestling in the foundations.

But he was in the dark, out of the range of the bullets. For a moment, he was safe.

Drevin hardly seemed to notice. He fired at the house until the gun clicked uselessly in his hands. It took him a while to realize that he had run out of bullets. Then, with a curse, he threw the gun down and staggered over to his son. Paul wasn't moving. In the distance, he heard shouting. A buggy was approaching through the rainforest. Drevin turned and ran across the beach towards the waiting plane.

Lying on his stomach, Alex looked out through the gap between the bottom of the house and the sand. He saw Drevin reach the water's edge and knew that he wasn't coming back. Slowly, dreading what he was going to find, he crawled back out into the open and went over to Paul.

There was a lot of blood. Alex was certain that the boy was dead, and he was overwhelmed by a feeling of sadness and guilt. But then, to his surprise, Paul opened his eyes. Alex knelt down beside him. Now that he was looking closely he could see that, beneath the blood, the damage might not be as bad as he had feared. Paul had been shot in the shoulder and the arm but the rest of the bullets must have passed over his head.

"Alex..." he rasped.

"Don't move," Alex said. "I'm really sorry, Paul. This is all my fault. I should never have come here."

"No. I was wrong..." Paul tried to speak but the effort was too much.

Alex heard the sound of the Cessna's engine and turned round in time to see the plane moving away from the jetty. Drevin was piloting it. Alex could make out the crazed, distorted face behind the controls. At the same time, a buggy screeched to a halt in front of the house and Ed Shulsky and two men jumped out. Alex was relieved to see that Tamara was with them, still pale but looking stronger than when he had last seen her.

"Alex!" she called out, then stopped, seeing Paul.

Shulsky signalled, and the two men sprinted over to the wounded boy, pulling out medical packs as they ran. "What happened here?" he asked.

"Drevin," Alex said. "He hit Paul instead of me."

"How bad is it?" Shulsky addressed one of the two men.

"I think he's going to be OK," the man replied, and Alex felt a surge of relief. "He's lost blood, and we're going to have to helicopter him out as soon as possible. But he'll live."

Shulsky turned to Alex. "We've taken control of the island," he told him. "Drevin's men didn't put up much of a fight. But we lost Drevin. Where is he?"

Alex pointed. The Cessna 195 had reached full speed and was rising smoothly out of the water. Bizarrely, impossibly, two canoes had risen up behind it, as if following it out of the sea and into the sky.

"What the—" Shulsky began.

It was the only thing Alex had been able to do in the time he'd had. Using the tow ropes from the waterskiing equipment, he'd tied the canoes to the seaplane's floats. He had thought about securing the Cessna to the jetty, but Drevin would have spotted that. Part of him had hoped that the plane wouldn't be able to take off, but he was disappointed. It was already high up, a bizarre sight with the two canoes dangling underneath it. Alex wondered if Drevin had even noticed. Well, whatever happened, it would make the plane easier to spot, and when it landed, with a bit of luck, the canoes might cause it to overturn.

But then Drevin made his last mistake.

Alex would never know what was in the Russian's mind. Did he think his son was dead? Did he think Alex was to blame? It seemed he had decided to take revenge. The plane swung round and suddenly it was heading back towards them. With no warning, before there was even any sound, the sand leapt up all around them and Alex realized that Drevin was firing at them, using a machine gun mounted somewhere on the plane. The detonations came a moment later. Everyone dived for cover, the two male agents crouching over the injured boy, protecting him with their own bodies. Bullets smashed into the side of the house;

wood splintered and one of the great glass windows frosted and cascaded down. The plane roared overhead and continued towards the rainforest. The canoes bumped and twisted just behind.

Drevin had missed them on the first pass but Alex knew they wouldn't be so lucky on the second. He looked at Shulsky, wondering what the CIA agent was planning to do. They might be able to make it into the house. But what about Paul? Moving him too quickly would kill him.

The plane began to turn. The canoes dipped down. Drevin was directly over the forest. He hadn't seen the canoes, so had no idea how low they were. There were two trees close to one another. As Alex watched – with a shiver of horror – the canoes collided with the trunks and became stuck between them, caught sideways on.

The plane came to an abrupt halt. It was as if it had anchored itself in mid-air. There was the sound of breaking wood. The canoes had smashed – but so had the floats. In fact, the entire undercarriage of the plane had been torn away, and Drevin was left sitting on thin air, surrounded by half a plane. One moment he had been flying forward. The next he simply rotated ninety degrees and swooped vertically down towards the ground. There was a scream from what was left of the engine; the Cessna's propeller turned uselessly. Alex saw the plane disappear into the forest. There was a crash and then, seconds later, a ball of flame. It leapt

301

up into the sky almost as if it was trying to escape from the devastation below. Two more explosions. Then silence.

For what seemed like an eternity, Alex stared towards the crash site. A fire still raged among the trees and he wondered if it would spread across the island. But even as he watched, the flames started to flicker and die down, to be replaced by a plume of smoke that rose up in the shape of a final exclamation mark. Drevin was dead. There could be no doubt about that.

Alex felt an immense weariness. It seemed to him that everything that had happened, from the moment he had met Nikolei Drevin at the Waterfront Hotel in London, had somehow been leading to this moment. He thought back to the luxury of Neverglade, the go-kart race, the football match that had ended in murder, the flight to America. Drevin had been a monster and he'd deserved to die. Washington was no longer in any danger. *Gabriel 7* and the bomb it was carrying would be blown up long before it reached Ark Angel.

But Alex couldn't feel any sense of victory. He looked back at Paul Drevin. The two agents were busy working on him, one of them wrapping pressure bandages around his wounds while the other fed an IV needle into his arm. Paul's eyes were closed. Mercifully he had slipped into unconsciousness and so hadn't seen what had just happened.

Alex turned back and watched the smoke spread through the air, and suddenly he wanted to be far away from Flamingo Bay. He wanted to be with Jack. The two of them would take a plane home.

It was finally over.

He realized that Ed Shulsky and Tamara were staring at him.

"What is it?" he asked.

The two CIA agents exchanged a look. Then Shulsky spoke. "I wish you hadn't done that," he said. "We wanted to have a word with Mr Drevin."

Alex shrugged. "I don't think he was planning to hang around for a chat."

"You may be right," Shulsky agreed. "But we still needed to speak to him." He paused. "You remember that red button I was telling you about?"

Alex nodded. "Yes."

"Well, it seems I was wrong. There isn't one. We can't blow up *Gabriel 7*. There's nothing we can do to stop it."

"What?" Alex's head spun. "But you just said that you're in control of the island. There must be something you can do."

Tamara shook her head. "After the launch, Drevin locked down all the computer systems," she explained. "He was the only one with the codes. It's not your fault, Alex. By the time we'd caught up with him it probably would've been too late. But right now *Gabriel 7* is on its way and we can't communicate with it. We can't bring it back and we can't divert it. It's going to dock with Ark Angel in less than three hours from now. The bomb is on a timer. It's all going to happen exactly as Drevin planned."

"So what are you going to do?" Alex asked.

Tamara didn't have the heart to say it. She glanced at Shulsky.

"Alex," he said. "I'm afraid we need your help."

ARK ANGEL

"No," Alex said. "No way. Forget it. The answer is no!"

"Let's go over this again," Ed Shulsky suggested.

They were sitting in the control centre on the western stretch of Flamingo Bay. Alex had been driven there from Drevin's house and it was clear that Shulsky's men were in command. Very little damage had been done. The guardhouse and the gate had been blown up – that was the explosion Alex had heard – but it seemed that Drevin's men had surrendered quickly. None of them had known what Drevin was really planning. They had been paid to help launch a rocket into space: Drevin had never told them what the rocket actually contained.

At least Paul Drevin was out of it. He had been flown to the Queen Elizabeth Hospital in Bridgetown, on Barbados. Alex was relieved to hear that he was going to be all right. He had already been given blood and the doctors were waiting for his condition to stabilize before he was flown to America. His mother was apparently on her way to see him. Alex wondered if the two of them would ever meet again. Somehow he doubted it.

Now there were just four people in the room, surrounded by computers, video screens and the blinking lights of the electronic display board. A series of blueprints had been spread out on the large conference table. They showed the overall design of Ark Angel with the different modules – a dozen of them – extending in every direction, up and down. It was like an enormously complicated toy.

Alex was slumped in a chair, his face grim, still dressed in the borrowed combat clothes. Ed Shulsky and Tamara Knight were sitting opposite him. Tamara looked exhausted, grey with pain and fatigue. She'd accepted a shot of morphine but nothing else. She wasn't leaving Alex until a decision had been made.

The fourth person in the room was Professor Sing Joo-Chan, the man in charge of the *Gabriel 7* launch. The flight director seemed a completely different person. He had lost his calm and self-possession and looked as if he was on the verge of a heart attack. His face was pale and he was sweating profusely, dabbing at his forehead with a large white handkerchief. Like everyone else, he claimed to know nothing about the bomb, nothing about Drevin's real plans. He had promised to cooperate, to do anything the CIA required, and for the time being Shulsky was giving him the benefit of the doubt. But Alex wasn't so sure. The professor had been recruited by Drevin; he had been in charge of the operation from the very start. Alex was certain he knew more than he was letting on.

"This is the situation," Shulsky said. "*Gabriel 7* will dock with Ark Angel at half past two this afternoon. It's carrying a bomb which will go off exactly two hours after that." He glanced at Alex. "Drevin told you that himself."

Alex nodded. "That's right. Half past four. That's what he said."

"Now, as I understand it, there are three docking ports on Ark Angel." Shulsky pointed to the diagram. "Two of them are positioned at the very centre ... here. But that's not where *Gabriel 7* is heading, because if the bomb blew up there it would simply rip the whole space station apart." He reached out and tapped a section on the other side, at the end of a long corridor. "*Gabriel 7* will dock here," he explained. "Right on the edge."

"Yes – the very edge!" Sing agreed. Alex noticed that the professor's eyes were wide and unfocused. He was taking care not to look at anyone directly. "That's how it was decided. That's what Mr Drevin insisted."

"The bomb must be inside the observation module," Shulsky said. "And I guess it'll be in exactly the right position. Most of the force from the explosion will go outwards. It'll have the effect of a push in the wrong direction, propelling the entire space station back to earth." He took a deep breath and for a moment something like panic flashed in his eyes. "The hell of it is, there's nothing we can do to stop it. We can't blow up *Gabriel 7*. And according to Professor Sing here, we can't access the computers to reprogram it."

"You can't!" The white handkerchief was out again. "Only Mr Drevin had the codes. Only Mr Drevin—"

"I've checked it, Alex," Tamara said. "It's true. The entire system has been shut down. It would take us days – possibly even weeks – to hack into it."

"I know it sounds crazy, but that leaves us with just one option," Shulsky went on. "We have to send somebody up to Ark Angel. Believe me, Alex, it's the only way. Someone has to find the bomb and neutralize it – by which I mean switch it off. And if that isn't possible, then they have to move it. They have to carry it into the middle of the space station and leave it there. That way, the force of the explosion will have a completely different effect. It'll destroy Ark Angel. What pieces are left will scatter and burn up in the outer atmosphere."

"You will destroy Ark Angel!" Professor Sing whispered the words as if he couldn't believe what he had just heard.

"I don't give a damn about Ark Angel, Professor!" Shulsky almost shouted the words. "My only concern is Washington."

"Move the bomb or switch it off – what difference does it make?" Alex asked. "How is anyone going to get there?"

"That's the whole point," Shulsky said. "The Soyuz-Fregat is ready for launching. It was all set to carry Arthur into space." He paused. "But there's no reason why it shouldn't carry you."

"Me? You really want to send me into outer space?"

"Yes."

"I'm not an orang-utan."

"I know. I know. But you have to understand! What we're talking about here, it's not as complicated as you think. I mean, a rocket is a pretty simple piece of machinery. It's just like a tank. It's not as if you have to control it or anything – that's all done from here." Shulsky gestured around the room. "We still have access to the flight programs for the Soyuz-Fregat. The computers marked COMMAND tell the rocket what to do. The docking, the re-entry ... everything. And those marked TELEMETRY allow us to monitor the health and well-being of the passenger. You."

"Not me."

"There is no one else," Shulsky said, and Alex could hear the desperation in his voice. "That's the whole point, Alex. We're adults. We're all too big!" He turned to Professor Sing. "Tell him!"

Sing nodded. "It's true. We planned to put Arthur – the ape – into space. I made all the calculations personally. The launch, the approach, the docking – all of it. But the first differential is the weight. The weight of the passenger. If the weight changes, then all the calculations have to change and that will take days."

"What makes you think I weigh the same?"

The professor spread his hands. "You weigh *almost* the same, and we can work within a margin. It's possible. But it's not just the weight. It's the size."

"The capsule has been modified and none of us would fit inside," Shulsky explained. "There isn't enough room. You're the only one who can go, Alex. Heaven knows, I wouldn't ask you otherwise. But there is no other way. It has to be you."

Alex's head was swimming. He hadn't slept for almost thirty hours; he wondered if this whole conversation wasn't some sort of hallucination. "But how would I even find the bomb?" he asked. "And if I did find it, how would I know where to put it?"

"You put it here." Again Shulsky pointed at one of the modules in the diagram. "This is the sleeping area. You'll pass through it on your way to

310

Gabriel 7. It's the very heart of Ark Angel. This is where the bomb has to be when it blows up. I've gone over it with the professor and he agrees. If it happens here, Washington will be safe."

"I'm just meant to carry it from one place to another?"

"It'll weigh nothing at all," Sing reminded him. "You see – it's zero gravity!"

Alex felt weak. He wanted to argue but he knew that nobody was listening. They had all made up their minds.

Tamara reached out and took his hand. "Alex, I'd go if I could," she said. "I'm just about small enough and I guess I weigh the same as you. But I don't think I'd make it. Not with this bullet wound..."

"I thought most kids would give their right arm to go into outer space," Shulsky added unhelpfully. "Haven't you ever dreamt about becoming an astronaut?"

"No," Alex said. "I always wanted to be a train driver."

"Statistically, the Soyuz has an excellent reliability record," Tamara said. Alex remembered seeing her reading about space travel on Drevin's plane. "Hundreds of them have gone up, and there have been only a couple of hiccups."

"How long will it take him to get there?" Shulsky asked. As far as he was concerned, Alex had already agreed to go.

"He'll be launched along the plane of orbit," Professor Sing replied. "I can't explain it all to you now. But he'll follow a trajectory that exactly matches the inclination of Ark Angel. Eight minutes to leave the earth's atmosphere. And he will dock in less than two hours."

"And the Soyuz-Fregat is ready?"

"Yes, sir. It's ready now."

That struck Alex as odd. He knew that the second launch had been brought forward – but why had Drevin been preparing to send the ape into space at all, just hours after *Gabriel 7*? If his plan had worked, Ark Angel would have been destroyed soon after the second rocket arrived. Not for the first time, Alex was aware that there was something they didn't know, something that everyone had overlooked. But his thoughts were in such confusion that he couldn't work out what it was.

Tamara was still holding his hand. "I know it's too much to ask," she said. "I know you don't want to do it. But, believe me, we wouldn't ask you if there was another way. And you'll be safe. You'll make it back. I know you will."

Suddenly everyone was silent. They were all looking at him. Alex thought of the bomb that was closing in on Ark Angel even now. He thought of an explosion in outer space, and the space station plunging towards Washington. What had Drevin said? Four hundred tonnes of it would survive. The shock wave would destroy most of the city.

He thought of Jack Starbright, who was somewhere in the middle of it all, visiting her parents. And he knew that – just like Arthur – he didn't have any choice.

He nodded.

"Let's get you suited up," Ed Shulsky said.

After that, things moved very quickly. For Alex, it was as if his world had disintegrated. He was aware of bits and pieces but nothing flowed. From the day he'd managed to get himself caught up with MI6, he had often found it hard to believe what was happening to him. But this was something else again. He seemed to have lost any sense of his own identity. He was being swept along, out of control, edging closer and closer to something that filled him with more horror than he had ever known.

He was made to shower and dress in the clothes that he had seen in the building where he and Tamara had been imprisoned: a white T-shirt and a blue tracksuit with the Ark Angel logo stitched onto the sleeve. Straps passed under his feet to hold the trousers in place and there were six pockets fastened with zips. Suddenly he was surrounded by people he had never met, all of them giving him advice, preparing him for the terrible journey he was about to make.

"You need to watch out for what we call the breakaway phenomenon!" This from a man in glasses with hair on his neck. Some sort of psychologist. "It's a feeling of euphoria. You may like it so much up there that you won't want to come back."

"I somehow doubt it," Alex growled.

"We'll be attaching EKG and biosensor leads..."

"We're going to give you an injection." This was a blonde-haired woman in a white coat. She was holding a large hypodermic syringe. "This is phenergan. It'll make you feel better."

"I feel fine."

"You'll almost certainly throw up when you reach zero gravity. Most astronauts do."

"Well, that's something you never see on *Star Trek*," Alex muttered. "All right." He rolled up his sleeve.

"Not your arm, Alex. This goes in your butt..."

He wondered why they hadn't given him a proper spacesuit, the sort of thing he'd seen in old films of the moon landings. Professor Sing explained.

"You don't need it, Alex. Arthur, also, wouldn't have worn a spacesuit. You will be inside a sealed capsule. If there was a leak, it's true that you would need a spacesuit to protect you; but that's not going to happen, I promise you. Trust me!"

Alex looked at the dark, blinking eyes behind the spectacles. He knew that Sing was ingratiating himself with the CIA, trying to persuade them that he had been innocent from the start. He was sure that Ed Shulsky and Tamara would be watching him throughout the entire launch. But he still didn't trust the professor. He was certain there was something he wasn't being told.

They gave him a headset and radio and wired up his heart. It seemed impossible to Alex that anyone could go into space like this, without months of training. Tamara never left his side, trying to reassure him. A fourteen-year-old was more adaptable than an adult, she said. It was going to be a bumpy ride, but he would come through it comfortably *because* he was young. And maybe Ed Shulsky was right. It would be something to talk about. An experience he would never forget.

And then he was in an electric buggy with Tamara and Professor Sing, feeling strange in his tracksuit, the material soft against his skin. The rocket was ahead of him. He looked at it but didn't see it. It was as if the connection had been severed between his eyes and his brain. It was huge. The capsule that would carry him into space was at the very top of a silver tank as tall as an office block, suspended between two gantries. Water was cascading down. Was it raining? No, the water seemed to be coming from the rocket. He could hear the metal creaking as if it needed a huge effort just to keep it in place. There were clouds of white steam pouring out – boil-off from the propellant. Alex saw a deep trench running from the launch pad towards the sea; he guessed it would carry the flames from the solid rocket boosters. It seemed impossible to him that this oversized firework could actually rise up and carry him into space.

In a lift, climbing higher and higher, still with Tamara and the professor. He could see the whole island, the sea stretching out an amazing blue – and there was Barbados in the distance. He was still being given advice. So many words. But they didn't actually penetrate. They just flitted around him like moths.

"...do everything lightly, do everything slowly. Don't look directly at the sun. It'll blind you. Don't even look at the clouds around the earth. The sun reflects... Some parts of Ark Angel will be hot; some will be cold. There have been problems with the air-conditioning... You're going to feel strange. Don't worry if your face becomes puffy or swells up. If your spine stretches. If you need to go to the toilet. It's the same for all astronauts. Your body has to adapt to zero gravity..."

Who was talking? Were they really being serious? How could anybody expect him to do this?

"You'll need to access the observation module of *Gabriel 7* to get to the bomb. There's a hatch. You saw it on the diagram. You move it to where Ed showed you and then you get back into the Soyuz's re-entry module. Don't waste any time. We'll control everything from here. You'll feel it disengage..."

And then he was inside. They had certainly been right about the amount of space. No adult would have been able to fit into it. He was lying on his back in a metal box that could have been some kind of complicated washing machine or water tank, his feet in the air and his legs so tightly packed in that his knees were touching his chin. There were tiny windows on either side but they were covered with some sort of material and he couldn't see out of them. There were no controls. Of course not. Arthur the orang-utan wouldn't have needed controls. Professor Sing was wiring him up. More monitors. Now Alex was the one who was sweating. They had told him he would sweat even more when he was in outer space. Because of fluids moving up, the body's salt concentration being upset. Alex tried to put it out of his mind. He didn't even believe he would get there. He didn't think he would survive the journey.

Tamara Knight leant over him. He was strapped into his seat. His stomach was clenched tight and he had difficulty drawing the air into his lungs. He could move his arms but nothing else. He was already cramped and he hadn't even started. Her face was very close to his, filling his field of vision.

"Good luck, Alex," she whispered. Nothing more. She waved a hand with fingers crossed.

"You will hear the countdown," Professor Sing said. He was somewhere behind her. "You have nothing to worry about, Alex. We will guide you through it all. You'll hear us over the radio. We'll look after you."

They sealed the door. Alex felt the air inside the capsule compress. He swallowed, trying to clear his ears. Apart from the sound of his own breathing, everything was silent.

He was alone.

"T-minus thirty." A crackle and a hiss of static. The disembodied words had come through the headset. What did they mean? Thirty minutes until blast-off. In thirty minutes' time he would be leaving the planet! Alex tried to make himself more comfortable but he couldn't move.

"How are you doing, Alex?" It could have been Ed Shulsky talking. Alex didn't know. The voices echoed inside his head and they all sounded the same.

"T-minus twenty-five... T-minus twenty..."

He could only sit there, doubled up on himself, as the countdown continued. The strange thing was, it felt that time had gone wrong too. A minute seemed like half an hour. Yet half an hour was passing in only minutes. He concentrated on his breathing.

"T-minus fifteen."

Inside the control room Ed Shulsky was watching Sing and his team of thirty as they went through the final preparations. He walked over to the professor. He was wearing a gun in a holster slung over his shirt.

318

"I don't mean to worry you right now, Professor," he muttered. "But I want you to know that if Alex Rider doesn't come out of this in one piece, I will personally rip your guts out."

"Of course!" Sing smiled nervously. "There's nothing to worry about. He'll be fine!"

Tamara Knight sat motionless in front of the observation window. Smoke was still rising from the rainforest where the Cessna had crashed. There were no birds to be seen. The whole island seemed to be tensing itself for the moment of launch.

"T-minus five."

What had happened to T-minus ten? Alex was feeling sick. The injection he'd been given hadn't worked. He could hear something in the distance. Was it his imagination or was something rumbling far below him?

"T-minus four ... three ... two ... one."

It began.

At first it was slow. Alex felt a shuddering, vague to start with, but soon it was all-consuming. The entire capsule was shaking. He wasn't sure if he was moving or not. There was a thud as the clamps holding down the rocket were automatically released. The shuddering got worse. Now the whole capsule was vibrating so crazily that Alex could feel the teeth being shaken in his skull. The noise level had risen too; it was now a roar that pounded at him with invisible fists and, lying on his back with his legs bent in front of him, there was nothing he could do. He was defenceless.

And still it got worse.

He was definitely rising; he could feel the force of the rocket's thrust. He was being pushed into the seat – not pushed, crushed! His vision had almost gone. His eyeballs were being mercilessly squeezed. He tried to open his mouth to scream but all his muscles had locked. He felt as if his face was being pulled off.

And then there was a deafening explosion and he was slammed forward in his seat, his neck straining, the belts cutting into his chest. Alex panicked, thinking it had all gone wrong, that part of the rocket had blown up and any moment now he would be either incinerated or sent plummeting back to earth. But then he remembered what he had been told. The first stage of the rocket had burnt out and been ejected. That was what he had heard and felt. God help him, he really was on the way. From nought to seventeen and a half thousand miles an hour in eight minutes.

Everything had been calculated. There should have been an ape inside the orbital module – instead there was a boy. To the computers it made no difference. At exactly the right second, the next stage ignited and once again he was thrown forward, the g-forces pulverizing him. How long had passed since the countdown had ended? Was he in outer space yet? It seemed to him that the shaking was more violent than ever. The whole capsule had become a distorted mass of jagged, flickering lines, like the image on a broken TV screen. He was at max Q, sitting on four hundred and fifty tonnes of explosive, being rocketed through the sky at twenty-five times the speed of sound. The main engine was burning fuel at over one thousand gallons a second. If the Soyuz was going to blow up, it would happen now. He was on fire! Blinding light suddenly crashed into the capsule. A nuclear explosion. No. The fairings on the windows had come free. They weren't needed any more. He was looking at the sun, which was streaming in, dazzling him. Was that blue sky or the sea? How much longer could his body stand the battering it was receiving? It occurred to Alex that nothing in the world, no amount of training, could have prepared him for an experience like this.

The rocket stopped. That was what it felt like. The noise fell away and Alex felt a quite different sensation: a sick, light-headed floating that told him he had, in an instant, become weightless. He was about to test it but then the third stage kicked in and once again he was propelled forward on this impossible fairground ride. This time he closed his eyes, unable to take any more, and so didn't see the moment when he broke through the onion peel of the earth's atmosphere and went from blue to black.

At last he opened his eyes. He wanted to stretch but that was impossible. Alex looked out of the window and saw stars ... thousands of them. Millions. Once again, he had no sense of movement. Was he really weightless? He fumbled a hand into one of the pockets in his trousers and brought out a pencil a few centimetres long. He let it go. The pencil floated in front of him. Alex stared at it. Before he knew what he was doing, he was laughing. He couldn't stop himself. It really was like one of those cheap special effects in a Hollywood film. But there were no hidden wires. No computer trickery. It was happening right before his eyes.

"Alex? How are you? Are you receiving me?" Ed Shulsky's voice crackled in his ear, and the strange thing was that it sounded no different, no further away – even though Alex was already almost a hundred miles from the earth's surface.

"I'm fine," Alex replied, and there was a tone of wonderment in his voice. He had survived the launch. He was on his way.

"Congratulations. You've just broken a world record. You're the youngest person in space..."

He was in space! With the shock of the launch behind him, Alex tried to relax and enjoy the view. But the windows were too small and in the wrong place. The earth was behind him and out of sight, but there were the stars and the infinite blackness all around. How strange it was, this sense that he was going nowhere. The pencil was still in front of him. He touched it with his finger and watched it spin. Round and round it went. Alex was hypnotized by it. Nothing else seemed to be moving. This wasn't a ride at all. He felt as if everything, his entire life, had stopped.

And then he saw Ark Angel.

At first he was aware of something shaped like a spider appearing in the periscope attached to the window inside the capsule. It looked like a star, but much brighter than the others. Gradually it drew closer. And suddenly it became clear, an awesome construction of silver modules and corridors, interlocking, criss-crossing, hanging from what looked like the tower of a crane, with massive panels stretching out in every direction, absorbing the energy of the sun. It was huge; it weighed almost seven hundred tonnes. But it was floating effortlessly in the great emptiness of space, and Alex had to remind himself that every piece of it had been laboriously constructed on earth and then carried up separately and assembled. It was an engineering feat beyond anything he had ever imagined.

Slowly Ark Angel filled his vision. Both he and the space station were travelling at seventeen and a half thousand miles per hour, so fast that to Alex it made no sense at all. But he seemed to be going very slowly. Then a booster rocket fired and the Soyuz accelerated, moving in on the central docking port. It was the only way Alex could measure his progress through outer space ... a few metres at a time, getting closer and closer. The rockets were controlled from Flamingo Bay but they were accurate to a fraction of a millimetre. Alex saw the curving metal plates, the intricate panel work that made up the space station. He saw a painted Union Jack and the words ARK ANGEL printed in grey.

The last part of the journey seemed to take for ever. The space station was swallowing him up and he had to remind himself that if something went wrong now it would have the impact of a bus smashing into a wall.

There was a slight jolt – nothing compared to what he had felt earlier. That was it. A voice crackled in his headset and he thought he heard applause – unless it was radio static. Whatever his misgivings about Professor Sing, it seemed that the flight director had been true to his word. Alex had arrived.

He looked at his watch. Someone had given it to him when he got dressed for the launch. Three o'clock. He had one and a half hours to find the bomb and either turn it off or move it. But there was something wrong. For a second Alex panicked. Had the oxygen supply stopped? He swallowed hard, three or four times, gasping for air. He could feel his heart hammering and he was certain he was going to die. But it wasn't that. There was still air in the module – he just had to draw it in. Alex forced himself to calm down. What was it?

Of course. The silence. Nobody was talking to him. Either he was on the wrong side of the planet, out of range of the control centre, or the radio had broken down. The silence was total, absolute. He had never felt more empty, more alone. But it didn't matter. He didn't need anyone to talk to him.

He knew what he had to do.

He unstrapped himself and reached for the circular hatch just above his head. It was his first experience of zero gravity and he knew at once that he'd made a mess of it. He rose out of the seat far too quickly and his head thudded into the metal wall, knocking him back down again. He ended up where he had begun – but with a bruised forehead and the taste of blood in his mouth. A bad start.

Everything had to be done slowly. He reached up again and found the handle. He pulled it out and turned it. The hatch swung outwards.

Alex braced himself. If there was any error, if the airlock wasn't secured, he would be exposed to the most lethal environment known to man. And he would die the most horrible death. The air would be sucked out of his lungs and his blood would boil. All his internal organs would seize up and he would be ripped apart by the total vacuum of space. He tried not to think about it. It wasn't going to happen. In less than ninety minutes he would be on his way home.

He found himself looking into a tunnel, about

eighty centimetres wide and a couple of metres long. This was the entrance – they called it the node – between his capsule and the reception area of Ark Angel. Reconditioned air, cold and dry, blew into his face. He pushed up with his feet, the lightest movement possible. Effortlessly, he rose. It was just like he had seen in countless films. He was flying.

The node led into the first module. Ark Angel had been built for tourists. It called itself a space hotel. But of course, it was in truth a space station very similar to Mir or the ISS, with very little room and every available inch crammed with cupboards, lockers and all the wires, pipes, dials, gauges, switches, circuits and other essentials needed to keep its inhabitants alive. Each section was a cylinder about the size of an ordinary caravan, lit with a harsh white light and jammed with equipment and handrails on three sides. There were more handrails and Velcro straps on the fourth. Alex understood that to stop himself floating off he would have to hook his hands or feet into the floor.

He had expected the interior to be silent. Instead he was aware of the humming of the air conditioners, the throb of pumps circulating liquid coolants through the walls, the grinding of metal against metal ... tonnes of it bolted together even as it spun round in orbit. He breathed in deeply. The air was very dry. He wondered how it was produced. Did it come out of a bottle or was there a machine?

Alex floated – or tried to. Once again, he pushed too hard with his feet and the entire chamber turned upside down as he spun helplessly around, totally out of control. Despite the injection, he was suffering from what NASA called space adaptation syndrome. In other words, he was about to throw up. He tried to steady himself. One of his hands caught the wall, sending him spinning the other way. He no longer knew what was up and what was down. He couldn't even see the capsule that had brought him here.

He reached out and managed to hook a finger into one of the straps. That slowed him. But the whole experience so far had been horrible. Alex had seen *Star Wars*. He'd watched the Millenium Falcon blast its way across the universe, and like millions of others he'd bought into the dream. The reality was nothing like it. His body was sending his brain weird signals. He was sweating. The balance of his inner ear had gone. His bones, no longer needed, were leaking calcium. His back was aching because of the elongation of his spine. Inside his stomach, his guts were floating helplessly, and because of the shift in his fluid level, he felt a desperate need to go to the toilet.

And it got worse. Alex stopped spinning and found himself floating in the very centre of the module. Either he was moving very slowly or he wasn't moving at all. The rails and Velcro straps were now uselessly high above his head. He stretched out his arms and discovered that the walls were a couple of centimetres out of reach. It was like some terrible nightmare. Every time he strained forward, his body moved back. He was quite literally stranded, floating helplessly, going nowhere.

What now? How did he make himself go up or down? He jerked his body and pedalled with his legs. It didn't help. He tried waving his arms like a bird in a bad cartoon. Nothing.

Alex started to panic. Nobody had warned him about this. He was stuck in zero gravity and he began to wonder if he wasn't doomed to remain like this until Ark Angel blew itself apart. He couldn't move!

It took him what seemed like an eternity to work it out. It was amazing really that a physics lesson on a damp Wednesday at Brookland School should suddenly come to mind and save his life. He took off his shoes and threw them with all his strength. The forward motion produced an opposite reaction, a bit like the recoil from a gun. Alex was thrown back and managed to grab hold of a handrail. He clung there for a moment, breathing heavily. It had been a nasty moment and he would have to be very careful it didn't happen again.

He had to get moving. He hadn't been able to see the observation module and the remaining stages of *Gabriel 7* on the far side of the space station, but he knew they were there. The rocket had docked automatically almost an hour ago and had brought with it an activated bomb. He looked at his watch again. Twenty-five minutes had passed! There was barely an hour left. If the bomb exploded at the right time and in the right place, he would be vaporized, and a four hundred tonne missile would begin its deadly journey back to earth. Alex thought back to the map of Ark Angel he had been shown and knew that he had to navigate his way through an interlocking series of modules to reach his destination. He remembered what Ed Shulsky had told him.

"Don't try to defuse it unless you're sure you know what you're doing, Alex. You press the wrong button, you'll be doing Drevin's work for him. Just move it into the sleeping area. That's all you have to do. Move it and then get the hell out. Fast."

It was ticking right now. Alex could imagine it. Just the two of them. Him and a bomb on a space station orbiting the earth.

He was about to set off when he heard something. The clang of a hatch closing. It was quite unmistakable. He stopped and listened. Nothing. What next? Martians? He must have imagined it. Alex pushed off with his feet, as gently as possible, trying to steer himself towards the next module. Once again he had pushed too hard. His shoulder hit the roof – or the floor – of the node and for a second time he found himself spinning out of control.

He reached out with his hands to steady himself and found himself holding onto a lever that jutted out of the wall. It was a shutter release. Unable to contain his curiosity, he opened it, wondering if it would give him a view of the earth. But the space station was facing the wrong way. Alex reeled back, almost blinded, as brilliant light burst into the module. Professor Sing had warned him not to look directly into the sun. Even in that brief instant, Alex had almost blinded himself.

He closed the shutter again and waited for his sight to return, then continued, gently flying into the sleeping area, the bunks attached vertically to the wall with straps to keep the crew members or guests from drifting off. In space you could sleep sideways, standing or upside down; it made no difference. There was a long, brightly lit corridor straight ahead – four or five modules bolted together. Everything was white. This was the very heart of Ark Angel, with the dining room, the exercise room, the showers and lavatories, a living room and two laboratories all laid out next to one another. *Gabriel 7* would have docked at the far end.

Alex tensed himself, preparing to make the next leap. He reached out with the palms of his hands. And froze.

A man had appeared in front of him, dressed in

an identical suit to his own. The man was wearing a skullcap but, seeing Alex, he tore it off, revealing a mirror image of the world three hundred miles below.

Kaspar. Of course.

Alex had forgotten about him. So had everyone else. But Professor Sing must have known that Kaspar had been on board *Gabriel 7* – that was the one piece of information he had been keeping to himself. Why? Had he been so scared of Kaspar that he couldn't bring himself to reveal the whole truth?

It looked as if Alex would never know. Kaspar had seen him. He was only twenty metres away, at the other end of the corridor. He hadn't spoken a word but now – expertly, as if he had been trained – he pushed forward, floating through the air towards him. He was confident, in perfect control.

And he was holding a knife.

RE-ENTRY

It was something straight out of a nightmare. It was every nightmare rolled into one. The hideously tattooed face, the knife, Ark Angel, outer space... Alex could only watch helplessly as Kaspar headed towards him, flying, arms outstretched, legs trailing behind.

What was he doing in the space station?

And suddenly Alex understood.

The second rocket, the orang-utan, Drevin's so-called experiment in weightlessness – they had all been part of the plan. There was no experiment. There never had been.

Kaspar had gone up in *Gabriel 7*. And Alex knew why. His own experience of the launch should have made him see that it would have been completely insane to try sending an armed bomb into space. The terrible vibrations would have set it off before it had even left the atmosphere. Only when it was in space could it be armed, and that had meant sending someone up with it. Kaspar. But now he needed to get back again. That was the point of the second rocket. Professor Sing must have known all along. The Soyuz had been sent up to collect him. And Kaspar would surely have left instructions behind. If anything went wrong, if the rocket didn't arrive, the professor would have been killed. No wonder he had looked so nervous! In the end, he had made a choice. Send the rocket and let the two of them fight it out.

That was something else Alex understood. There were now two of them in the space station. But there was only one seat home.

Kaspar passed through the first node, where he was bathed momentarily in soft, pink light before he emerged into the glare of the next module. He seemed to be adept at manipulating himself in zero gravity. He had aimed carefully and pushed off lightly. One hand touched a wall to correct himself; the other still clasped the knife. He was taking his time – but then he knew Alex had nowhere to hide. Just seconds remained before they would come face to face in a module barely large enough for them both.

Alex searched around him for a weapon, anything he could use to defend himself. But everything was packed down too neatly. The cupboards and lockers were closed. He was still feeling sick and disorientated and every movement he made threatened to propel him in the wrong direction. If he lost control and went into another spin he would be finished. Kaspar would cut him to pieces.

Kaspar passed through the next node. In a few moments he would arrive in the same module as Alex. The sleeping area. This was the place Professor Sing and Ed Shulsky had shown him on the map. The heart of Ark Angel. It seemed an appropriate meeting point. Maybe he could reason with Kaspar. The mission was pointless now – surely he would see sense?

But Alex doubted it. Kaspar's eyes looked empty, mad. There was a twisted smile on his lips. The knife he was holding was a Sabatier, the blade a single piece of high carbon stainless steel, hand-honed and about ten centimetres long. Where had he got it from? He couldn't possibly have brought it with him. Then Alex remembered. Ark Angel was a hotel. One day it might have a chef cutting sirloin steak for some American multimillionaire, and someone had made sure he was properly equipped. Kaspar must have picked up the knife as he passed through the kitchen.

As Kaspar entered the sleeping area, Alex did the only thing he could. He crouched low, then kicked out, propelling himself along, a few inches above the floor, as if he were swimming underwater in a pool. His movement caught Kaspar unawares, and the man sailed past above him. Alex realized that there was one thing you couldn't do in zero gravity: change direction. Kaspar continued to the far wall, but as he passed him he slashed down with the knife. Alex felt the tip cut into the suit between his shoulder blades. He was lucky. Another few millimetres and it would have drawn blood. It had sliced the suit's material but hadn't pierced his skin.

Kaspar reached the far wall and clung onto one of the handholds. Alex continued through into the next module and managed to stop himself. He found himself surrounded by gym equipment: a treadmill, a pair of chest expanders, a rowing machine – but nothing he could throw at Kaspar. Where were the weights? Of course, there was no point having weights in a weightless environment. Alex scrabbled for one of the lockers and the door fell open. There were tools inside. A hammer, a curiously shaped ratchet, some sort of bolt tightener. He grabbed the hammer, pulled it free and held it in front of him.

Alex turned and saw Kaspar preparing to launch a second attack. The man seemed crazed, as if he were on drugs. Perhaps he was. Or perhaps he found the experience of being in space as terrifying as Alex did.

"Kaspar!" Alex wasn't sure what to call him. What was his real name? Magnus Payne? But that wasn't how the two knew each other. "It's over," he went on. "There's no point in this. Drevin is dead.

335

The CIA's in control on Flamingo Bay."

"You're lying!"

"How do you think I got here? There's nothing for you to do. Dropping Ark Angel on Washington – there's no point. Drevin's dead."

"No!"

Two continents twisted in anger and disbelief as Kaspar kicked off, this time travelling diagonally down. Alex knew there was no point trying to reason with him. Whatever had happened on Flamingo Bay, Kaspar needed the Soyuz. Alex stood in his way. So Alex had to die.

Kaspar flew towards him. Alex brought the hammer round and threw it with all his strength. For a moment he thought it would travel in slow motion. Wasn't that what happened in films? But it didn't. The hammer spun at full speed through the air and hit Kaspar on the shoulder. But would the hammer do any damage if it weighed nothing? Once again Alex thought back to his physics class, starting work on his GCSEs. The hammer picked up energy because of motion; the energy was dispersed when it came to rest. In this instance, it came to rest because it had hit Kaspar square on. Kaspar howled and dropped the knife. Energy dispersed equalled pain!

But the forward motion was enough to send Alex stumbling back, and for a moment he lost control. His shoulders crashed into a wall. Or perhaps it was the ceiling or the floor. It made no difference. Kaspar had leapt forward. He plunged down as if he had been fired from a gun, and a second later he was on top of Alex.

The blue and green skin of the man's face was just inches away. Eyes full of hatred glared at him. Kaspar's hands closed around his throat and began to tighten. The man was strangling him. And there was nothing Alex could do. He had no gadgets, no weapons. He couldn't even move. He could feel metal plates against his shoulders, one of the lockers pressing into his back. Kaspar was floating horizontally above him, connected to Alex only by his hands. The breath was no longer reaching Alex's lungs; the grip was too tight. He felt dizzy. In a few seconds he would pass out.

Barely knowing what he was doing, he scrabbled behind him. His knuckles brushed against some sort of lever. What was it? Even as his consciousness began to leave him, Alex remembered. He knew what the lever did. But now he couldn't find it. Desperately he lashed out and his flailing hand caught hold of it. He pulled down.

The shutter opened and the light that had almost blinded him before exploded into the module a second time, shafting in over his shoulder. The window was facing directly into the sun and the light had a physical force as it burst in. Alex could feel it burning his neck and shoulders. The whole capsule seemed to disintegrate into a brilliant chaos of white and silver, all other colours sucked out.

Kaspar screamed as the light seared his eyes. It was as if he had been punched in the face by the sun itself, and his hands fell away, instinctively coming up to protect himself. Alex brought his legs up and kicked; his feet slammed into Kaspar's stomach. Alex's back was against the wall, and Kaspar was sent hurtling towards the other side of the module.

The Sabatier knife was right behind him.

It had been hovering there, its deadly point aimed at Kaspar's neck. As Kaspar travelled backwards it went with him, but then the handle came into contact with the wall. The blade entered the city of Beijing and continued its journey, burrowing into the world's surface. Kaspar's body jerked as if he had been electrocuted. Then he was still.

Lying underneath him, Alex watched in disbelief. Kaspar's arms were hanging down towards him. He was in the middle of the module, not touching any surface, suspended there. A string of bright crimson marbles appeared and began to orbit around his head. They grew larger. Now they were golf balls, trailing away, glistening red.

The knife had severed an artery. Kaspar's blood hung around him like a grotesque Christmas decoration.

Alex had had enough. The module was heating up rapidly, still exposed to the sun, and he reached out and closed the shutter. A shadow fell across Kaspar's face. The marbles darkened.

With his skin crawling, wanting to get away from the obscene, floating body, Alex dragged himself into the next module using a series of Velcro grips. He found himself next to a space toilet, a grey plastic box with some sort of cone device floating at the end of a pipe. He needed to use it. He was going to be sick. Grimly he swallowed, forcing himself to stay calm. He didn't want to find out what vomit looked like in outer space.

The bomb...

How much time did he have left? Alex looked at his watch. One minute past four. Just twenty-nine minutes left. He had to move quickly. To have come so far, to have been through so much, only to die now! He forced himself to concentrate, to control his movements. He remembered the map he had been shown in the control centre. He knew where he had to go.

The hatch leading into the capsule that had brought Kaspar into space was open, and Alex saw the bomb at once. It was shaped like a torpedo, black, with six tiny switches and a glass panel with a digital read-out. The whole thing was strapped to the wall, held in place with Velcro. With a ghastly sort of fascination, Alex lowered himself into the module and floated next to it. There was a six-figure display, rapidly counting down: 27:07:05. Alex checked it against his watch. Yes. Three minutes past four. He had just twenty-seven minutes left.

Could he turn it off? Alex examined the switches but there were no symbols, nothing to tell him what function they performed. Did he dare press one? If he made a mistake, he'd be blown to smithereens. He reached out a finger. His mouth was dry. Being so close to the bomb filled him with horror. But he had to try, didn't he? Drevin might have perverted the genius of Ark Angel but, even so, the space station was a technological miracle, completely unique, the world's first hotel in orbit around the earth. Could Alex really allow it to be destroyed? His finger rested against the top switch. All he had to do was flick it. It might deactivate the bomb, but it might set it off. The question was, did he dare take the risk?

The numbers in the display were still counting down. Now they showed 25:33:00.

Alex swore. Why didn't they have some sort of rubbish chute? Then he could get rid of the bomb, jettison it into outer space. There probably was an airlock on Ark Angel, but he had no idea how to operate it. Anyway, there was no time. His finger was still touching the switch. One of six switches. A one in six chance of getting it right.

Not good enough.

Alex let out a long, shuddering breath and withdrew his hand. He took hold of the still-ticking bomb and gently unfastened it, then eased it up through the hatch and back into the centre of the space hotel. Ed Shulsky had told him where to leave it, but Alex made the decision for himself. The toilet. Somehow it seemed a fitting end. He lowered the nose of the torpedo into it and left it there.

It was time to go.

He pushed himself off as gently as he could and was rewarded with a slow, careful progression back towards the waiting module of the Soyuz. He passed underneath Kaspar, taking care not to look up. In a few minutes' time, the dead man was going to be given one of the most spectacular cremations anyone could ask for. It was more than he deserved.

The docking station was ahead of him – but there was one last thing he had to do. He looked at his watch. Eleven minutes past four. There were just nineteen minutes remaining, and Alex knew it was madness to waste even a few seconds. But he would never have this opportunity again. He found another window on the opposite side from the sun, opened the shutter and looked out.

And there it was.

Planet earth. Seen from outer space.

His first thought was how big it was; his second, how small. Of course, he had seen images of the earth taken by astronauts. But this was different. He was seeing it with his own eyes. And he was moving. As he crouched in front of the porthole, he was travelling so fast that it would take him just ninety minutes to go all the way round. No wonder it seemed small. And yet the earth filled his vision. All the life in the universe, five billion people, was concentrated there. And the thought of that was enormous.

He was struck by the colours. No photographs could have prepared him for the sheer iridescence of the planet. It looked as if it were lit from inside. At first it seemed that everything was blue and white – most of the planet was water – and Alex remembered lying on his back when he was small, staring at a perfect summer sky. If he could have turned the sky into a ball, that was what he was seeing now. But as he gazed down he began to make out the shape of the coastlines, a thin line of emerald green; and then Ark Angel turned the corner of the world and there was Africa – all of Africa ahead of him – and suddenly he was seeing intense gold, yellow and red ... mountains and deserts but no cities. Nothing moving. And he wondered, if he was an alien and came upon the earth, could he pass by without being aware of the teeming life below?

But then day became night and he found himself over the western Mediterranean seaboard, and even from three hundred miles away he could make out thousands of electric lights that had to be man-made. Spain and Gibraltar, Turkey, Tunisia, Algeria and Lebanon – all of them were visible at once, the tiny lights blinking like fireflies. There were storms over Europe. Alex saw the lightning shimmer through the clouds.

It wasn't just that there was life on earth. The whole earth was alive. Alex could feel it pulsating beneath him, and suddenly he knew that for all its technology, Ark Angel was a sterile, dead place and he didn't care that soon it would no longer exist. He had made the right decision. At that moment, Alex felt a sense of loneliness he would remember for the rest of his life. He wanted to go home.

He made his way back to the Soyuz module, trying to control his progress but still crashing into the walls. Only by holding onto the handrails did he prevent himself from going into another sickening spin. He had a raging thirst and wished he'd found himself something to drink before he left. What happened when you opened a can of Coke in space? He would never find out.

Somehow he reached the entrance and folded himself in. He was operating on automatic. All he wanted was to get away. He reached up and closed the hatch, turning the lever to lock it before blast-off. This was the compartment he had travelled up in. But it was going to stay behind. There was a second hatch underneath him and he opened it, passing into the re-entry module below. There was more room here. Of course. The re-entry module had to be big enough for Kaspar. He strapped himself into the seat, found another headset and put it on, wondering if it would work.

"Alex? What is your status?" It was Tamara's voice. He had never been happier to hear anyone.

"The bomb is still active," he said. He looked at his watch. Twenty-five past four. "Professor Sing lied to us," he went on. "Kaspar was here. And now I've only got five minutes left. Get me out of here."

Another burst of static. A disembodied voice was muttering half-words that made no sense. There had to be something wrong with the radio. Alex wondered what would happen next. How long would he have to sit here before he disengaged? And what would happen if he didn't? The second hand on his watch ticked round. It seemed to be taunting him, moving faster than it should. The time now was twenty-eight minutes past four.

Already he was sweating. Hunched up on his back with no view, he had no idea where he was, how much further he was around the world. Twenty-nine minutes past four. Had he reached the last sixty seconds of his life?

He felt a sudden jolt. For a terrible moment, he thought that the bomb had detonated. Then he realized that was impossible. He hadn't heard anything but he was suddenly aware that the module's retro-rockets must have been fired. He twisted his head round and peered through the periscope. Ark Angel was already a mile away, vanishing into space like a pebble dropped into a well.

And then it exploded.

The bomb blew up, a burst of orange flame that ripped the entire space station apart, sending the different modules spinning in different directions. The arms with the solar panels fell away. There were two more explosions. A shower of brilliant sparks and a dazzling burst of white light that stretched out in silence.

Alex felt a sense of euphoria. He had succeeded! He had put the bomb in exactly the right place, and instead of propelling Ark Angel towards Washington, it had simply destroyed it. There was nothing left. A few pieces were falling through space but they would quickly burn up. At last it was over.

He fell.

The crackle on the radio stopped abruptly. Alex found himself in the grip of a silence so complete that for a moment he thought he might have died, and he had to remind himself he wasn't home yet. He was plummeting down, feet forward, moving at eighteen thousand miles an hour. Five miles a second. This was the most dangerous part of the entire journey. If the control centre had miscalculated, he would be incinerated. Already he was aware of a pink glow outside the window as the module began to rub against the earth's upper atmosphere.

And then he was on fire. The whole world was on fire. The very air was breaking up, being smashed to pieces, the electrons separating from the nuclei.

345

The module had become a fireball, and Alex knew that his life depended on the hundreds of thermal tiles that surrounded him. He was in the heart of a living hell.

He yelled out. He couldn't help himself.

Then the red disappeared, like a curtain being torn apart.

He saw blue.

There was a second, back-breaking jolt as the parachute deployed. The world seemed to shimmer on the other side of the window and Alex saw the Pacific Ocean spread out before him.

A splash. Steam. Waves lashing at the windows. Sunlight turning the water into diamonds.

And at last silence.

He was rocking back and forth, a hundred miles off the eastern coast of Australia. The wrong side of the world – but that didn't matter.

Alex Rider was back.

**Read the next mission
in the Alex Rider series:
Snakehead**

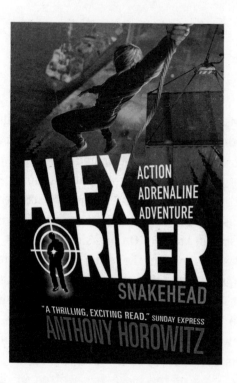

Can Alex Rider survive the poison of
the Snakehead?

Turn over for a short taster...

"DEATH IS NOT THE END"

It was the sort of building you could walk past without noticing: three storeys high, painted white, with perfectly trimmed ivy climbing up to the roof. It stood about halfway down Sloane Street in Belgravia, just round the corner from Harrods, and was one of the most expensive addresses in London. On one side there was a jewellery shop and on the other an Italian fashion boutique – but the customers who came here would no longer be needing either. A single step led up to a door painted black, and there was a window which contained an urn, a vase of fresh flowers and nothing else.

The name of the place was written in discreet gold letters:

Reed and Kelly
FUNERAL DIRECTORS
Death is not the End

At half past ten on a bright October morning, exactly three weeks before Alex landed in the Pacific Ocean, a black Lexus LS 430 four-door saloon drew up outside the front entrance. The car had been carefully chosen. It was a luxury model but there was nothing too special about it, nothing to attract attention. The arrival had also been exactly timed. In the past fifteen minutes, three other vehicles and a taxi had pulled up briefly, and their passengers, either singly or in pairs, had got out, crossed the pavement and entered the parlour. If anyone had been watching, they would have assumed that a large family had gathered to make the final arrangements for someone who had recently departed.

The last person to arrive was a powerfully built man with massive shoulders and a shaven head. There was something quite brutal about his face, with its small, squashed nose, thick lips and muddy brown eyes. But his clothes were immaculate. He was wearing a dark suit, a tailored silk shirt and a cashmere coat, unbuttoned. There was a heavy platinum ring on his fourth finger. He had been smoking a cigar, but as he stepped from the car he dropped it and ground it out with a brilliantly polished shoe. Without looking left or right, he crossed the pavement and entered the building. An old-fashioned bell on a spring jangled as the door opened and closed.

He found himself in a wood-panelled reception

room, where an elderly, grey-haired man sat with folded hands behind a narrow desk. He looked at the new arrival with a mixture of sympathy and politeness.

"Good morning," he said. "How can we be of service?"

"I have come about a death," the visitor replied.

"Someone close to you?"

"My brother. But I hadn't seen him for some years."

"You have my condolences."

The same words had already been spoken six times that morning. If even one syllable had been changed, the bald man would have turned round and left. But he knew now that the building was secure. The meeting that had been arranged just twenty-four hours earlier could go ahead.

The grey-haired man leant forward and pressed a button concealed under the desk. At once, a section of the wooden panelling clicked open to reveal a staircase leading up to the first floor.

Reed and Kelly was a real business. There once had been a Jonathan Reed and a Sebastian Kelly, and for more than fifty years they had arranged funerals and cremations until, at last, the time came to arrange their own. After that, the undertaker's had been purchased by a perfectly legitimate company, registered in Zurich, and it had continued to provide a first-class service for anyone who lived – or rather, *had* lived – in the area. But that was no longer the only purpose of the building in Sloane Street. It had also become the London headquarters of the international criminal organization that went by the name of Scorpia.

The name stood for sabotage, corruption, intelligence and assassination: its four main activities. The organization had been formed some twenty years before in Paris, its members being spies and assassins from different intelligence networks around the world who had decided to go into business for themselves. To begin with, there had been twelve of them. Then one had died of cancer and two had been murdered. The other nine had congratulated themselves on surviving so long with so few casualties.

But recently things had taken a turn for the worse. The oldest member had made the foolish and inexplicable decision to retire, which had, of course, led to his being murdered immediately. But his successor, a woman called Julia Rothman, had also been killed. That had been at the end of an operation – Invisible Sword – which had gone catastrophically wrong. In many ways this was the lowest point in Scorpia's history, and there were many who thought that the organization would never recover. After all, the agent who had beaten them, destroyed the operation and caused the death of Mrs Rothman had been fourteen years old.

However, Scorpia had not given in. They had

taken swift revenge on the boy and gone straight back to work. Invisible Sword was just one of many projects needing their attention, for they were in constant demand from governments, terrorist groups, big business ... in fact, anyone who could pay. And now they were active once again. They had come to this address in London to discuss a relatively small assignment but one that would net them ten million pounds, to be paid in uncut diamonds – easier to carry and harder to trace than banknotes.

The stairs led to a short corridor on the first floor with a single door at the end. One television camera had watched the bald man on his way up. A second followed him as he stepped onto a strange metal platform in front of the door and looked into a glass panel set in the wall. Behind the glass, there was a biometric scanner which took an instant image of the unique pattern of blood vessels on the retina in his eye and matched it against a computer at the reception desk below. Had an enemy agent tried to gain access to the room, he would have triggered a ten-thousand-volt electric charge through the metal floor plate, instantly incinerating him. But this was no enemy. The man's name was Zeljan Kurst and he had been with Scorpia from the beginning. The door slid open and he went in.

He found himself in a long, narrow room with three windows covered by blinds, and plain white walls with no decoration of any kind. There was a glass table surrounded by leather chairs and no sign of any pens, paper or printed documents. Nothing was ever written down at these meetings. Nor was anything recorded. There were six men waiting for him as he took his place at the head of the table. Following the disaster of Invisible Sword, there were now just seven of them left.

"Good morning, gentlemen," Kurst began. He spoke with a strange, mid European accent. The last word had sounded like "chintlemen". All the men at the table were equal partners but he was currently the acting head. A new chief executive was chosen as fresh projects arrived.

Nobody replied. These people were not friends. They had nothing to say to each other outside the work at hand.

"We have been given a most interesting and challenging assignment," Kurst went on. "I need hardly remind you that our reputation was quite seriously damaged by our last failure, and as well as providing us with a much-needed financial injection following the heavy losses we sustained on Invisible Sword, this project will suffice to put us back on the map. Our task is this. We are to assassinate eight extremely wealthy and influential people five weeks from now. They will all be together in one place, which provides us with the ideal opportunity. It has been left to us to decide on the method."

His eyes flickered around the table as he waited for a response. Zeljan Kurst had been the head of the police force in Yugoslavia during the 1980s and had been famous for his love of classical music – particularly Mozart – and extreme violence. It was said that he would interrogate prisoners with either an opera or a symphony playing in the background and that those who survived the ordeal would never be able to listen to that piece of music again. But he had guessed that one day his country would break up, and he had decided to quit before he was out of a job. And so he had changed sides. He had no family, no friends and nowhere he could call home. He needed work and he knew that Scorpia would make him extremely rich.

"You will have read in the newspapers," he continued, "that the G8 summit is taking place in Rome this November. This is a meeting of the eight most powerful heads of government, and as usual they will talk a great deal, have their photographs taken, consume a lot of expensive food and wine … and do absolutely nothing. They are of no interest to us. They are, in effect, irrelevant.

"However, at the same time, another conference will be taking place on the other side of the world. It has been arranged in direct competition with the G8 summit, and you might say that the timing is something of a publicity stunt. Nonetheless, it has already attracted much more attention than G8. Indeed, the politicians have almost been forgotten.

Instead, the eyes of the world are on Reef Island, just off the coast of north-west Australia in the Timor Sea.

"The press have given this alternative summit a name: Reef Encounter. A group of eight people will be coming together, and their names will be known to you. One of them is a pop singer called Rob Goldman. He has apparently raised millions for charity with concerts all over the world. Another is a billionaire, considered by many to be the richest man on the planet. He created a huge property empire but is now giving his fortune away to developing countries. There is an ex-president of the United States. A famous Hollywood actress, Eve Taylor. She owns the island. And so on." Kurst didn't even try to keep the contempt out of his voice. "They are amateurs, do-gooders – but they are also powerful and popular, which makes them dangerous.

"Their aim, as they put it, is 'to make poverty history'. In order to achieve this, they have made certain demands, including the cancellation of world debt. They want millions of dollars to be sent to Africa to fight Aids and malaria. They have called for an end to fighting in the Middle East. It will come as no surprise to those of us in this room that there are many governments and businesses who do not agree with these aims. After all, it is not possible to give to the poor without taking from the rich; and anyway, poverty has its uses.

It keeps people in their place. It also helps to hold prices down.

"A representative from one of the G8 governments contacted us six weeks ago. He has decided that Reef Encounter should end the moment it begins – certainly before any of these meddlers can address the television cameras of the world – and that is our assignment. Disrupting the conference is not enough. All eight are to be killed. The fact that they will all be in one place at one time makes it easier for us. Not one of them must leave Reef Island alive."

One of the other men leant forward. His name was Levi Kroll. He was an Israeli, about fifty years old. Very little of his face could be seen. Most of it was covered by a beard and there was a patch over the eye which he had once, by accident, shot out. "It is a simple matter," he rasped. "I could go out this afternoon and hire an Apache helicopter gunship. Let us say two thousand rounds of 30mm cannon fire and a few Hellfire air-to-ground laser-guided missiles, and this conference would no longer exist."

"Unfortunately it isn't quite as straightforward as that," Kurst replied. "As I said in my opening remarks, this is a particularly challenging assignment because our client does not wish the Reef Island eight to become martyrs. If they were seen to be assassinated, it would only add weight to their cause. And so he has specified that the deaths must seem accidental. In fact, this is critical. There cannot be even the tiniest amount of doubt or suspicion."

There was a soft murmur around the table as the other members of Scorpia took this new information on board. To kill one person in a way that would arouse no suspicion was simple. But to do the same for eight people on a remote island that would doubtless have a tight security system – that was quite another matter.

"There are certain chemical nerve agents..." someone muttered. He was French, exquisitely dressed with a black silk handkerchief poking out of his top pocket. His voice was matter-of-fact.

"How about R5?" a man called Mikato suggested. He was Japanese, with a diamond set in one tooth and – it was rumoured – yakuza tattoos all over his body. "It's the virus we supplied to Herod Sayle. Perhaps we could feed it into the island's water supply."

Kurst shook his head. "Gentlemen, both of these methods would be effective but still might show up in the subsequent investigation. What we require is a natural disaster, but one that we control. We need to eliminate the entire island with everybody on it, but in such a way that no questions will ever be asked."

He paused, then turned to the man sitting opposite him at the end of the table. "Major Yu?" he asked. "Have you given the matter your consideration?"

"Absolutely."

Major Winston Yu was at least sixty years old and although he still had a full head of hair, it had turned completely white – unusual in a Chinese man. The hair looked artificial, cut in a schoolboy style with a straight fringe above the eyes and the whole thing perched on top of a head that was yellow and waxy and that had shrunk like an over-ripe fruit. He was the least impressive person in the room, with circular glasses, thin lips and hands that would have been small on a young boy. Everything about him was somehow delicate. He had been sitting very still at the table, as if afraid he might break. A walking stick with a silver scorpion entwined around the handle rested against his chair. He was wearing a white suit and pale grey gloves.

"I have spent a great deal of time working on this operation," he continued. He had a perfect English accent. "And I am happy to report that although, on the face of it, this seems to be a rather difficult business, we have been blessed with three very fortunate circumstances. First, this island, Reef Island, is in exactly the right place. Five weeks from now is exactly the right moment. And finally, the weapon that we require just happens to be here in England, less than thirty miles from where we are sitting."

"And what weapon is that?" the Frenchman demanded.

"It's a bomb. But a very special bomb – a proto-type. As far as I know, there is only one in existence. The British have given it a code name. They call it Royal Blue."

"Major Yu is absolutely right," Kurst cut in. "Royal Blue is currently in a highly secret weapons facility just outside London. That is why I chose to hold the meeting here today. The building has been under surveillance for the past month and a team is already waiting on standby. By the end of the week, the bomb will be in our possession. After that, Major Yu, I am placing this operation in your hands."

Major Yu nodded slowly.

"With respect, Mr Kurst." It was Levi Kroll speak-ing. His voice was ugly and there was very little respect in it. "I was under the impression that *I* would be in command of the next operation."

"I am afraid you will have to wait, Mr Kroll. Once Royal Blue is in our hands, it will be flown to Bangkok and then carried by sea to its final des-tination. This is a region of the world where you have no working experience. For Major Yu, however, it is another matter. Over the past two decades he has been active in Bangkok, Jakarta, Bali and Lombok. He also has a base in northern Australia. He controls a huge criminal network – his *shetou*, or snakehead. They will smuggle the weapon for us. Major Yu's snakehead is a formidable organization, and in this instance it is best suited to our needs."

The Israeli nodded briefly. "You are right. I apologize for my interruption."

"I accept your apology," Kurst replied, although he didn't. It occurred to him that one day Levi Kroll might have to go. The man spoke too often without thinking first. "Major?"

There was little left to be said. Winston Yu took off his glasses and polished them with his gloved fingers. His eyes were a strange, almost metallic grey with lids that folded in on themselves. "I will contact my people in Bangkok and Jakarta," he muttered. "I will warn them that the machine will soon be on its way. The delivery system has already been constructed close to Reef Island. As to this conference with its high ideals, you need have no worries. I am very happy to assure you that it will never take place."

At six o'clock in the evening, two days later, a blue Renault Megane turned off the M11 motorway, taking an exit marked SERVICE VEHICLES ONLY. There are many such exits in the British motorway system. Thousands of vehicles roar past them every hour and the drivers never give them a second glance. And indeed, the great majority are completely innocent, leading to works depots or police traffic control centres. But the motorway system has its secrets too. As the Megane made its way slowly forward and came to a shuddering halt in front of what looked like a single-storey office compound, it was tracked by three television cameras and the security men inside went into immediate alert.

The building was in fact a laboratory and weapons research centre, belonging to the Ministry of Defence. Very few people knew of its existence and even fewer were allowed in or out. The car that had just arrived was unauthorized and the security men – recruited from the special forces – should have instantly raised the alarm. That was the protocol.

But the Renault Megane is one of the most innocent and ordinary of family cars, and this one had clearly been involved in a bad accident. The front windscreen had shattered. The bonnet was crumpled and steam was rising from the grille. A man wearing a green anorak and a cap was in the driving seat; there was a woman next to him with blood pouring down the side of her face. Worse than that, there were two small children in the back, and although the image on the screen was a little fuzzy, they seemed to be in a bad way. Neither of them was moving. The woman managed to get out of the car, but then she collapsed. Her husband sat where he was, as if dazed.

Two of the security men ran out to them. It was human nature. Here was a young family that needed help; and anyway, it wasn't that much of a security risk. The front door of the building swung shut behind them and would need a seven-digit code to reopen. Both men carried radio transmitters and 9mm Browning automatic pistols underneath their jackets. The Browning is an old weapon but a very reliable one, a favourite with the SAS.

The woman was still lying on the ground. The man who had been driving managed to open the door as the two guards approached.

"What happened?" one of them called out.

It was only now, when it was too late, that they began to realize that none of this added up. A car that had crashed on the motorway would have simply pulled onto the hard shoulder – if it had been able to drive at all. And how come it was only this one car, with these four people, that had been involved? Where were the other vehicles? Where were the police? But any last doubts were removed when the two security men reached the car. The two children on the back seat were dummies. With their cheap wigs and plastic smiles they were like something out of a nightmare.

The woman on the ground twisted round, a machine gun appearing in her hand. She shot the first of the security men in the chest. The second was moving quickly, reaching for his own weapon, taking up a combat stance. He never had a chance. The driver had been balancing a silenced Micro Uzi sub-machine gun on his lap. He tilted it and pulled the trigger. The gun barely whispered as it fired twenty rounds in less than a second. The guard was flung away.

The couple were already up and running towards the building. They couldn't get in yet, but they didn't need to. They made their way towards the back, where a silver box about two metres square had been attached to the brickwork. The man was carrying a toolkit which he had brought from the car. The woman stopped briefly and fired three times, taking out all the cameras. At that moment, an ambulance appeared, driving up from the motorway. It drew in behind the parked Megane.

The next phase of the mission took very little time. The facility was equipped with a standard CBR air filtration system – the letters stood for chemical, biological and radiological. It was designed to counter an enemy attack, but now the exact opposite was about to happen as the enemy turned the system against itself. The man took a miniaturized oxyacetylene torch out of his toolbox and used it to burn out the screws. This allowed him to unfasten a metal panel, revealing a complicated tangle of pipes and wires. From somewhere inside his anorak he produced a gas mask which he strapped over his face. He reached back into his toolbox and took out a metal vial, a few centimetres long, with a nozzle and a spike. He knew exactly what he was doing. Using the heel of his hand, he jammed the spike into one of the pipes. Finally he turned the nozzle.

The hiss was almost inaudible as a stream of potassium cyanide mixed with the air circulating inside the building. Meanwhile, four men dressed as paramedics but all wearing gas masks had approached the front entrance. One of them pressed a magnetized box no bigger than a cigarette packet against the lock. He stepped back. There was an explosion and the door swung open.

It was early evening and only half a dozen people were still working inside the facility. Most of them were technicians; one was the head of security. He had been trying to make an emergency call when the gas had hit him. He was lying on the floor, his face twisted in agony. The receiver was still in his hand.

Across the entrance hall, down a corridor and through a door marked RESTRICTED AREA: the four paramedics knew exactly where they were going. The bomb was in front of them. It looked remarkably old-fashioned, like something out of the Second World War: a huge metal cylinder, silver in colour, flat at one end, pointed at the other. Only a data screen built into the side and a series of digital controls brought it into the twenty-first century. It was strapped down on a power-assisted trolley and the whole thing would fit inside the ambulance with just inches to spare. But that, of course, was why the ambulance had been chosen.

They guided it back down the corridor and out through the front door. The ambulance was equipped with a ramp and the bomb rolled smoothly into the back, allowing room for the driver and one passenger in the front. The other three men and the woman climbed into the car. The dummies were left behind. The entire operation had taken eight and a half minutes. Thirty seconds less than planned.

An hour later, by the time the alarm had been raised in London and other parts of the country, everyone involved had disappeared. They had discarded the wigs, contact lenses and facial padding that had completely changed their appearance. The two vehicles had been incinerated.

And the weapon known as Royal Blue had already begun its journey east.

READ OTHER GREAT BOOKS BY

ANTHONY HOROWITZ...

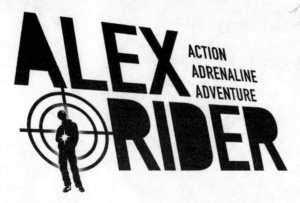

WELCOME TO THE DARK SIDE OF
ANTHONY HOROWITZ

BOOK ONE

He always knew he was different. First there were the dreams. Then the deaths began.

BOOK TWO

It began with Raven's Gate. But it's not over yet. Once again the enemy is stirring.

THE POWER OF FIVE

BOOK THREE
Darkness covers the earth.
The Old Ones have returned.
The battle must begin.

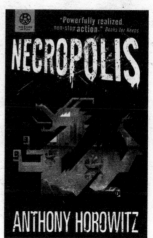

BOOK FOUR
An ancient evil is unleashed.
Five have the power to defeat it.
But one of them has been taken.

BOOK FIVE
Five Gatekeepers.
One chance to save mankind.
Chaos beckons. Oblivion awaits.

THE CHILLING POWER OF FIVE SERIES

NEXT IN THE SERIES:

Necropolis

Oblivion

Heading for an exciting new life in London, Tom
Falconer is ambushed by the murderous Ratsey.
Helpless and alone, the orphan gallops towards
the great city, where a number of mortal dangers
await him. But on the first night of a new play –
The Devil and his Boy – Tom discovers that the
fate of Elizabethan England rests in his hands.

"A cracking historical adventure... Thrilling." *TES*

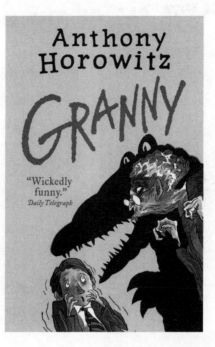

Joe Warden isn't happy. He has rich, uncaring
parents and he's virtually a prisoner in the huge
family mansion, Thattlebee Hall. But his real
problem is his granny. Not only is she physically
repulsive and unbelievably mean, she seems to have
some secret plan – and that plan involves him.

Can Joe thwart Granny's evil scheme before he's
turned into neoplasmic slime?

"Wickedly funny." *Daily Telegraph*

"Hugely popular ... I can hear Horowitz fans
drooling." *The Times*

COLLECT ALL OF THE HILARIOUS

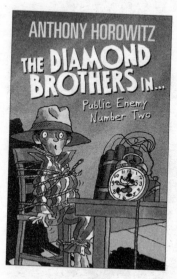

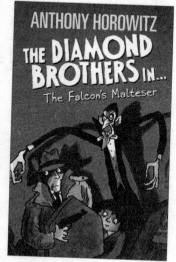

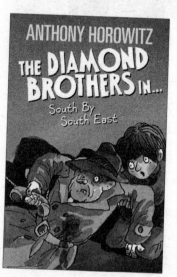

"Horowitz is the perfect writer. His dialogue crackles with hardboiled wit."

Frank Cottrell Boyce, *Guardian*

DIAMOND BROTHERS INVESTIGATIONS

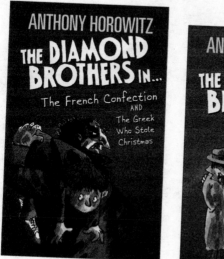

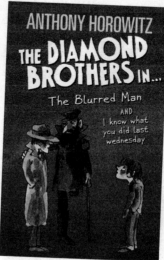

Tim Diamond is the world's worst private detective, and unfortunately for his quick-thinking brother, Nick, the cases keep coming in. What connects them? Murder! And if the Diamond Brothers don't play their cards right, they could be next!

LOOKING BACK, Henry Parker could honestly say that he had never wanted to hurt anyone. Certainly, it had never occurred to him that he would one day plan and then execute the perfect murder of an internationally well-known children's author ... even if that was what actually happened. To begin with, all Henry wanted to do was write...

Photograph © Jon Cartwright

Anthony Horowitz is the author of the number one bestselling Alex Rider books and The Power of Five series. He has enjoyed huge success as a writer for both children and adults, most recently with the latest adventure in the Alex Rider series, *Russian Roulette*, and the highly acclaimed Sherlock Holmes novel, *The House of Silk*. His latest novel, *Moriarty*, is also set in the world of Sherlock Holmes and was published in October 2014. Anthony was also chosen by the Ian Fleming estate to write the new James Bond novel which will be published this year. Anthony has won numerous awards, including the Bookseller Association/Nielsen Author of the Year Award, the Children's Book of the Year Award at the British Book Awards, and the Red House Children's Book Award. In 2014 Anthony was awarded an OBE for Services to Literature. He has also created and written many major television series, including *Injustice*, *Collision* and the award-winning *Foyle's War*.

You can find out more about Anthony and his work at:
www.alexrider.com
@AnthonyHorowitz